Running Coyote
and
Fallen Star
and other stories

Gavin Boyter

First published by Sword Press 2021

An imprint of Gugnug Press

www.unforeseentales.com

Cover Art by Ian Boyter

Running Coyote and Fallen Star first appeared in Tigershark, *Duet* appeared in The Ice Colony, *A Clearing* in The Periodical, Forlorn, *Antbots* in The Closed Eye Open, *A Cork on the Ocean* in Dreamcatcher, *Beeswax* in Every Day Fiction, *The Pact* in Constellations, *The End of Money* first appeared in The Abstract Elephant, *The Purple Heart* was published by Underwood Press, *Float Me Down the River* appeared in Dark Moon Lilith, *Eyes in the Dark* in Bluing the Blade, *Wheatfield with Crows* in Kithe Magazine, *10 Social Isolation Games* in High Shelf, *A Sign from Above* in Etched Onyx Magazine, *Crawling to the Endzone* in Progenitor Art & Literary Journal and *Keepsakes* was published by Bright Flash Literary Review.

A CIP record for this book is available from the British Library.

ISBN: 978-0-9571298-2-5

Set in Garamond 11pt (body text) and Corbel light 16pt (headers)

For my friends

(my most demanding readers)

Stuff your eyes with wonder, live as if you'd drop dead in ten seconds. See the world. It's more fantastic than any dream made or paid for in factories.

Ray Bradbury

Contents

Introduction

In February 2020, with remarkable timing, I quit my administrative position in the NHS to seek other opportunities. In part, I found myself in a management position entirely unsuited to my temperament. I was also growing to realise that it was absurd to be working in a job that didn't use any of my skills. I thought it might not be unreasonable to find a job where I might capitalise on my writing abilities.

Of course, we all know what happened next – Covid-19 appeared, a malignant viral invader, seemingly intent on throwing the planet into chaos.

I'd planned to spend a few weeks at my parents' house in Edinburgh, my hometown. First, I thought I'd have a week or two in the West Highlands, revisiting some places I'd not seen since my childhood. This notably included Sandaig, the beach near Glenelg where writer and naturalist Gavin Maxwell once lived (after whom I was named).

I loaded up Roxy, my self-converted Mazda Bongo campervan and set off. The first few days were quite lovely. I relished driving through snowclad mountains at Glencoe and parking on the top of the steeply winding Mam Ratigan, while wild winds buffeted the van and pale winter sunshine contrasted with fast-moving banks of cloud. At night, the sparkling skein of the Milky Way was alarmingly vivid, in a way you never experience in London.

Then one morning I picked my way along the rocky foreshore to Glenelg, blasted by furious horizontal rain and increasingly angry wind, finally appreciating how challenging it must have been for Maxwell to build a home there. After a couple of days of brutal weather, I decided to cut short my Highland idyll and head to Edinburgh.

Once I got to the capital, Scottish First Minister Nicola

Sturgeon, reacting quicker than her English counterpart to the spreading pandemic, announced a stay-at-home lockdown. Overnight I found that my voluntary trip to visit my parents, Ian and Kath, had become a sort of house arrest.

I'm exaggerating of course. It was in fact lovely to catch up with my folks and my sisters (socially distanced, outdoors, and often through a fence) but it also felt weirdly lonely and regressive – like I'd stepped back into childhood at the age of 49.

I needed a purpose. I couldn't really look for work down south when everyone was being furloughed and encouraged to work from home. I had sufficient savings to get by for a few months and no real inclination to apply for jobs I didn't really want out of a sense of obligation.

I decided to write. I had a novel to work on (*Stutter*, still unfinished) and I also thought I might start writing short stories again. As a teenager and young man, I used to love making these brief forays into imaginative worlds, often in the genres of science fiction or the surreal. Somewhere along the line, I lost the habit and I'd been told by more than one contemporary that this was a great shame. Spending time in the family home might allow me to tap back into that youthful wellspring of imagination. There was just one problem. I had no ideas for stories.

From out of nowhere appeared the thought that perhaps I could use some random process to generate stories. I had some precedent for this. In recent months I'd entered the NY Midnight short story competition (in fact, A Sign from Above, featured here, was originally written for it). The premise of this contest is to use randomness to inspire creativity. The organisers randomly assign a location, object, and genre, all of which you must incorporate in your tale.

I'd always found such challenges entertaining and inspiring. I'm also a big fan of the OuLiPo writers of the 1960s, including George Perec, who famously wrote an entire book without including the letter "e" (brilliantly translated into English by Gilbert Adair as *A Void*). The OuLiPo movement, which began in

France, used deliberatively restrictive rules to inspire creativity. I wondered if I might borrow from some of their practices.

The notion developed into the concept of writing and reading aloud (on my YouTube channel) 1000-word short stories inspired by and incorporating five random words. I visited the website textfixer.com to come up with the words, which proved particularly challenging. The American site tossed up such unique terms as "goldbricker" and "Badlands".

In true OuLiPo fashion, I decided the stories had to be exactly 1000 words long, not a word more or less. I began writing these stories daily, each of them inspired by the random associations of words thrust upon me by an unknowable algorithm. Many of these stories are contained in this book.

As time went on, I began to relax the arbitrary restriction on length. For the purposes of this book, the initially 1000-word stories have been edited without this constraint.

The title story and *Beeswax* are two examples of my original conceit. The former was inspired by ferment, duke, murderous, sanitary and Badlands. The latter incorporated gland, brood, queen, wrestle, and captain. I've provided an appendix of the stories included in this volume generated by this unusual technique, alongside the words which inspired them.

There are other, more long-form tales in this book, written without using this strategy, as well as some noticeably miniature pieces composed for publications with their own brutal length restrictions (including *Antbots* and *Arrhythmia*). I hope their variety provides an opportunity to find a tale for each slice of time you'd like to fill, however short.

My rediscovery of the joys of short stories has proven a great comfort in the often lonely and fearful year we've all lived through. I feel I owe a debt to the masters of the form who have inspired me, amongst them Bernard Malamud, Ray Bradbury, Alastair Gray, Angela Carter, Donald Barthelme, Guy de Maupassant, M.R. James, and Raymond Carver.

I would also like to thank my parents, Ian and Kath, for

putting up with my crazy creativity (as well as for designing this book's cover, in my father's case). Gratitude is also due to my sisters Katy and Fiona and their families, for their ongoing support, as well as my friends Guy, Sara, Aradhna, Indy, Francesca B and Rob H, to whom I read some of these tales. Of course, I'm delighted that so many were published, and am indebted to the editors and readers of all the journals and websites listed in the frontispiece, for their belief in these stories.

I hope you'll enjoy this profusion of crazy tales. Many of them surprised even me with the paths they led me down, as well as the characters I met along the way. In part, I suppose, I was looking for people I could safely spend time with, without masks, social distancing, or hand sanitiser. I certainly found diverting company, and I hope that you do too.

London, 2021.

Running Coyote and Fallen Star

Leopold Wainwright III, lifelong off-grid eccentric and illegal distiller of unreasonably strong spirits, woke to the sound of his front door being mercilessly assaulted. It must be early – Duke the rooster had not yet crowed in that insistent way that would send Leo lurching downstairs with momentarily murderous intent, particularly on mornings after he had sampled a new batch of moonshine.

Leo tore open his front door and shouted at the trespassers, who were triply indistinct because he couldn't find his spectacles, was hungover and the screen door pixelated everything.

"Who in Satan's name are you? What are doing on my porch?"

Two figures, both slender and petite. Women?

"Mister, please, you gotta let us in. We ran out of gas."

Leo wasn't falling for that. Nine months previously, Mrs Gantry, who ran the pet store in town, was robbed at knifepoint after she took pity on a drifter with an empty guitar case that he filled with all her valuables (precious little, as it happened, so he took her head too).

"I have a loaded shotgun and I don't see well enough to wing you!" he replied.

Leo heard a vehicle approaching along the dirt track that led up from the highway. Given his deliberately remote location, Leo knew the second car was unlikely to betoken anything good.

"Round the back so I can get a look at you", Leo ordered, grabbing the shotgun he kept by the door, which hadn't fired properly for several years.

The mystery couple raced around the building as the approaching car skidded to a halt. Leo squinted through the back-door spyhole and saw two dishevelled women, one with bright blue hair, the other sporting a nose ring and a fierce expression. They looked like bad news but the sudden rap upon the front door sounded worse. The dark-haired woman, who looked half Native American, was cradling something in her arms. A baby? Might be a scam, thought Leo, a doll swaddled to elicit sympathy.

"Please, we need somewhere to hide. The Feds want to take my baby."

Leo shuttled through a series of assumptions and counter-assumptions. He was fiercely anti-establishment, plus the woman's story was so peculiar it might just be true.

"FBI! Let us in." The tone and mandatory warning were familiar. Leo had just seconds to act. He opened the back door on its chain. The women were scarcely in their twenties, desperate and afraid.

"Lean-to out back. Take a couple of jars, fill your tank. Now run!"

The door burst in behind Leo as he heard the fugitives race away.

Running Coyote made it to the sheds first, with the baby held firmly to her chest. Melanie limped behind her, wondering how her day had gone so horribly wrong. A social worker who'd undertaken a routine evening call to visit single mum Coyote, she'd taken one look at the baby and had known that the hysterical story the native American had told her might just be true. They'd driven through the night before the Feds had caught up with them.

Coyote pulled open the first door, revealing a cloud of flies and a stench that was far from sanitary. The john. She gagged and joined Mel as she entered the larger shed, which was dark and dank. There must be cans of gasoline somewhere. Mel found a switch; a dim bulb flickered on. The lean-to contained only a home-made still and a shelf of demijohns full of clear liquid. The air was thick with the ferment of mashed barley.

Mel unplugged a jar and recoiled at the smell of 80-proof alcohol.

"Jeez – man, this'll blind you."

Coyote looked panicky, her baby growing restless, gurgling slightly. "There's no gas, is there? He tricked us," she said, wondering why Mel was smiling.

"Nope," said Mel, holding out a hammer and a six-inch nail. Can you get to their vehicle unseen if I take the kid?"

Now it was Coyote's turn to run the risks. She nodded, handing Fallen Star over. Raised voices issued from the shack. It wouldn't be long before the Feds checked the outhouses.

Coyote used the skills her grandfather had taught her, dashing with grace and speed between rocky red outcrops until only a 20-yard sprint stood between her and the Feds' black sedan. A whirl of windblown dust provided the necessary cover. Moments later she crouched behind the car, took a deep breath, and drove the nail into the tyre. It burst with a low pop and Coyote raced to her own car, a ramshackle 1972 Oldsmobile, where Mel was emptying a second demijohn into the tank.

"Will this work?" Coyote hissed, climbing behind the wheel as Mel tossed the jar aside and slid into the passenger seat, holding firmly onto Fallen Star, who was mewling softly.

Coyote gunned the engine, which spluttered inconclusively. The front door of the shack opened and two impressively tall men in dark suits emerged, eyes shaded behind standard issue Ray Bans.

"Stop where you are!" shouted one, raising his gun. Coyote turned the key again. The starter struggled, then the engine abruptly rumbled into life.

A warning shot blasted over their heads.

"They won't risk harming him!" Mel reassured Coyote as she spun the Oldsmobile, throwing up a spiral of dust. The Feds had jumped into their own vehicle.

"They'd better fucking not!" yelled Coyote, as they tore away down the track, through the baked red brutality of the Utah Badlands.

Growing restless in Mel's arms was the beautiful, strange hybrid Coyote had brought into the world, his wings struggling to unfurl, his green lizard eyes alive with intelligence, his voice like the music of distant nebulae – not crying so much as singing his frustration. Mel turned to see the Fed's car skid as it skittered three-wheeled behind them, losing pace.

They would make it to the border, where their strange little family could spread its wings, Fallen Star literally. Evolution couldn't be stopped – love would have its way.

Aloha

Professor Martin McCullers finally yielded to his twelve-year-old daughter Rosalie's insistent demands and agreed to show her the facility where the signal had first been detected. Nothing more, nothing less than the first detected utterance by an alien being. A single word containing both promise and ambiguity: *welcome*.

McCullers' pass-card still functioned, because he hadn't returned it as he'd been instructed to, and nobody had yet noticed. McCullers also hadn't informed either his daughter or his wife Melissa that he'd been fired from the Mount Braddock SETI project. Secrecy had become a way of life to Professor McCullers, or Marty, as he insisted his students address him.

"Go on, Dad, you promised!"

It hadn't so much been what Rosalie said, the habitual whine of an adolescent insisting on parental justice, as how she'd said it, with that plaintive head tilt and wide-eyed stare Marty could never say no to. So it was that on the evening of 12th February 2036, he drove his daughter from their home, nestling on the edge of the forest, up the winding single track roads to the rocky mountaintop facility.

Originally just an observatory, Mount Braddock was at the vanguard of quantum entanglement research. Just three weeks previously, a breakthrough had occurred which would change humanity's understanding of its place in the universe forever. Except, that is, if the government had its way.

McCullers' team at the facility had solved a problem that had bothered SETI researchers for some time. If extra-terrestrial life were ever detected from alien signals broadcast across the universe, the distances involved would mean that the civilisations originating those signals would most probably have died out or significantly evolved in the thousands or even millions of years it had taken their signal to reach earth, let alone any reply. Conversations would become impossibly attenuated by the vast distances involved. McCullers explained this to his daughter.

"You know when there's a news broadcast and the presenter asks someone in another country a question, there's a delay before they hear the presenter's voice and can respond?"

"Yes. It's really annoying and they look really dumb."

"Well imagine that times a million million. Every light year, by definition, adds a year in signal transmission delay. If we get a signal back from Proxima Centauri, the nearest star to ours, then that signal was sent over four years ago. That's the best we can do, unless we somehow intercept an alien ship buzzing our solar system."

"So, talking to the aliens is pointless?" Rosalie asked, as they stood at the gates of the Braddock facility and Professor McCullers let them in with his passcode and thumbprint scan.

"Well, the usual method – monitoring likely electromagnetic signals – is really a branch of archaeology. The only meaningful message you could send that way would be 'Aloha'. Hello and goodbye in one expression. Now, our new method... well, that's where the magic lies."

"Quantum entanglement," Rosalie piped up. She evidently had been reading the pile of books he'd placed by her bedside.

"That's right," he replied, proudly. "We take a cloud of

particles in a Bose-Einstein condensate."

"A what whatty?"

"Just a bunch of really cold particles," he explained, as they entered his laboratory. Fortunately, nobody was still working this late. A strict 10pm curfew had been instituted recently – something to do with work-life balance. McCullers started flicking switches, booting up the "call box" as they colloquially called it. They didn't have long. He was sure they must have tripped a silent alarm somewhere.

"At just a fraction of a degree above absolute zero, we can make these particles act as if they are all identical. This means if we separate them and then alter one of them in some way, the other spatially-distinct particles all respond exactly like the one we're directly affecting."

"Like Newton's Cradle?"

McCullers shook his head. "No – that's the transference of kinetic energy between solid objects and it takes time. It looks instantaneous, but it takes a few microseconds before the ball at the far end moves in response to the first ball hitting the second. Quantum entanglement changes really do happen instantaneously, no matter how far apart the particles are removed from one another."

Rosalie looked confused as she slid into a swivel chair in front of one of the consoles.

"But nothing travels faster than the speed of light?"

"That's right. But there's nothing travelling in this scenario. The particles really do become, to all intents and purposes, the same particle. Anyhow, this is how we came up with the Quantum Entanglement Communicator, or Queck. We have a lattice of entangled particles we can form into patterns – basically ones and zeroes. We've made an 8-bit communicator. A galactic pager. It's humanity's greatest invention since, well, the wheel."

"Cool. Lemme see…." Rosalie said, spinning her chair as McCullers finished powering up the device.

"We can probably only be here for a minute or two before they send someone," McCullers warned, "but we might get one of the Oglers online if we're lucky."

"Is that what the aliens are called?"

"That's just our nickname for the first race we identified. We classified their planet OGLE-2014-BLG-0124L. I know – catchy isn't it?" McCullers flicked one last bank of switches on and stood back.

A screen flickered into life and a cursor winked amidst the black. McCullers handed his daughter a wireless keyboard.

"Go on then, type."

What he was doing was an outrageous breach of protocol, but McCullers no longer cared. The US government had voted to cut funding to the program, and arrest anyone who spoke of it, under national security provisions. This seemed short-sighted, immoral, and deeply unfair to Rosalie's generation, who ought to know the wonderful truth that there were many civilisations out there in the vastness of interstellar space, and none of them had heard of Jesus, Jehovah, or Allah.

None of the intelligent species so far discovered, still had the concept of God. Earth alone had retained that hypothesis. The government felt that this knowledge would prove devastating to Earth's estimated five billion believers, and so it was deemed wisest to pull the plug. When McCullers had argued vehemently in a closed congressional hearing that this was wrong, he had been unceremoniously released from both his research role and his professorship.

What McCullers had done next was fuelled by frustration and rather too much Jack Daniels. He'd gone on Facecast, the instant video broadcasting platform, prepared a nest of juicy tags – aliens, alien life, SETI, religion, god, atheism, religion – and had released an eleven-minute rant which had instantly gone viral. No, scratch that, it had gone pandemic.

...they think you're sheep, moon-faced imbeciles who can't handle the truth. And it's a beautiful truth – we are NOT alone! There are incredible civilisations out these – tens of thousands of them. Wouldn't you trade that for your invisible space wizard? I mean, sure, you could make up a convoluted reason why God never mentioned these other planets, these infinite reaches of teeming life, but why would you want to? Throw away a bucket of pearls for a handful of sand? Anyway, you want proof, visit the following site...

He'd given a link to some of the early transmission recordings, from that first welcome to the higher dimensional mathematics that would keep human geniuses busy for decades. The illicit info-dump included the video feed in which a clever colleague had transposed the three-dimensional shapes that comprised Ogler language into musical chords, to help convey some of the wonder of their strangeness. It produced the most beautiful, bizarre, and lushly avant-garde music – Arvo Pärt, György Ligeti and Sigur Ros jamming together across the aeons.

Of course, the powers that be had algorithms to shut down such seditious ideas and his broadcast eventually sank like a stone and was lost. But not before the ripples in the human pool were felt. People managed to access the material McCullers had leaked. Now they knew something that could not be unknown – nowhere in the vast reaches of space was there room for their tiny God.

There were riots, bible burnings, mosques and synagogues bombed, monks tearing off their cassocks in mass renunciations, priests hanging their dog collars on the handrails of bridges (and sometimes themselves from those selfsame bridges). Opposing this was a retrenchment amongst some religious communities – a refusal to look at the evidence, a refusal to admit that evidence meant anything at all, when stacked against the monolithic consolations of faith.

To keep the peace, the government had declared SETI research a kind of intellectual terrorism. Some ideas, evidently, were just too dangerous to promulgate.

McCullers had largely sobered up by the morning after his diatribe, though not entirely. He immediately realised the danger he was in when he turned on the television. Chaos on the streets of the world's major cities. Endless pontification as to who was to blame for the explosions of anarchy and nihilism.

The Ministry would come for him, and that was okay. McCullers couldn't, however, let his beloved daughter remain in ignorance. That was really why they had gone back to the observatory, against his wife's wishes. Melissa was calling him even now. McCullers could feel his earlobe vibrate as the callclip registered the signal. He touched the back of the device to reject the call. He'd explain later.

That morning, Melissa had packed their bags and formulated a plan. After dark, a family friend was going to smuggle them out of town in his truck. Although McCullers had disguised his appearance and voice in his rant, as well as his location, he knew MoRSE would find him sooner or later. They really ought to get going.

Rosalie, who from infancy had grown up with text communication as a natural way of engaging with other minds, was typing furiously. McCullers stopped her with a gentle hand upon her wrist.

"They've only just learned English. You'll have to us fewer words."

Rosalie hit the delete button and bit her lip, thinking intently.

"How far away are the Oglers?"

"Twenty-five thousand light years," McCullers replied. "You won't be meeting face to face anytime soon. I don't, to be honest, know if they even have faces."

Rosalie began typing again, more slowly this time:

HELLO! I'M ROSALIE. WHO ARE YOU?

They waited. Nothing happened.

"Might just not be online," McCullers replied. "Or they may just perceive time entirely differently from how we do. But that's a whole other con…"

His mental flow was interrupted by a cascade of letters appearing onscreen:

WE ARE LITHRICOPUS ANTANAA, WE ARE HAPPY OF SPEAK YOU

"They haven't quite got our grammar yet but bear in mind it's been only three weeks since we started talking," explained McCullers. Rosalie was already typing back.

HI LITHRI. HOW ARE YOU TODAY?

A much quicker response came through.

WE AM NOT TODAY, AM LITHRI

McCullers laughed. "You have to be really explicit, rather than ambiguous. I don't know if it's a linguistic or psychological barrier. The don't seem to have irony or idiomatic expressions or metaphor or anything like that."

Rosalie thought carefully, then typed:

ARE YOU WELL TODAY?

This proved much more successful. The reply appeared momentarily.

WELL THIS DAY, MANY GRATITUDES. SUNS ARE IN THE SKY, DROONITS ARE FLYING.

"They have three suns, would you believe?" McCullers whispered, as if somehow, the Oglers might hear him.

"Nuts!" said Rosalie. "What are droonits?"

"We think they're something like birds and something like pillowcases. We haven't been able to send anything like a drawing or a photograph yet. That was going to be our next project."

As McCullers finished talking, he heard the faint sound of tyres on gravel. Here we go, he thought. Rosalie hadn't noticed anything; she was far too focused. She would have made a brilliant analyst. McCullers felt his eyes moistening, so saddening was the small-mindedness of the imbeciles shutting all this down. Whole new branches of science would be strangled at birth – the analytical study of an alien race would create whole new fields of study in sociology, psychology, biology and pretty much any discipline you could shove an exo- in front of.

McCullers felt he wanted to warn the Ogler, Lithri, that there might be no more communication for a while. While Rosalie considered what to type next, he quickly tapped out:

COMMUNICATION MAY BE INTERRUPTED. WE ARE SORRY.

And the reply came immediately:

WHY INTERRUPTED?

"I have no idea how to answer that," admitted McCullers, as half a dozen heavily armed soldiers led by Professor Lysander Street, McCullers' ex-boss. Street, in her early forties, stood an imperious six foot two and had a military bearing that would have been imposing even if she didn't have an armed guard with her. Rosalie ducked instinctively behind her father.

"What the hell do you think you're doing, McCullers?" demanded Street.

McCullers found himself shaking but managed to growl defiantly: "I am saying goodbye to our guests."

Street sighed, then turned to her reinforcements.

"A clear-up team will be here to strip it in an hour. For now, just render it inoperable, Captain."

The Captain, who looked scarcely thirty, seemed bewildered by the array of computers and gadgetry surrounding him. His uniform featured an unusual insignia: MoRSE – the Ministry of Religion and Spiritual Enlightenment. .McCullers was impressed by how quickly a squad from the Ministry had got here.

"Destroy the consoles, man!" she ordered. "Use your rifle butt."

Professor McCullers couldn't believe he'd been fooled by Street for so long. She'd always been reluctant to outline her scientific credentials when he'd tried to engage her in conversation, so he'd just written her off as an administrator. Now he realised she'd been a government plant from day one, most likely a MoRSE spy. These men were her Ministry's ground troops.

Street advanced on McCullers, confused.

"Do you really not see why depriving the world of its source of consolation and hope, is a terrible idea?"

McCullers shook his head. "False consolation, illusory hope."

"Nevertheless…" began Street.

An explosion of sparks leapt from a bank of computers as the soldiers went to work. McCullers and his daughter backed away, aghast at the destruction. McCullers couldn't help but protest.

"The condensate will heat up! The particles will disentangle. This is cultural vandalism!" McCullers shouted, to no avail, as the screen containing Lithri's last words faded and blurred out to eternal darkness. It had taken four years for Voyager II to carry its payload of entangled particles out to the centre of the galaxy, awaiting an advanced civilisation to pick up the receiver, so to speak.

Now that connection had been irretrievably broken, and as far as Street and her goons were concerned, first contact with an alien species was consigned to a historical footnote, no doubt to be redacted out of existence. Well, that was the idea, at least.

McCullers knew the Oglers were themselves in contact with over three thousand other races. The outer reaches would not be silenced for long.

"Dad," whispered Rosalie from behind his shoulder, "That was amazing. I'll remember that forever."

If they let us live, thought McCullers, before dismissing the thought as melodramatic. Deep down, the forces of retrograde solipsism must know their days of self-enforced ignorance are numbered. He decided to let Rosalie into one more secret, whispering back:

"I didn't keep all the particles here. I sent batches of condensate out to a dozen other labs, in India, China, Britain, Switzerland, South Africa, and the international space station. They can't stop this."

Rosalie smiled a secretive smile and McCullers had a fleeting vision that she would one day lead the world towards universal unity, the ultimate goal of the Queck project – permanent links between all galactic civilisations and a realisation that we are not alone, and never will be again.

Marty McCullers gripped his daughter's hand tightly, as the technology fizzled and buzzed out of existence. The Luddites hadn't stood a chance and nor would Street and her MoRSE thugs. Communication was McCullers' religion, and the heretics would not be silenced.

"Aloha," Rosalie whispered. Goodbye and hello.

Merry Go Round

Alice's dates were amongst the saddest experiences she'd ever had. As a forty-five-year-old double divorcee, she'd had her share of disappointment. Somehow the four encounters Alice squeezed into the pandemic-restricted month of November 2020 felt desolate in a particularly demoralising way. Firstly, all of her dates were outdoors since meeting inside was disallowed. Secondly, because nothing was open, Alice was left with drizzly walks around local parks or through deserted city streets. Sometimes she'd get a takeaway coffee or cup of soup just to keep her hands warm.

Lastly, the kind of men who'd agree to meet a stranger for a melancholy stroll around a park, wearing surgical masks and dodging puddles and non-compliant strangers, were men seemingly lacking something vital. Chris, the tax auditor, had spoken entirely in non sequiturs, mostly about his narrowboat. Adam had been barely five feet tall, his deep booming voice oddly incongruous coming from such a slight frame. Rajinder was animated at first, and since he too was a designer, they had at least something in common. Then he got onto the subject of his children, who lived with their mother in Mumbai, and he simply burst into tears. Alice spent the remainder of their date boosting Raj's spirit, while she felt her own dwindle away.

Today she was with Karl, who was a doctor and a medical examiner, a job she hoped would be filled with excitement and intrigue.

"It's mostly certifying cause of death for RTA victims, cancer patients and suicides," Karl confessed ten minutes into their wander down the South Bank.

"Tragic stuff," was all Alice could think to reply, half wishing she were back home, working on the academic book jackets she'd been putting off. The agency had been good to her, giving her a whole series to work on. She ought to be prioritising work.

"Not entirely, " said Karl, whose German accent was subtle and whose sensitive features now betrayed a flicker of amusement. "Last week I was called out to certify a fisherman who was removed from the Solent with a harpoon through his neck."

Alice wasn't sure if she was supposed to laugh at this, and Karl wasn't offering any social cues. It seemed that he hadn't finished his anecdote.

"But he didn't drown, and the harpoon wouldn't have killed him either. In fact, he died from anaphylactic shock from a peanut butter sandwich he'd taken a bite out of shortly before loading the harpoon gun. I had to explain this to his grieving widow."

Again, there was no indication that a humorous response was required.

"But my role is rarely as droll," said Karl, sinking back into a silence he seemed happy to let continue indefinitely. They had reached the peculiar chromium sculpture near the Hayward Gallery. Alice watched their figures warp and stretch across its surface. Raindrops ran down the scuffed metal in erratic rivulets.

"You don't enjoy it much," Alice said, cradling her latte. Karl took a sip of his green tea. He had long, delicate fingers and for a brief moment Alice wondered if he would touch her as gently as he handled his silver Thermos cup. She shook away the thought and awaited his answer.

"It's fulfilling, in a sense," he began. "I get the feeling I'm doing something useful. And I suppose I'm good at it, or I wouldn't be one of the few full-time examiners." Karl sounded like he was trying to convince himself as much as her.

"Not much joy in it though?" Alice asked rhetorically.

"That's it!" Karl said with surprising vigour, as they passed the closed bookshops and restaurants under the South Bank Centre. "I bring people the answers they need, but not the comfort they want."

Alice had a strong impulse to grab and squeeze his hand encouragingly. Karl was at least sensitive and thoughtful, qualities sorely lacking in both of her husbands. Sadly, the logistics wouldn't work, since they were both carrying drinks and umbrellas. She settled for a broad smile instead. Karl's eyes crinkled with amusement. He looked at least ten years older than his Tinder profile picture, but his slightly jowly face still had a handsome structure underpinning it. For some reason, the Shakespearian phrase chopfallen flitted into mind.

Then she realised Karl wasn't smiling at her. He was looking at the whirling colour and noise of a distant merry-go-round. His brown eyes reflected the rotating horses as they approached from the desolate Christmas market under the Jubilee Bridges.

"We had such an amusement in my hometown, when I was a boy," he said. "I loved it."

Alice realised she hadn't asked him where he was from. Perhaps she could have a surreptitious look at his profile.

"It'd appear during Oktoberfest and stay until New Year".

Alice looked around at the serried ranks of wooden

sheds, with single strings of bright yellow bulbs looped between them. Even if they were open, this place wouldn't hold a candle to any of the German Markets she'd seen in magazines.

"I've never been to a proper German Market", Alice said softly.

"You must go," Karl said, his face suddenly brimming with enthusiasm. The 'you' filled Alice with more sadness than she knew she could contain.

"Fancy a ride?" she said, half-joking.

"Yes," he said simply, with a look of gratitude on his face. Alice could suddenly see the boy this fifty-five-year-old man had once been. Stuffing his face with candyfloss, skipping through puddles with trailing shoelaces.

Buying two tickets from the surly-looking attendant, and concealing their possessions behind a bollard, they climbed upon the brightly painted horses, whose faces were frozen in manic expressions of equine joy. Wurlitzer music chimed out Good King Wenceslas as Alice and Karl rose and fell upon their steeds. One minute into the ride, Alice realised she was grinning from ear to ear, as was her beau.

Well, this is all right, Alice thought as Karl reached across recklessly to squeeze her shoulder. She realised, with a shock of surprise, that she'd never been on horseback. There were just too many things Alice hadn't done; perhaps that would change.

Ten minutes later, feeling more than a little queasy from a combination of candyfloss, glühwein and needless rotation, Alice accepted Karl's gloved hand as she clambered down off her painted steed. They spent a very pleasant thirty minutes walking along the South Bank and then went their separate ways. Karl actually bowed as a socially distant equivalent of a cheek kiss. Alice would have preferred a handshake or even one of those awkward elbow bumps she'd seen Boris Johnson doing on the news.

Walking back to her flat, Alice realised they hadn't arranged a second date. She hadn't really expected to, but still felt a little disappointed that Karl had not seized the initiative. Weren't Germans supposed to be super organised, or was that assumption a bit xenophobic?

It came as a shock of relief therefore, as Alice got home, threw off her heavy coat, scarf, and gloves, to discover that Karl had texted already. What he had written made her laugh out aloud, in an involuntary response that would normally have made her idiotically self-conscious.

Have you ever been to a 1980s roller disco?

Alice had, and she had loved it with a vehemence entirely out of proportion with the reality of rolling round a darkened room wearing a tutu and deely-bobbers. She still had a pair of skates hidden in the back of her wardrobe, assuming they hadn't rusted away or been consumed by moths. Was Karl really suggesting they go roller-skating together? Alice closed her eyes and tried to imagine it. Strangely, the image came quickly into focus and was remarkably convincing.

Karl and Alice whooshed by, arm in arm, emerging from a cloud of dry ice. Alice wore an expression of nervous excitement, Karl remained incongruously serious, as they attempted not to collide with the couple in front of them. Together they circuited a darkened room, illuminated by sweeping lasers, to the sound of 'Hey Mickey' by Toni Basil.

Alice found herself typing furiously.

Of course. And I loved it. What do you have in mind?

She had spent years of her life lost in the mistaken belief that love was a serious endeavour. The world had just revealed to her how inherently ridiculous the pursuit of a soulmate really is.

And Alice was okay with that. As she waited for Karl's reply, she went through to the bedroom, knelt before her walk-in wardrobe, and reached behind the coats. She had to stretch out with the fingers of her left hand.

There it was. The dull, ball-bearing-aided whirl of a rubberised wheel.

She would have to find some WD40.

Duet

Three months into lockdown Stella had settled into a comfortable, and comforting, routine. Stuck in her compact third floor flat in a line of Victorian terraces in West London, she was concentrating on writing songs for her debut album.

Her day began at eight am with coffee and toast and some vocal warm-ups before she kept her voice in shape with a few covers, performed to backing tracks she'd found online. Stella would video some of these for her YouTube channel which gratifyingly had received a spike in subscribers in the last few weeks – she had recently celebrated her ten thousandth follower. Eclectic in taste, her three biggest tracks were Al Green's 'How Can You Mend A Broken Heart', 'No Surprises' by Radiohead and Adele's 'Hello'. Her own songs tended towards the melancholy, particularly since her break-up with boyfriend of the past five years, Tony.

Two weeks ago, as Stella had been preparing to record a version of 'Let's Go Out Tonight', a little-known heartbreaker by cult Scottish band *The Blue Nile*, when she heard a rich, velvety voice from the flat next door, singing something operatic and Italian. Singing remarkably well, despite the accompaniment of an occasional crashing she could only imagine was the sound of a large, clumsy man putting pots and pans away. In part this image was aided by the fact that Stella had a couple of times bumped into her new neighbour a week or so before the pandemic started, both times in the hallway outside their flats.

On the first occasion, the man, in his early fifties and

very overweight, had been struggling upstairs with an armful of plants. From the nearby garden centre, Stella guessed. He'd fought to fish his keys out of his pocket and Stella had been too slow to offer to help. The second time she'd seen Mr Adamson (Stella had seen his name on his mail) he'd been rushing downstairs, immaculately dressed in a tuxedo and white bow tie. Stella had offered 'nice suit', in passing, a daft understatement meant as a genuine compliment. Her neighbour had grinned, taking the comment in the spirit in which it was intended.

Now, listening to Mr Adamson sing, Stella suddenly understood the meaning of the tuxedo – her neighbour was an operatic tenor, presumably on the way to a concert, in the vintage Alfa Romeo she'd seen parked outside.

Now, as she listened to the tenor's aria, a melancholy floating, drifting melody, she later discovered was Donizetti (after much Googling), Stella's initial annoyance that her latest video couldn't be recorded gave way to grudging admiration. Mr Adamson could really sing. Her Googling had not thrown up any famous tenors of that name, so she guessed, like her, he was firmly in the category of gifted amateur, albeit one able to play the kind of gigs that required dress shirt and tails. Someone she had first dismissed as an eccentric old goat was recast in her imagination in an entirely new light.

The following day, Stella heard Mr Adamson doing her own warm-up exercises, a series of rising and falling scales in a variety of keys. She wondered if, like her, he had perfect pitch, or whether he used an app or tuning fork to hit the right starting note. She found herself falling into unison with him, rising and falling in sync with his notes, albeit a register higher. After a few minutes of this, Mr

Adamson seemed to stop mid-scale. Had he heard her? Stella decided she didn't care and finished the set of scales anyway.

Later that afternoon, Stella heard Mr Adamson singing the same Donizetti aria on his balcony. She felt a little too shy to step out there to listen, so she stood behind the billowing curtain in the overheated room and listened to the street applauding his efforts. Even the workmen digging up the street below had downed their tools, Stella could see, peering through her curtains. Of course, she added her own applause to the impromptu audience's.

Suffering as she did from both Crohn's Disease and a mild form of agoraphobia, Stella had scarcely been out for days, but later that evening, she decided to venture out onto her own balcony, which she mostly used for drying laundry. Pushing the rack of skirts and skimpy tops to one side, she closed her eyes, leaned against the doorframe, and sang 'If You Go Away', the English lyrics of the magnificently over the top Jacques Brel song she'd played on constant rotation in the week following her break-up. The street outside was quiet and Stella didn't really care if anyone was listening or not.

Halfway through the song, a strange low descant seemed to join her voice. Stella realised it was Mr Adamson, humming a low accompaniment, above which her own voice floated, like a seabird drifting upon a dark ocean. It was strangely self-effacing, given what Stella knew his voice was capable of, but it really added a powerful underscore to the song. After the last 'if you go away…' faded, a rapturous applause followed and Stella opened her eyes to see, with astonishment, a small gathering of people on the balconies across the street, or on the pavements below. All were looking up at her and clapping. Stella turned to applaud Mr Adamson, who was standing beaming broadly on his own tiny balcony.

"Take a bow, my dear, you were magnificent," he said, making Stella's day.

Thus, they finally broke the ice between them and began chatting, daily, between their balconies, about music, performance, lyrics, work, and many more unrelated topics. Mr Adamson gifted her one of his plants, a small rosebush. In return, Stella loaned him the cookery book in which she'd found the recipe for cheese scones, after he commented on the delicious smell wafting out of her kitchen window (she later passed over a Tupperware box containing three scones).

They began to duet, across their balconies, on pop songs, after Stella confessed that she couldn't read music. "What a shame," Mr Adamson said. "I have the perfect Donizetti duet." Stella was flattered but bemused by the very idea of singing opera. After all, she had no formal training in such music and knew little or nothing about it.

"Hush dear, you're a natural," her neighbour said, "but we can stick to Simon and Garfunkel if you prefer."

They essayed 'Bridge over Troubled Water', 'The Boxer' and 'America' before moving on to Cole Porter, 'Something Stupid' and 'Body and Soul'. Stella didn't try to foist anything too modern on Mr Adamson, whose popular music tastes didn't extend much into this millennium, and Mr Adamson didn't try to push any Italian opera on Stella, although she loved hearing him sing it.

Like Stella, seemingly like a lot of people in the transient neighbourhood of Earls Court, Mr Adamson lived alone, and presumably he was also having a hard time with this period of self-isolation, being a confirmed bachelor (Stella suspected he was gay and that there was tragedy in his romantic history, but she didn't pry). Knocking on his door to offer him a cup of tea might be forbidden but they could at least converse across their respective balconies, in words, and via their shared love of song.

Then, one day in early June, the duets stopped. Stella no longer saw Mr Adamson around and she wondered if he had moved away, or taken advantage of things opening up a little, to go and visit friends or relatives. It was only when she heard unfamiliar voices from the apartment next door that she decided to investigate. Venturing out into the hall, she tiptoed to the door of flat 7 and listened intently. A male and a female voice could be heard, talking in low tones.

"I guess the rest can go to charity."

"Whatever. Look, do you want the filing cabinet?"

Before knowing quite why, Stella knocked on the door. When it was opened, Stella found herself face to face with a large-boned and rather plain girl in her mid-twenties who was clearly Mr Adamson's daughter, a fact that was both incontrovertible and surprising. The likeness unsettled Stella a little and made her fumble her words. She backed away to an appropriate distance.

"Em, I'm... sorry to disturb. I'm from next door. I haven't seen Mr Adamson around. Is he okay?"

As soon as Stella finished her question, the answer was evident from the girl's expression. The girl, Sophie, re-vealed that her father had suffered breathing difficulties in the middle of the night a couple of weeks previously and had been taken by ambulance to hospital and there dia-gnosed with Covid-19. He was put on a ventilator and treated assiduously by his nurses but died after several days of struggling on life support.

Adamson's funeral had been held yesterday. Today Sophie and her fiancé Mike were going through his possessions and deciding what was to be done with them. Hearing this, Stella felt a strange sense of dislocation – her last memory of Mr Adamson was of him in full voice, belting out a rendition of Amazing Grace that drew an audience of several dozen wildly applauding neighbours and passers-by. To imagine those fine lungs choked and ruined by a virus in a matter of ten days, seemed bizarre and frightening. True, she had heard some coughing now and again through the wall between their flats, but it hadn't seemed unusual or life-threatening.

Stella found herself ending the conversation rather abruptly, with a promise to keep in touch (Sophie and Mike had some notions about holding a memorial concert for their father and perhaps Stella could sing). Sophie and Mike seemed lovely and said they recognised her from the YouTube links their father had sent them. The had been meaning to knock on her door to thank her for enriching their father's last days. Stella felt touched but a little embarrassed too. It wasn't as if she'd got to know her neighbour especially well, save for their shared love of music. Nevertheless, she agreed to contribute to the memorial and then decided to pay him a personal tribute.

Of course, there was only one composer she could choose to celebrate her neighbour. As she couldn't read music and had little practical knowledge of singing in an operatic style, Stella set about learning new techniques and memorising a piece of Donizetti by ear. It was a beautiful and sad aria from his opera about Lucia of Lammermoor and involved only a limited range of vocal pyrotechnics. Nevertheless, Stella took a full two weeks to reach a standard she felt able to submit to public scrutiny and even then, on just the first three and a half minutes of the piece.

She set up her phone on the balcony, propped up against some books and plugged in her vocal microphone. Then she started the video recording and said the following:

"This song is for my neighbour, Mr Adamson, who sadly passed away from Coronavirus a few weeks ago. I wanted to perform a piece by one of his favourite composers and although I'm not an operatic soprano, I'll try my best to do it justice."

Then she began to sing, filling her lungs with life-giving air, forcing it through her straining vocal cords, letting the notes resonate deeply in her chest. Stella sang like she never had before, and people stopped in the street and squinted up against the sunlight. She could still feel Adamson's eyes on her, somehow, although she didn't turn to look at his balcony, for fear of seeing him there, or for sorrow at his absence.

Stella's high, pure voice cut through traffic and building work sounds, it stopped people in their tracks and echoed in the terraced streets. Stella sang of tragic loss and regret and her voice bore testimony to her loss, and the world's.

A Clearing

Running saved me. It sounds hyperbolic but I wouldn't still be here, engaged in the banal act of assembling an Ikea bookcase (or avoiding doing so, if I'm honest), if it weren't for the simple act of putting one foot in front of another, at speed, through the English countryside.

When my marriage fell apart, it prompted a period of retrenchment and isolation. My wife and I had been gnawing away at one another for years, our arguments increasingly futile, repetitive, and vitriolic. She wanted me to be more decisive, to take more responsibility or, at the very least, to appreciate how much slack she picked up in our partnership. I wanted her to relax more, fret less, let go of past failures and accept that we will never achieve more than a fraction of our overweening ambition.

In effect, we were saying to one another 'I wish you could be a different kind of person'. There was of course, a ready solution to this intransigent dilemma – we split up and found other people. Diane met a young man whose online fabric retail business was booming in a way my career as a novelist clearly was not. I found someone else to spend quality time with – myself.

We sold the house and divided the proceeds, I took the campervan we rarely used, she kept the car. We went our separate ways, Diane to move immediately in with Masood, which I smugly knew was a mistake she'd greatly regret, me to a folly on the Kentish coast, a ramshackle barn I'd decided to renovate, whilst living in the van. I think the audacity of this decision is in part explained by my desire to show that I could have been the man of action and responsibility that Diane had always wanted, as if this would somehow prove a sweet revenge, rather than an onerous and expensive ordeal.

Nine months later, I'd project managed the three-hundred-year-old barn, which overlooked a ragged crescent of seashore, into a barely watertight bolt hole. Storms and seasons did what they could to reduce my ambitions to rubble but, watching my savings dwindle away to nothing, I finally moved into my new home as autumn began to give way to the inevitable chill of winter. Only the bathroom and one bedroom were complete but at least I didn't feel like a vagrant squatting in an unheated van at the edge of a building site. The workmen went about their days, nodding amiably to me as I went about mine – answering long-avoided emails and trying to plot out a new book.

One problem immediately presented itself. I'd successfully distracted myself from the depressing realities of my life but now that the house was becoming habitable, memory and regret moved in with me. They were not convivial housemates.

When I needed to escape the solitude and the seething tumult of memories and regrets, I'd go for a run, rediscovering an activity from my youth I'd long abandoned. I started with the occasional jog along the coastal path, adding a mile or two each week. My first run ended with me collapsing onto the pebbles covering the beach with lungs ablaze and heart thundering like a herd of rhinos. I coughed compulsively for over an hour – the detritus of eight years of juvenile smoking catching up with me. My bad habits ended with my marriage. Or perhaps I should say that new ones took their place.

From this first agonising jog, I gradually built up my

stamina until I could manage seven or eight miles in the space of an hour. Then, looking for variety, I discovered a drove path leading up into the hills and skirting a small patch of woodland I felt immediately drawn to. It had the evocative name of Weirwynd Wood and was evidently listed in the Domesday book (or so a helpful tourist information plaque informed me). A stile and finger post invited me in, and I clambered over and quickly lost myself in a crisscrossing network of paths and streams ribboning their way down the hillside to the sea below.

From the forest, the perpetual wash of surf was mixed with the rustling of the leaf canopy and the grace notes of birdsong, ceaseless and varied. On that first forest run, I could name very few of the birds that perched in the branches above me as I ran, but after just a few weeks I knew them by their melodies. They were my unseen companions and I even tried to mimic their music in a faltering whistle, to no great effect.

After six months, satisfied that my home was watertight and windowed and leaving the workmen to electrify, plaster and plumb, I began to take longer and longer morning runs. In part this was to get away from the incessant hammering and drilling, as well as the necessity of a small talk that didn't come naturally to me. The builders came from as far away as Latvia and Lesotho, but I didn't want to become their friend and couldn't abide their well-meaning but banal questions. So, I was a writer – wow. Where did I get my ideas? What was I working on now? Would I have written anything they'd know? I had answers for all of the above – from the junkyard of my memories, a middling, derivative thriller, and no, I have not – but I knew these would sound glib, dismissive and self-loathing. Instead of failing to connect, I absented myself.

I kid myself that these daily long runs were building towards something – perhaps I'd enter a marathon or undertake some sort of adventure – running the coast of Britain, perhaps. I told myself that although I wasn't writing my book, and hadn't really worked effectively for weeks, my subconscious was laying the groundwork. Ideas were percolating, plot lines taking shape. In truth, I was running from the tyranny of a blank screen and avoiding my agent's calls.

As autumn gave way to winter, and the trees of the forest shed their crisped parchment leaves, I ran with memories gasping to catch up with me. The way Diane would spontaneously massage my shoulders after a long day at my desk. The window box garden I surprised her with when she returned from a business trip overseas. Drinking wine and listening to Joni Mitchell, making love in the attic in a nest of dusty old blankets.

One morning I tore open the mail, nodding a terse thank you to Keith, the local postman, as he wobbled away on his bike. Inside a crisp white A4 envelope was a sheaf of papers, signed and expensively letterheaded. Brickman, Lewis and Partners. Decree Nisi. So, this was it. I'd known it was coming. We'd decided not to wait for the formalities before disentangling our lives but somehow seeing it in print made my knees weaken and my chest tighten with anxiety. I considered having a drink, but I'd always told myself that so long as I didn't start morning drinking, I was still a civilised member of the human race, no matter how attenuated my circumstances became. I laced up my running shoes, choosing the Saucony trail pair I'd just worn in. I had to run. Nothing else could take me away from the spiralling sadness beginning to fill me.

Almost angrily, I set off along the coastal path, ignoring puddles and patches of mud, revelling in the fact that I could just splash and slosh through them. It felt like a minor superpower at times, this ability to race through terrain hikers and dog walkers would pick their way around. I loved the fact that my legs were soon streaked with mud up to the knees. It didn't bother me that my feet were soaking wet. I wanted this run to be extreme, to take me to a place where the physical intensity of my movement obliterated the clamour my head. I achieved this about four miles in, when pausing to gasp for breath at a familiar gate, I had to decide whether to turn back or head up the footpath to Weirwynd Wood. As I weighed the pros and cons, something cold and wet touched my cheek. For an absurd moment, I thought it might be a tear, until I realise that it was something rarer still – a snowflake. I looked up and a swirl of flakes was falling from a sky that had whitened without me noticing.

The weather made my decision for me – it would be wonderful to run in the forest in the snow. I climbed the fence and headed up the tussocky slope to my left, making for the gnarled nest of bare trees that decorated the hillside. As I got closer, breathing laboured but refreshed by the newly icy air, the trees looked somehow forbidding and inviting at once – a challenge and a promise of the kind of intensity I was seeking.

As I squeezed through the narrow gap in the fence surrounding the wood, I saw that the snow had already salted the ground with a thin layer that was quickly accumulating, obscuring the chilled earth and mouldering leaves beneath. Seasons don't so much supplant one another here as crossfade. The winter would preserve some of those autumn leaves well into spring and impetuous crocuses would start appearing through the frost on the sun-facing slopes in a matter of weeks.

I ran the now-familiar outer loop of the forest, splashing through the streams and watching my breath gust out around me, as if I were generating the mist that was beginning to settle on the hillside. I dug into the forest, following my instinct, and soon found myself in a region I'd not visited before, where the trees thinned out into a clearing at the top of a small rise. A horseshoe of oaks and maples faced me, a large, gnarly yew in the centre, its corded trunk twisted into a profusion of branches. I slowed to a walk, catching my breath, emerging from my own cloud. I walked up to the yew and felt its ancient bark. I'd read somewhere that yews are amongst our oldest trees. I guessed that this one might be hundreds, even thousands of years old. Carved into its thick bark were dozens of letters and dates. Carved initials, hearts, and declarations. Josie 1975. B & L '22. Others that could no longer be deciphered – the decades had eradicated their promises.

Two letters were carved inside a near-perfect circle, decorated with diamond patterns. An E and an S. I guessed these were the initials of the artist but what he or she had meant by their handiwork, I couldn't guess. Perhaps simply to assert that 'I was here' in an age before everyday identity was immortalised, fixed, and copied endlessly in a digital realm. ES had no web presence, but he had this.

I took a swig from the bottle of water I carried with me, turned, and ran back down the slope, taking a different route, with the intention of emerging on the high edge of the wood. But somehow, I found myself looping alongside an impenetrable hedge and back down, over a slope of tangled roots, then taking a sudden turn through a dense thicket and back into... the same clearing I'd just left. I laughed at my error and decided to retrace my footsteps and leave Weirwynd the way I entered it. The snow was now lying two inches deep and making everything look different from how it had upon my arrival. Boughs dipped low with their burden and there were no footsteps to follow.

Nevertheless, I reversed the sequence of turns I'd taken to get here – left, right, right, left, over the fallen log and finally.... no, that's not right. I'd reached a fork in the pathway. I must have missed it on my way into the wood, but I now realised I had no idea which way to go.

Just then a muffled sound could be heard, its source apparently some way down the left path – a girlish laugh, perhaps, although it had been brief. That decided it, I'd run that way and if I met a local, so much the better – he or she could redirect me if I'd gone astray. I felt the first finger of a chill grip me – the sweat cooling against my skin. The thin jacket I'd worn was now completely ineffectual against a rising wind that blew directly into my face, swirling flakes up my nostrils as I ran. I'd normally have enjoyed the extremity of it all, but something felt wrong, and not at all entertaining.

Surely, I'd been running for far too long now. No more peals of laughter sounded, and I met nobody, but it didn't matter – I should definitely have reached the edge of the woods by now. And yet, the gently curving path ahead of me, though encouragingly wide, seemed impossibly long.

Had I somehow got turned round? Perhaps I should head back to that junction. My forehead felt cold, and I could sense a headache coming on. Why had I chosen to wear a thin cap instead of a proper woolly hat? I turned and looked back, just in time to catch a hint of movement, a rustling in the underbrush.

"Hello?" I called, not expecting a reply from what was probably just a badger or fox.

The trail of my footprints was already filling in with fresh snow. How quickly the world erases us, how indifferently our flickering lives register against the centuries, I thought, filing the phrase away for future use. I took a few long, icy breaths to calm myself and ran on. It didn't matter which way I was heading now. I had to keep moving. Something was gripping me, something familiar I hadn't felt since the drive south after the separation. I felt fear – a kind of grinding terror that everything which made sense was slipping away. As if the reality I'd built was tissue thin and I might tear through it with one ill-timed stumble.

I came to a narrowing in the path and squeezed between two trees, only to realize that the tree to my right was the now-familiar yew tree with the carved initials. I was back in the clearing again. This time I didn't laugh. Something was happening here – either inside me or beyond my understanding. I couldn't decide which option was more terrifying. I backed away from the yew, into the centre of the clearing and looked up into its spindly branches, which stretched into a seemingly impenetrable nest about twenty feet above my head.

Climb. The word seemed spoken aloud, but I knew its source was within my head. A young female voice, gently insistent. Should I? I used to love climbing trees and besides, I might be able to see out over the canopy and find my way out of this green and white labyrinth. As I took the first handhold, I realized that the birds had stopped singing. Huddled against the snow or holding their breath? Waiting to see if I would dare venture into their domain, perhaps.

My muscles were aching from the run, and the cumulative effect of the many months of manual labour and long, soul-cleansing runs. Nevertheless, I found the nub of a cut branch low enough to get my leg over and pulled myself up with both hands until I flopped over the lowest limb. I was an ungainly climber, very different from the monkey-like child I'd once been. Each tentative step onto a higher branch now came with an inner admonishment – this is dangerous.

Quickly though, I was high enough to grab hold of the lower branches of the tangled nest that crowned the tree. I must have been about fifteen feet from the ground, but it felt like a hundred. I stretched a foot out but couldn't quite make the necessary next step. I'd have to jump. This was stupid. I should climb down. If I fell, I'd surely break something, and nobody would find me until morning.

I leapt, slipped, and slapped my knee against the trunk, grabbing serpentine branches to arrest my fall. Pain flared under the patella. I would pay for this misadventure. My misstep only made me more determined, and I stretched up with both hands and pulled myself into the heart of the tree.

Unfortunately, I was several feet yet from being able to see out over the treetops. I stopped to catch my breath and watch it billow out before me. For a second, it almost seemed to take the shape of a face, a female one, then it dissipated. A trick of the light, or of the dark, for certain.

Three or four minutes later, I had shinned up the next stout section of trunk, and was holding on for dear life, as the tree gently swayed back and forth over the forest canopy.

I stepped out onto a limb, braced myself, and looked. I was right in the middle of the forest, but I could see the road beyond the southern perimeter, and a thin blue-grey line of sea beyond the distant cliffs, although the whole scene was blurred by the incessant snow, tumbling down from a white sky turning pink along the horizon. It must be close to four o'clock; nightfall wasn't far off. Encouraged that I now knew where I was going, I was about to begin the challenging descent when I froze. I'd felt a tiny puff of warmth at the back of my neck. Wet warmth. Something unmistakable – breath.

I span round, but nothing was there. I listened. There was a slight gasp, as of indrawn air. Was someone holding his or her breath – someone other than me? Of course, I was alone in the tree, my imagination running rife against the background hum of nameless fear, the primal, animal sense of foreboding we can feel in wild, natural places.

I began stiffly to climb down, being especially careful to have three solid foot- or handholds, before choosing the fourth. I made it back down to the nest of branches and was squinting down through the boughs, choosing a safe route down, when something moved below, something pale and oval – a face, with straw-blonde hair half-hidden under a lacy bonnet and eyes stark, wide, and terrifyingly green. Skin almost translucently white, like the snow. A sorrowful stare, moving behind a trellis of branches and then slipping away into darkness.

I panicked, knowing instinctively that the person

watching me was not quite of this world. My left foot slid off a limb caked with snow and green moss and I thudded down onto an unyielding bough, grasping blindly for a branch. The one I grabbed broke entirely away from the nest, through which I inevitably tumbled, crashing to the ground on my upper back and shoulders and rolling onto my side. A spike of pain and a cold stab of fear suffused me. I opened my eyes, curled in a foetal position among the roots of the yew and found I was still grasping the broken branch.

But when I looked at it, planning to use it as a crutch to lift myself to my feet, I discovered it wasn't a branch. It was a bone – probably a shinbone – grey-green with lichen and the dirt of ages. It was then that I must have passed out, the last sound I heard a ripple of girlish laughter.

"Ah, he's coming to now, poor lad."

A kindly voice insinuated itself into my consciousness and I opened my eyes to find a stout, concerned woman in her sixties dabbing my brow with a warm cloth, soaked in something stringently herbal. I started instinctively.

"Don't worry dear, you're amongst friends now," my nurse said.

I turned my head, saw a sideways confusion that resolved into a cosy cottage interior – a slightly chintzy attic bedroom, with a sloped ceiling on one side. A familiar, stick-thin figure tottered into the room from the top of a staircase carrying a tray loaded with tea things. The village postman – Keith – out of uniform but instantly recognisable from his gait. He winked, his angular, weathered face mischievous.

"I told you running in all weathers wasn't good for

you," he admonished, setting down the tray. "This is Margery, my wife."

I sat up a little against plump cushions and attempted a smile of gratitude, although I was both bewildered and in an alarming amount of pain.

"Here, take these," Margery said, popping two pills into my mouth and letting me wash them down with a sip of water from a glass she held out. "Painkillers – got them for my back. They work wonders."

I didn't bother to work through the sense, or lack of it, of swallowing the mystery medication – I was in too much agony not to comply. And wonderfully, within twenty minutes, the pain did lift, and I was able to sit up against the pillows.

Over a cup of tea (I am something of a caffeine addict, so this intervention was much appreciated) Keith explained how I'd come to end up in his spare bedroom. He'd been cycling back from his rounds, eager to get back to the warmth of home, when he'd seen something unusual – what looked like a body slumped against a hawthorn hedge on the fringes of the forest.

I stopped him there. "Did you say on the edge of the forest?"

"That's right," he explained. "Where the burn vanishes into the culvert. "Just off the road."

"And how was I lying?" I asked. Keith frowned as if this was rather beside the point.

"You were sort of sitting up, in that bit that overhangs. Were you trying to get out of the snow?"

I shook my head, baffled. I'd fainted under the tree, hadn't I?

"Anyways," Keith continued. "I thought you were a

goner. You were still breathing but shivering all over and not responding to me at all. I called Marge and she drove down, and we got you back up here in the car. Doc's on the way but he's coming from Margate – only the coastal road's open. It's fair coming down out there."

Margery then elaborated on my recovery, an improvised process involving an electric blanket, hot water bottles and a balaclava. Apparently, I'd been delirious for a couple of hours before finally falling into a comfortable sleep. It was now nine o'clock and I gratefully accepted the Cloughs' offer to stay the night. After a hot bath that finally thawed the last remnants of the cold from my bones, I sat down to dinner with Keith and Margery. As his wife ladled hot stew onto my plate, Keith suddenly bolted, long-limbed, from the room. He returned holding something silvery.

"I nearly forgot… you were clutching this in your hand. I could barely get your fingers off of it."

He dangled a piece of jewellery at me – a silver locket, antique, on a thin chain. I took it, quite sure I'd seen it before but uncertain where. On its front, the locket had an unusual design – a snake coiled in a circle, eating its tail.

"Ouroboros," Margery said, surprising only me.

Keith nodded proudly. "She does the crossword every day. Is she a relative of yours?"

Keith was indicating the locket. I pressed the tiny catch on its side and opened it up. Inside was a blurry photograph – the defiant face of a young girl, fair-haired and pale, with a penetrating gaze.

"I don't know her," I lied.

It was several days until I felt well enough, and the roads were clear enough, for me to venture into town. Keith drove me home the afternoon after my accident. The barn, although watertight, now proved itself to be far from airtight, as icy winds howled through the boards of the angled ceiling. I had the same dream for three nights in a row – I'm running in the wood and a girl (or perhaps two girls) are running after me and laughing. When I turn around, I see nobody, only my own footsteps fading away into nothingness. Sometimes it felt more like a memory than a dream.

My head was ablaze with questions and I was almost feverish with the need to know more about the wood and its uncanny inhabitant. More prosaically, I knew I had to report the mysterious shinbone to the local police. I had two house calls to make.

Walking into town to exercise my aching limbs, I wandered into Remington's Antiques House, a cornucopia of ancient tat whose window I'd examined several times since I moved to the village, although I'd never been in. A bell rang above the door as I entered a musty, dusty storehouse of forgotten things.

An ornate dresser was heaped with mother-of-pearl inlaid jewellery boxes. A chaise longue was the resting place for a pyramid of greying books. A stack of old tennis racquets leaned against an ornate Japanese screen. In pride of place was a fully rampant stuffed bear, wearing a lady's hat, wide-brimmed and decorated with purple paper roses.

One the far side of the room, lit by a shaft of tobacco-stained sunlight, was a glass counter under which sparkled a dragon's horde of bangles, necklaces, tiaras and cufflinks. Behind this was the round, jovial face of a woman I'd passed in the street several times and smiled back at.

"You'll be the new tenant at Forgehead Farm," she

said, extending a ruddy hand.

"Owner actually," I said. "For my sins. I'm sorry, I don't know…"

"Jill Remington, daughter of the famous Bill," she replied.

I assumed I was supposed to know who the famous Bill was but didn't ask for clarification.

"I've been meaning to come in for ages," I lied. "I found something in the wood, and I wondered if you might be able to shed some light on it."

I felt a flicker of hesitation about handing the locket over, then a suggestion of breath on my neck (but it was merely a two-bar heater with a fan, stationed nearby on a pile of old magazines).

Jill studied the locket, pushing a pair of reading glasses further up her nose. She didn't speak for almost a minute and I began to wonder if something was wrong. I was about to clear my throat, but abruptly, Jill straightened and announced:

"You're in luck. As well as running this place, I'm the chairperson of the village historical society, and I know exactly who that is. Her name is Elizabeth Bailey."

Jill then proceeded to tell me an extraordinary story. Elizabeth has been the youngest daughter of the Hedgecombe family, who had owned Forgehead Estate. The one-hundred-acre estate had once included the farmhouse whose haybarn I was currently renovating. The manor on the Northern side of the hill, beyond the forest, was in fact still under the ownership of a branch of the venerable Hedgecombe dynasty. Their lineage went back at least four centuries.

Elizabeth had lived in the manor with her two older

brothers, mother, father, and several enormous deerhounds. The Hedgecombe daughter was born around 1895, Jill thought, although some of the parish birth records appeared to be incomplete in that period. What could be gleaned from the meticulously maintained household ledgers is that, as well as the usual transient servants and old retainers, the family obtained the services of a French au pair and live-in tutor around the turn of the century, Madame Bouvier. The Madame brought with her from Epernay, her own daughter Elodie, just two years Elizabeth's junior. The innovative notion was that the girls would be co-educated by Madame Bouvier and learn one another's languages and cultures.

The two became fast friends, and in their teens scarcely separable. So much so that when they were finally separated, following Madame Bouvier's dismissal for instilling unwholesome morals in the girls, and an unnamed outrage the local newspapers would not elaborate upon, both girls wept for days. Two weeks later, as Madame Bouvier packed her things in a local guesthouse, with the plan of returning home to France, her daughter Elodie vanished. She was never seen again, without even a letter to explain her whereabouts or any witnesses to shed light on the disappearance. The village feared the worst and to their credit, the Hedgecombes paid for a thorough search involving the police, coastguard and every able-bodied man and woman in the locality. It was to no avail.

"And what happened to Elizabeth?" I asked.

Jill sighed, as if delivering recent bad news.

"I'm afraid she went quite mad, had to be committed and caught the Spanish flu from a fellow inmate. She died the day before her sixteenth birthday."

I shivered, despite the heater liberally roasting my rear nearby. I looked at my watch, hastily thanked Jill for her information and headed uphill to the little local police station.

The following morning a cherry-picker was arranged, and a screen assembled around the yew tree. I was allowed inside to direct the forensic team and the arborealist they had called upon to oversee the removal of Elodie Bouvier's remains from the tree. Photos were taken of the position of the bones, which I found surprising – were the police really going to investigate a century-old tragedy?

Also at hand was a well-dressed and shivering aristocratic man in his fifties. He introduced himself as Alasdair Hedgecombe, and he was the great, great grandson of Elizabeth's elder brother Michael.

"I felt it fitting to draw a line under this… smear upon our family. I believe my ancestors did this poor girl a grave disservice."

I wasn't exactly sure what he meant until the forensic team carried the bones down from the yew and laid them upon a tarpaulin. They had also found an empty bottle of a popular opiate, once used to alleviate gout, and quite lethal if drunk in a large enough dose. To think that a vibrant soul now amounted to little more than this collection of forgotten fragments seemed deeply sad. What made the tears come, however, were the words Elodie had written in her faltering English on the scrap of miraculously preserved paper in her pinafore pocket.

My heart lies here because my love will not. Elizabeth you were my beloved and if they don't accept, is the world's loss. I will always be your cherie.

51

I remembered a detail Jill had told me about the ouroboros design on the locket, now clearly a love token.

"The Victorians we're obsessed with symbols," she had said, "and you need to be careful how you decode them. Nowadays we see the snake eating its tail as an emblem of futility, of something sinister, of doom even. At the turn of the century it meant unending love, the circle of life, an eternal pledge."

I didn't give the locket to Jill, or to the police. I wear it around my neck whenever I run in the Weirwynd Wood, as I am no longer afraid to do. I wear it to remind me that some loves never end, even though mine did. I wear it to remember Elodie and Elizabeth, to grant them the forgiveness they were never allotted in life.

No living relative locatable, the remains of Elodie Bouvier were interred in the Hedgecombe family plot, within sight of the house and the woods they loved to explore together. Elizabeth's grave was within touching distance of Elodie's. The burial was a fitting and graceful ceremony, attended by a handful of villagers, including Keith, Margery, and Jill, and presided over by Michael Hedgecombe, who I noted was accompanied by his husband Louie. I now realised why the tragic suicide of his ancestors' *amour fou* meant so much to him. I wasn't entirely clear why it meant so much to me.

Except, delirium and hallucinations notwithstanding, I somehow believed I knew Elizabeth and Elodie. I had looked into the deep green eyes of one, felt the other's breath. Elodie had entrusted me with her keepsake, and I believed Elizabeth had saved my life by bringing me, somehow, to the edge of the wood.

As I watched a light smirr drift over the graves of the

two girls, I knew that, touching as the ceremony had been, the thwarted lovers didn't really lie here, in the family grave-yard. Well, not the part of them that mattered. Their souls were surely still laughing, chasing one another forever round the maze of little lanes around Weirwynd Wood. I ran with them, and with my own ghosts, and we were at peace.

Antbots

Antbots all over my workshop, in various stages of assembly. I'm drowning in antennae and mandibles. Endless repairs and custom jobs. People love their antbots like they love their pets. We've taken on three new technicians: Antonella, Anthony, and Anton.

Antonella's the most skilled. She grinds micro-lenses for an ant's mind. Photons: focused, diffracted, reflected through porous nanocarbon, a quantum computer interpreting it all. Antbots are uniquely identical – individuals focused upon contributing to the good of the colony, AKA us – their human overlords.

I watch Antonella at work and realise with a shock of inevitability that we're engineering our replacements.

Antbots will inherit the Earth.

The Pact

"Did you ever get to the point where you thought… I can't go on?" Suzy asked Karl.

"Yes. More and more," he replied, "and it's tougher to come up with decent reasons to keep going."

Friends thirty years, Suzy and Karl had met at university, when Karl was completing his final year in English Literature and Suzy was starting her engineering course. He was 21, she was 18. Life seemed full of possibilities – how could it not? It was the late 1990s and spirit of optimism infused the country when Tony Blair, the upbeat new Labour Prime Minister seemed to offer a real alternative to the "me first" Toryism that had blighted their childhoods. Of course, disillusionment rapidly set in, both in politics and Suzy and Karl's prospects.

Karl found his literature degree virtually valueless in the jobs market. Having been asked by umpteen friends and family if he would become a teacher, Karl took the path of least resistance and got a teaching qualification. This led him to a sinkhole school in Glasgow and a job that often left him in tears at the end of a long week of being called a cunt to his face by twelve-year olds. He'd hoped to write a novel but after several false starts, Karl had to admit he probably didn't have it in him.

Suzy got a good job in an engineering firm, working on an offshore power project in Orkney. However, the Japanese financiers pulled out and half the workforce was laid off, Suzy included. Next, she fell into an emotionally abusive relationship with an architect who ground down her self-confidence and left her with an eating disorder and entirely reasonable commitment issues.

Meanwhile, Karl endured a succession of unsatisfying relationships, including one with a married woman which went nowhere. Then Karl was arrested for agreeing to hold stolen goods for an old school friend who promised to return for the designer watches but never did. Karl spent three months in prison, the severe sentence probably due to the fact that Karl was black, his lawyer ruefully admitted.

To celebrate his thirtieth birthday, Suzy and Karl got tattoos, their subjects chosen by one another, based on nicknames. This is why his left buttock sported a smiley lollipop while Suzy's midriff was decorated with the face of a werewolf.

By late 2020, Karl was pushing forty and Suzy, childless and regretful, was having problems convincing her sterile boyfriend Alan to adopt. Rather than commit to this once-shared goal, Alan broke up with Suzy on her forty-sixth birthday. Suzy ran to Karl. They shared a couple of bottles of wine, a bed, and their latest disaster stories.

"Do you remember our pact?" Suzy said.

"I was hoping you'd forgotten," he replied. "We were joking, weren't we?"

"I don't think we were, Karl. I'd never joke about something like that."

Karl sighed and turned to face Suzy in bed. She seemed flush with something between excitement and madness.

"Well, I guess we'd better get on with it," he said.

Eight months went by and it was never mentioned again, let alone acted upon. Then something happened to each of them that pushed them over the proverbial edge.

Suzy discovered a lump on her breast that, after examination, turned out to be malignant. Karl's mother died, tumbling down the stairs in her sheltered home and breaking her neck. He had not been to visit her for four months. Karl and Suzy called one another at practically the same moment, and they came to an agreement.

"I think it's time," Karl said.

"I agree," Suzy replied. "Will you pick me up?"

"Sure," he answered, as if arranging a delightful day trip. "4pm, after I've finished my marking."

Here they stood, on the bridge they'd driven to in Karl's clapped-out campervan, watching the sun set over a tumultuous, raging river. The Coronavirus summer in which each of them had been on lockdown alone, communicating only on Zoom and by text message, filled moments like this with a beautiful sense of freedom. However, for Karl and Suzy, it was just too little, too late.

They waited, holding one another for warmth, watching the torrential flow, until sunset gave way to dusk, then to windswept, rainy darkness. Karl took his umbrella down; the wind kept blowing it inside out. The rain came down with biblical violence.

"I'm getting cold, let's do it. "

No cars coming and no pedestrians in sight. They climbed over the handrail and stood in the little gutter on the far side, holding hands, as the river raged fifty feet below.

"It's now or never," Karl said.

Suzy nodded. "Three... two... one..."

They jumped. The moment of falling seemed to stretch like caramel, or tar... before the icy tumult took them, feet first, and prepared to swallow.

The terms of the pact were clear. If they both survived this moment, then it meant they were clearly meant to struggle on. If either of them died, the other would then commit suicide. If both of them perished then, so be it. The river would decide their fates.

The dark currents tried to drag them apart, but Karl and Suzy held on tight, as they were spun and rinsed, floated, and bobbed down the dark watercourse, past gnarled trees, harboured boats, darkened cottages, eventually breaking the surface after a seeming eternity of tumbling and twisting in the unrelenting water. Karl felt a rock scrape his back – it would leave an everlasting scar. He stretched out, reflexively grabbing a branch, and pulling them both into the shelter of a tiny spit of sand, beneath willow trees.

They were alive. Freezing cold, teeth chattering, bodies aching, numb and yet strangely elated as they stumbled back to the car.

"Well, that's that then," said Karl as they grabbed towels from the back seat. It paid to be prepared.

"I guess it is," Suzy said, with a smile so radiant, Karl almost mistook it for the dawn.

A Cork on the Ocean

Margaret McLeod, as she sometimes still thought of herself, sat in her Wagon-Lit sleeping compartment aboard the Orient Express, wondering if she'd have someone to share it with. A deep sadness had come over her, a feeling that she was rootless and adrift – a cork bobbing upon the ocean of history.

Margaret, or as she was known professionally, Mata, felt that it was time to settle down somewhere, although where she couldn't say. She no longer felt welcome in Paris. Recent reviews of her *Moulin Rouge* show were middling. It was true she had begun to put on a little weight, and that fashion had moved away from the exoticism of her Javanese dances, but the mean-spirited fashion in which the critics turned on her was shocking. These men, and they were inevitably men, seemed to view her sensuality, no, let us be frank, her sexuality, as a threat. Margaret was certain Isadora had never had to put up with this. She must get around to writing to her.

Three loud bangs issued from the hallway. Margaret popped her head out, in time to see a conductor chasing two small boys down the aisle. The boys, a string of Chinese firecrackers trailing behind them, collided with a sharp-suited young man who crouched to scold them and apologise to the conductor.

His accent was perhaps Eastern-European. "I told you not to light those indoors," he said, confiscating the offending fireworks and ushering his charges into his compartment. Before he closed the door, the man tipped his hat to her. Margaret wondered if she'd see her debonair fellow passenger in the dining car later, hopefully minus the little saboteurs. Dammit – why couldn't she stop thinking about sex for one minute? The conductor strode back down the passage, offering a *désolé madame* in passing. Madame! She had until recently been a mademoiselle.

Margaret sat back amongst Wagon-Lit luxury, wondering which evening dress to wear. She settled upon the Chanel number a long-forgotten admirer had bought her. Poor thing had probably thought this was an extraordinary gesture. In truth, half of Margaret's wardrobe had been gifted, and even her Orient Express ticket to Constantinople had been the final token of a now-dissolved romance. Hand-me-downs and keepsakes, that was what her life had become.

Stop it! Margaret scolded herself. She was becoming a real moaning Minnie. She took a quick sponge bath in the little porcelain basin and dressed for dinner, donning long white gloves, pearls and one of the fascinators she'd hand-crafted. This evening they would arrive in Budapest and she'd have to decide whether to get off to go and meet the Hungarian Minister of the Interior who'd sneaked her a backstage note three weeks ago or remain on the train as far as Constanta. She did want to see the Carpathian Mountains and the idea of clearing her head by the Black Sea held much appeal. Margaret decided that by bedtime, she would have chosen her point of embarkation.

The dining car was almost full, and Margaret felt uncharacteristically shy. She wondered how many of the passengers recognised her – surely most of the French would. For perhaps the first time in her life, she felt an overwhelming desire to be anonymous –

"Mademoiselle, I must apologise for the racket

earlier."

Of course, it was her handsome near neighbour.

"Captain Vadim Maslov, at your disposal.   If you haven't found a table, do please share mine," he said.

He was terribly thin, and his moustache could do with waxing, but Margaret found him handsome, in a slightly underfed way.   They would have to do something about that.

"Where are the tiny terrors?" she asked.

"My nephews? I bribed the conductor to show them the engine. Should be good for half an hour of peace."

Nephews.   Not an errant father or husband then. Margaret had met enough of those to last a lifetime.

"Please, do sit."

She sat down opposite Maslov, who proved to be engaging company. A Russian pilot, on leave from his French squadron, ferrying his nephews from their Parisian boarding school back to their wealthy industrialist father in Budapest. He had wonderfully blue eyes and, like Margaret, was a man without a country, with no intention of returning home. Still – a question remained.

"Do you know who I am?" she said, as coyly as possible, sipping the champagne he'd ordered.

To his credit, he maintained eye contact. "None other than the infamous Mata Hari. I've seen you dance in Paris."

She laughed. "Infamous?"

He looked a little embarrassed.   Flirting in a second language could be tricky. Margaret, who spoke French and English in addition to her native Dutch, knew that better than anyone.

"Celebrated.   You have quite a reputation," he said. "As a dancer, I mean."

He couldn't be older than 23 or 24. In two years' time she would be forty.

"Did you like my dancing?" she said, spearing a quail's egg with a cocktail stick.

He nodded, firmly. "Very much so."

She touched his wrist, leaning in conspiratorially.

"Perhaps I'll do a little private show for you later, if you'd like."

Maslov looked like he'd just been electrocuted. He began to fidget with his collar.

"Hell, it's hot in here. Shall we open this?"

He stood and fiddled with the narrow upper window, yanking it open an inch. Other diners shot Maslov looks of disdain, which he ignored.

Margaret refilled Maslov's glass.

"It's okay Captain," she said, "I like a shy man… who knows what he wants."

Maslov laughed and seemed to relax. "If only I did. I know what I love, which is flying. My brother would like me to join him in business. My mother wants me to marry, my father believes I should see the world. I'm quite adrift."

"A cork bobbing on the ocean," Margaret said softly.

Maslov nodded vigorously. "Speaking of corks…"

He signalled for a waiter and ordered more champagne. Margaret felt her decision had been made.

Constanta could wait. In any case, she had always wanted to see Budapest.

Beeswax

Captain Montgomery Finch (retired) finished pouring pine needles into the bee smoker and switched off the television. He'd been disheartened to hear the lockdown was due to end. Boris Johnson and his government cronies were itching to open the country up again, lest a fatal economic downturn prove their undoing. Why this was *bad* news for Monty Finch involves a little unpacking.

Although he'd attained the rank of Captain in the Royal Navy, Finch had worked largely in logistics and procurement, dealing with as few people as humanly possible. He's never been a *people person*, to use that nauseating phrase. Finch was an introvert – an only-child content to live in his imagination, who'd made few friends and, at seventy-seven, was unlikely to make any more.

In this time of 'social distancing', being an introvert was a little like having a superpower. While others tore their hair out in boredom, Finch walked his dogs, read, played his clarinet, tended his hives and was content.

Finch dropped some lit tinder into the handheld metal canister, blowing gently until the wood caught. The twigs and needles should smoke nicely, and the sweet fragrance would prove soporific for the bees. He donned his overall and gloves and ventured into the warm May afternoon.

Finch walked through three acres of wildflowers, painstakingly nurtured. The hives stood at the bottom of the garden, by the hawthorn hedge. Beyond that lay a barn conversion that he'd heard a young couple were about to move into. Maddy, a busybody in the local fishmonger, insisted on filling him in on such gossip. His petty revenge was to call her Madeleine, as he had for twenty-seven years.

The hives were now three tiers high – he'd add one whenever the layer below became full, the combs' hexagonal cells waxed-over by the worker bees. He would inspect the honeycombs and the hives' colonies. In particular, he had to make sure the queens were in good health.

As grey-blue coils of smoke drifted up through the hives, a voice penetrated the hum of patrolling insects.

"Apiculture, eh?"

A young man was peering over the hedge. Had he climbed the ladder for that express purpose? No – the newcomer held shears and was levelling the top of the hawthorn. Finch could ignore him, but he wasn't a rude person by nature, he just didn't require the chatter upon which most people seemed to thrive.

"That's right", said Finch.

"Bit of a dumb question," said the man, who extended a hand then retracted it.

"Oops, keep forgetting!" grinned the neighbour. "Social distance, and all that. I'm Frank."

Finch sighed. It seemed he wasn't going to be left in peace.

"Monty Finch", he replied. "You might want to stand back."

Frank shook his head. "I'm not afraid of bees. Wasps – that's another thing entirely."

Here came the cliché about bees stinging less frequently, because they generally die, whereas wasps are serial stingers.

"I'm avoiding working on my novel. I'm a crime writer. Frank Latimer?"

"I mostly read books about beekeeping and naval history." Perhaps boring his neighbour off the ladder might work.

Frank seemed oblivious. "I'm completely blocked. I need a way a perfectionist serial killer can be caught out. The cops are trying to find his secret torture den, but he's a neat freak with an enormous IQ. He's always one step ahead. I'm afraid I've painted myself into a corner."

Finch wondered how long Frank would go on talking if he just went about his business, but his neighbour seemed to be awaiting some input.

"A thorny predicament. I'd better get on."

Frank nodded, sheepishly. "Sorry, of course. I must get back indoors and wrestle with my killer. Lovely to meet you."

"Likewise," said Finch, staring at Frank's outstretched hand. Frank slapped himself on the forehead.

"I'm such a dummy. Until next time."

"Looking forward," Finch lied.

The inspection went well. The workers were plentiful and fully engaged. One thing Finch admired most about bees was how compartmentalised and efficient they were. They had multiple special glands – hypopharyngeal glands produced royal jelly to feed the larval brood and enzymes to break down sugars. Another gland produced wax and, of course, bees had venom glands to repel invaders.

He hadn't always been alone. There had been Mary, the golden-haired secretary who won his heart with amusing little margin notes she scribbled on his memos. Eventually those notes contained little hearts and kisses. It had taken him far too long to take her out, but only four months of "stepping out" before he asked her to marry him.

Mary had been the only person he could stand to spend more than half an hour with, and they had enjoyed fifty-one years together, before the leukaemia. They'd never had children; he couldn't and she, remarkably, accepted that.

That night, as he lay in bed reminiscing, Finch had a sudden brainwave.

He leapt out of bed, headed to the pantry, and retrieved a jar of honey. He attached a note to the jar with an elastic band and crept out of the house.

Finch hoped that at 2am, during lockdown, nobody would see him sneaking around in his dressing gown. There was an upstairs light on in the renovated barn. He considered turning back, but something stopped him. This small gesture seemed important. Mary would have loved it. He quietly let himself into the Latimers' backyard and left the honeypot on their patio.

The note contained only one word. *Melissopalynology*. Melissopalynology was the analysis of the pollen content in honey. A clever scientist could identify the pollen grains and their relative distribution and perhaps even conjecture where that particular combination of flowers might be found. Say, for instance, in the meadows surrounding a killer's secret lair.

Frank was delighted, as Finch had known he would be. When Finch took his dogs for a walk the following morning, he found something had been left for him – a thick novel entitled "Shadow Boxers" by Frank Latimer.

It was inscribed, simply, "To Captain Finch, with eternal gratitude, Frank."

The End of Money

When the end of money came, it happened on both a microscopic and macroscopic scale. The Covid-19 crisis of 2020-21 and subsequent pandemics decimated world economies, reduced international monetary markets to chaos and caused stock prices to plummet for everything that wasn't tech-based. Hyper-inflation, previously seen in Germany before World War II, became the norm, with world governments having to convene regularly to agree the strategic devaluation (or re-valuation as it was euphemistically termed) of their respective currencies. Banknotes began to appear with mathematical formulae in place of lines of zeros. A loaf of bread would cost ten to the power of 8 dollars. Financial markets, struggling to function at all, would start bandying about the kinds of terms once used by overexcited children – one quintillion, five point eight sesquetillion. A Googleplex of pointless pennies.

Various desperate strategies were adopted. The world's first global currency was trialled – the Omnidollar. It bore nobody's face because nobody could agree who to put on it. Instead, it had a honeybee on one side (a symbol of industriousness) and a dove on the reverse (a symbol of hope). Issued in denominations of 1, 5, 10, 50 and 100, it lasted eight months before succumbing to hyperinflation too. Soon it became infinitely cheaper to wipe your bottom with Omnidollars than actually buy toilet paper with them.

There was a brief plan to return to the gold standard in the 2030s, lauded of course, by those economies who still boasted gigantic gold reserves. A group of anonymous techno-terrorists put an end to that, sending a vast swarm of nanobots to devour the US federal gold reserve. These minuscule machines crawled through ventilation ducts and keyholes, eating almost 5000 metric tonnes of gold, carried away in tiny particulates over the course of one holiday weekend and scattered to the wind. You could find gold dust on the beaches of California, blowing across the Nevada desert and silting up the swamps of Alabama. Diamonds were mooted as a replacement, but the power shift this would entail towards some fairly unpleasant African dictatorships put paid to that one.

A radical solution was proposed – simply to abolish money altogether and return to a barter system. Obviously the seriously wealthy opposed this most vigorously, since they had very little the general populace wanted, except access to their outrageous lifestyles. Farmers and food producers were the most vocally supportive of such a system, for obvious reasons. The general populace, when it wasn't starving in its billions, marching upon parliaments, deposing despots, forcibly crossing borders and rioting, simply wanted stability, enough food to eat, and a dry place to sleep. Was that really too challenging a list of demands?

By 2044, Earth's citizens were submitting to 'chipping', being fitted from birth with a device which measured and tallied their consumption and linked this directly to ability and readiness to work. Of course, there were widespread protests, by those libertarians who still believed freedom was the ultimate human right, superseding the right to equality and perhaps even the right to life.

You were born, chipped and thereafter allocated a weekly supply of food and spendable credit, which could be enhanced only within rigid parameters, based on conspicuous hard work.

All work was declared equal, from sewage engineers to architects to musicians to doctors to hairdressers. Jobs that nobody wanted were performed by all on an AI-controlled rota system, which had always worked well for jury duty and national military service. You worked in a particular allocated role in six month stints every five years, unless you were permitted a medical exemption. In 2044 everybody took turns working as a sewage engineer, a refuse collector, or a member of parliament.

Jobs that could only be done only by certain individuals – scientists, writers, sprinters, world leaders – were designated as protected and had to be applied for, but these were not rewarded with any additional life credits. You could be the president of the United States of America and you would still be entitled to only one loaf of bread per week.

Violations of these codes were dealt with severely – reduction of goods allocation or incarceration seemed to work reasonably well as incentives to good behaviour. Black market bartering was swiftly curtailed. Royalty was abolished, and its excesses redistributed. Buckingham Palace became a hotel, its rooms costing the same as all hotel rooms everywhere – one away-from-home sleep credit. Booking was available by lottery only. A popular YouTube video showed a Syrian child refugee, now in her forties, reclining in a palatial tub once occupied by the King of England. King William the Fifth was photographed sweeping up autumn leaves in Windsor Park, holding both thumbs aloft to the camera, doing his statutory work rotation.

It is true that totemic displays of human achievement diminished considerably during this time – giant dams, bridges and palaces were no longer built. But it was felt the world had plenty of those. A movement to celebrate the rejuvenation of the earth's biodiversity gained ground instead, as climate change diminished, and the world returned to a kind of observant stasis. Animals not seen in significant numbers for decades began to proliferate – herds of white rhino thundered across the African veldt once more.

After the initial decades of catastrophe and conflict, wars ended – after all, what was the point in fighting another group of people whose wealth was identical to yours, and from whom you could take literally nothing that you could keep? And if you couldn't benefit personally from subjugating another, why go to all the effort? Even a sociopath could see that it simply wasn't a worthwhile use of one's time.

Dissidents called this phase in human history 'the systematic self-destruction of the human race'. Idealists called it 'a new golden age'.

Kate Blackhurst called it 'ridiculous', crumpled up the piece of paper upon which she'd written the above fantasy scenario, and returned to her novel about Russian oligarchs having one another's families executed. After all, a writer had to pay the rent somehow.

Black Cubes

In a top-secret location in the Nevada desert lurked the Theoretical Incursion Centre. You submitted to a retinal scan, vocal and fingerprint identification to gain entry to the thirty-strong think-tank beavering away below.

What TIC did, in essence, was formulate strategies to deal with 'incursion events' or, if you were of a more optimistic bent, 'first contact scenarios'. These ranged from alien viruses (although 2020's Covid-19 crisis had shown Earth had plenty of microscopic enemies of its own) to repelling land-based, flying or water-dwelling invaders, all the way up to protocols for how to handle visits from intelligent species, friendly or hostile. Every sort of alien bogeyman you could think of, they had it covered. Or so they thought.

What nobody had envisaged, except, seemingly an alt-country singer-songwriter from Millerstown, Ohio, was giant, softly humming, unspeakably matt black cubes, floating several feet from the ground, in thousands of locations over the earth.

Joel Gittings Jr., farmer, and part-time musician, who'd never made it as far as Cincinnati, let alone Nashville, woke at 5.15am to milk his cows, only to discover two incredible things.

The first was a trio of black limousines outside his front porch. Even more alarming was a sixty-foot square black cube floating above his house. It hummed ominously and emitted a light crackle of static electricity. It absorbed all light. The only way you could tell it was a cube was by walking around it and seeing its outline change from a regular to an irregular hexagon and back again.

Joel did a circuit with the 'men in black', who seemed convinced he knew more about the extra-terrestrial object than they did. This would be absurd, were it not for the fact that a day before the black cubes had 'arrived', materialising out of thin air, Joel had written a song, based on an eerie dream, called 'Black Cube Blues', which he shared online.

> Black cubes in the morning
> Floatin' in the hazy light.
> Black cubes without warning,
> Made of shadows, made of night.
> Black cubes calling out to me,
> They sing a silent song.
> Black cubes gonna take me,
> And one day I'll be gone.

When Lieutenant Simons and Lieutenant Connor (man and woman respectively) said he needed to come with them, Joel thought he was in trouble. What for, he wasn't sure, but this was clearly no time to rebel.

Connor smiled and said, "Don't worry bud, we just want to pick your brains."

Joel chose to assume she was speaking figuratively.

Two car rides and a charter plane from a military base later, they arrived at the TIC site. Simons and Connor shepherded Joel down in a lift to a facility at least a quarter mile underground. It looked like mission control at NASA. There were people with a military bearing, others with the harried, intelligent look of scientists.

An angular gent, in a smart suit, walked over and shook his hand. The team seemed to defer to him, yet all eyes were on Joel.

"General Thorncliffe. Please have a seat and some refreshment."

Joel sat, sipped coffee, and waited to be told what the hell was going on.

Eventually, they briefed him on the 97,411 other cubes reported around the globe and their various unsuccessful attempts to communicate with the aliens.

"So… you want to brain-scan me, 'cause you think my song was some sorta prediction?"

Thorncliffe laughed. "Yes and no. We want you to dream."

"Sorry, you what?"

"We would like you to fall asleep so we can monitor your dreams."

As crazy as it seemed to Joel, Thorncliffe and his team were serious. Also, he guessed, desperate. So, he took the sleeping pills, was fitted with electrodes, bedded down in the isolation quarters, and slipped into a deep sleep. When he awoke, the scientists thanked him but revealed that his REM patterns had not demonstrated anything useful.

"So that's that?" Joel said.

Officer Connor approached to direct him towards the lift. "We'll call upon you again if we think of anything else. Needless to say, you didn't see any of this."

Joel nodded, like a good patriot. "Don't want to hear the rest of the song?"

"Sorry, the rest?" queried Thorncliffe, overhearing.

"I only uploaded two verses. Couldn't think of the final one. It came to me this morning. Thought it might be… useful in some way?"

Thorncliffe thought for a moment, his fingers together in a pyramid in front of his chin. Then he turned to the assembled TIC team.

"Can anyone get this man a guitar?"

Minutes later, Joel had tuned the Gretsch that someone had procured and, although its action was a little heavier than he was used to, he banged out a passable version of 'Black Cube Blues'. When he got to the third verse, after a brief instrumental interlude, which he felt was under-appreciated, Joel sang:

> Black Cubes vanished just like that,
> Said we just ain't ready,
> Took me where the ten moons rise,
> Left me there with Freddie.

"Freddie's my old deerhound," Joel explained, finishing with a strumming flourish.

There was a portentous silence. Joel began to feel exceptionally self-conscious. He also seemed to be fading slightly, his image fraying around the edges.

"General! We've got reports coming in…" said an excitable woman wearing a large pair of headphones. Mice clicked at laptops; large screens flickered into life. Scenes of cities, deserts, forests, and seashores around the world. There was absolutely nothing strange about any of the live feeds. Apart from one thing.

There were no black cubes.

The headphone-wearing scientist swivelled round in her chair.

"Sir, they've gone. Vanished into thin air."

Thorncliffe whirled round, his mind astir with questions for the lanky country singer.

But Joel Gittings Jr. was gone, his prophesy fulfilled, just a slight whiff of something metallic where he'd been sitting. With a small, nervous laugh, the General realised Gittings had managed to take the Gretsch with him. And presumably Freddie.

"I hope they like Hank Williams," he mused, to nobody in particular.

The Purple Heart

"Break-time's over lads! Come on Godfrey, put that out, you goddamn goldbricker!"

The way he conducted himself, you'd think work detail leader Brad Knight was a platoon sergeant in a WWII movie. Will Godfrey stubbed his cigarette into a nearby glob of something disgusting and stuffed the cotton wool balls back up his nose. Two more days of this and he'd finally be free from the dumb sentence the judge had ordered for Will's latest heinous crime. When the gavel had gone down in court three months ago, Will found himself laughing at the judge's order: a $1000 fine and twelve week-ends of working for the department of sanitation, all for emptying out a deep fat fryer into a public drain behind the restaurant where he worked as a pot-washer.

Admittedly he'd argued with a cop about it and called him a "fat fucker" and, fair enough, Will had a colourful rap sheet including brawling, breaking and entering and stealing a pretzel wagon (drunken teenage hi-jinks), but twelve weeks in a sewer, battling "fatbergs" and solidified drifts of toilet tissue, human excrement and hair was excessive. Godfrey considered appealing the ruling, but his attorney advised against it. In fact, he'd practically forbidden it: "Just do your service, pay your fine and put this behind you."

Good advice, for sure, but Will would love to see the judge down here in the horrific old Chicago sewer, prising used tampons and diapers out of a wall of yellow fat. Will had spent the first three days gagging and being sick. He had learned not to eat before noon.

As he set to work with his protective gear, high-pressure hose, and "harpoon", as he called the metal tool used to scrape free persistent agglomerations, Will was literally counting the hours. He hardly spoke to any of his fellow sewage workers, around half of them recidivists like himself. He just got on with the task in hand and showered for at least thirty minutes at the end of each day.

"Let's get this little honeypot broken up and go home, boys!" shouted Mr Knight, attempting camaraderie.

'This little honeypot' was a fatberg big enough to earn its own postal code. Will was hard at work, spraying it with a solvent that dissipated the fat, then prising chunks free. He was at the head of the line, on the far side of a brick bulwark, away from the others. Abruptly he lowered his hose, having seen something sparkle amongst the gristly grey berg. Will reached out to prise it free. It looked metallic. He managed to hook a piece of coloured fabric attached to it.

"Fuck me!" he felt the need to exclaim. He held in his gloved hand a surprisingly well-preserved Purple Heart, the unmistakable profile of George Washington standing out against the dark background. Quickly remembering what kind of individual he spent his days with, Will shoved the medal into the pocket of his jumpsuit and got on with his work, heart thumping.

The following Monday, as he sat in the public library going through the job advertisements, planning for his fat-free future, Will took the purple heart out of his pocket. On its reverse was an engraving motto: 'For Military Merit' and then, in a different typeface: Harold D. Buckley. Having a curious nature (part of the reason for his extensive rap sheet; Will couldn't resist letting himself in through open windows) Will googled the name.

There it was, in a list of awarded WWII servicemen. Buckley had been awarded the Purple Heart for his role in the 1945 Battle of Corregidor, in which US troops had re-taken the island from the Japanese. He'd led a group of men who'd attacked a Japanese gun emplacement shelling the island's military hospital. For his efforts, Buckley ended up in that self-same hospital, and had to have his left leg amputated, but the battle was won.

Learning this, Will felt a pang of guilt. He'd already searched several online auction sites and militaria suppliers, for the resale value of the medal, and had been disappoin-ted to discover he'd be lucky to get $40 for it. Over a mil-lion were issued during the second world war. Not only would it be far from profitable to sell the medal, Will real-ised that, given that it had been engraved and he knew who it belonged to, it would be wrong to do so. His natural in-quisitiveness and a new sensation he supposed was honour led Will to a firm conclusion – he would give the medal back.

It took just one more hour of online database re-search for Will to unearth the address of Buckley's widow, who could be found in assisted living accommodation in Lafayette, Indianapolis. Just a three-and-a-half-hour jour-ney on two Greyhounds; practically next door. Let's face it, what else did he have to do?

The next day, Buckley was in Lafayette, wandering up and down South Street, trying to locate the Seven Elms Retirement Village. He found it up a shady, tree-lined lane. Number 47 was a cute bungalow with a porch and wheel-chair ramp zig-zagging up to the front door. It took three insistent knocks before a hunched figure appeared behind the screen door, clutching a walking frame.

"Mrs Ida Buckley?" Will asked, half expecting a shake of the head and to have the door slammed in in his face. Instead, the sprightly nonagenarian invited him in for cookies and home-made lemonade. Will began to suspect Ida had mistaken him for her home help, but at least it got him in the door.

When he explained himself and presented her with the Purple Heart that had belonged to her long-deceased husband, Ida's face did not break into the radiant glow Will had imagined on the coach ride from the windy city. Instead, she scowled, her liver-spotted and gnarled hand batting Will's away.

"I threw that away for a reason. Don't want the darn thing back."

It transpired that Ida had attended a special celebration event for war widows in Chicago in 2015, to mark the sixtieth anniversary of the Far Eastern campaign. There she'd been shocked to meet a woman called Annabelle Nguyen, apparently her late husband's daughter by a woman called Rose he'd met in Manila during his six-month recuperation in 1945. For all his heroism, Buckley had fallen in love with his nurse, led a secret life, fathered a child, and Ida had known nothing about it. That night, in her hotel, she'd wept for the first time in years, and had flushed the medal down the lavatory, pushing it around the U-bend with her walking stick.

Two hours later, Will sat in a local bar, downing his fifth Bud and wondering if the awful country covers band would stop murdering Waylon Jennings songs anytime soon. It took another couple of beers before they did.

Nothing had gone according to plan and Will felt more than a little foolish. Didn't anyone want to be reminded of serviceman Harold D. Buckley's sacrifice?

Will was probably still a little drunk the following morning as he sat in an internet café and bought himself a return ticket to Manila, all but draining his bank account in so doing. He'd never previously journeyed further than Florida, and here he was going eight thousand miles on a probable wild goose chase. Still, it wasn't as if Will had a busy social calendar ahead of him. Why not have an adventure? Will obtained the necessary documents and shots, packed a raggedy suitcase and was an All Nippon Airways flight to the Philippines three days later.

Arriving at Ninoy Aquino International Airport on 31st June, Will was assaulted by a wall of moist heat. Taxi drivers jostled for his business, but he waved them away and grabbed a tuk-tuk to his mid-priced hotel in Makati, one he couldn't really afford but had chosen very carefully, nevertheless. Will didn't draw attention to himself on arrival, just crashed onto his bed with the air-con on full. Chicagoans aren't made for mid-thirties humidity. It would take Will several days to adjust to everything about this chaotic, fragrant, and beautiful country. He walked the lively streets, jogged along the Baywalk, visited Fort Santiago and some of the war memorials, drank sickly cocktails, bided his time.

Four days later, what Will had been waiting for finally occurred. A woman came into the hotel lobby where Will was sipping a coffee and pretending to read a three-day old New York Times. The woman was extraordinarily petite, not quite five feet tall, in her mid-twenties and wore wide-rimmed glasses that gave her pretty face an owlish cast. She began to tend to the plants in the lobby, removing dead leaves, spraying insecticide, watering everything. Will surreptitiously watched her, sliding along the banquette seating to allow her access to a bold display of orchids. As she was completing her rounds and packing away her equipment, Will lowered his paper.

"Cherry Nguyen?"

The woman's response was almost comic – she jumped back, pushing her glasses up her nose and looking panic-stricken.

"No, no," Will said quickly. "I'm a friend. Well, I come in peace. I mean… sorry, this is stupid. I have something for you. Something from your grandfather. Look."

Flustered, blushing unexpectedly, Will handed over the presentation box he'd sourced online. Christ, this was ridiculous. What was he trying to prove, and why had he sprung it on her like that?

Cherry took the gift with a perplexed smile and opened it, sitting down edge of a large circular planter. Inside, of course, was the Purple Heart, newly polished. Will had had plenty of time to work on its restoration, unpicking the seam on the ribbon so it could be separately dry-cleaned, then stitching it back together. When Cherry turned the medal over, she gasped audibly, and then she did something that helped Will understand that nothing he'd done in the last ten days had been stupid. She smiled, an expression of surprise and joy that filled Will with something he'd not felt for months – uncomplicated happiness.

"Amazing!", Cherry said, "Thank you so much. But… how?"

Will bade Cherry join him at his table, ordered them two cool drinks and told her his story, leaving nothing out, not even his crimes.

"I'm Will Godley," he began "and I have made many mistakes".

Float me Down the River

I've always loved wild swimming; it's what I miss most, since they banned visits to the countryside. Three more years, the government said. Three more years until the nanobots wind down and the last one drops lifeless to the earth. Around a million of the 'fleas', as they're nicknamed, remain, drifting the earth's moist places in search of prey, occasionally killing a careless farmhand or schoolboy crossing the fens.

I'm walking with Richard, hand in hand, daringly gloveless as we cross Grantchester Meadows in the direction of the river. The simple sensation of his hand in mine feels like an astonishing luxury. His touch is a gift I never dared ask for. With just a few nanobots left from the billion once released, and only a tiny fraction of those malfunctioning and delivering a fatal bite to a human, our chances of calamity are miniscule. We've been cooped up in the teeming city for years. It feels worth the risk.

Richard's fingers squeeze mine in reassurance. A breeze ruffles the tiny hairs on my forearm. I have rolled my sleeves up, recklessness taking over in the idyllic June afternoon.

This curve of the river would once have been loud with picnicking families and groups of half-naked kids hurling themselves into the deep pools of the languorously gliding river Cam. Today it is as quiet as a graveyard, although alive with the fluttering confetti of butterflies amongst the buttercups.

"Our usual spot?"

Richard's smile lacks even a trace of irony. I nod vigorously as we head for our once-familiar bend, where a willow tree shades a sandbank providing easy access into the deep green waters. We won't be swimming today. Not even I am that reckless.

We have a story prepared in case we're caught. I've got terminal cancer and this spot is where Richard proposed marriage to me years ago. An Environmental Protection Officer (EPO) would have to have a heart of stone to arrest us. Richard can cry on cue; I do a great line in shamefaced apology.

We spread our blanket on the springy grass and sit in dappled sunlight wishing we could take off our socks and shoes. How freighted with irony the EPO's role is. Where once the Office worked to protect the environment from us, it now has the reverse function. That's assuming you allow that the fleas are now part of the environment, which they surely are.

The fleas were going to save humanity. Well, a large swathe of it. They were engineered to capture mosquitos in their miniscule "holds", like those military aircraft that can swallow trucks, then neutralise their ability to transmit disease by injecting a bio-engineered enzyme into the captive insects. Within a year it was estimated that malaria, dengue fever and the zika virus would be eradicated. And it worked.

Unfortunately, the fleas' tiny AIs have one design flaw. They can't tell the difference between a mosquito-shaped blob and an actual mosquito. Quite a lot of things superficially resemble mosquitos, seemingly – biscuit crumbs, splashes of mud, moles. Lots of things that can trigger a bite and a squirt of an enzyme that, it transpires, is fatal to humans. Twenty-seven thousand accidental deaths, most of them amongst poor agricultural labourers. Woe-betide any contrarian who counters with the four and a half million malarial deaths that would otherwise have occurred.

We lay out the chicken wings, cherry tomatoes, Mediterranean dips, slices of pitta bread and crudities, and pour ourselves glasses of river-cooled rosé. Tears fill my eyes – a kind of aching happiness. I bury my face in Richard's broad chest. That's when I feel it, the sharp prick on my right underarm.

"Ouch!"

Richard panics. "What? Let me see. It's a tick."

He picks the silver speck from my arm. It isn't a tick. You can even see a tiny serial number printed on its underside. Richard squishes the flea and tosses it into the long grass.

"Fucking, fucking hell," is all he can think to say. Then, once rationality returns, "We need to get you to a hospital. Now!"

He wrenches me to my feet; already I can't put any weight on my legs. My consciousness is clouding. I look at a tiny smear of blood on my forearm. There's a tiny freckle I'd never previously noticed.

"Come on Sylvie! Lean against me."

I've never seen Richard, lovely lazy Richard, move so urgently. He begins to hobble across the meadow, dragging me alongside. The light is dimming, sound fading.

"That house! It's closer than our car."

I know I'm doomed. The ridiculousness of that word doesn't carry the requisite gravitas. I have five minutes at best. The nearest hospital is twenty minutes away. It's in my bloodstream now and that's that. Richard has a deeply logical brain – he's the proper adult in our relationship. He'll reach the same conclusion, eventually.

"Stop! Just stop, will you?"

He does. Turns my face to his. Tears stream down his cheeks.

"I want to swim", I whisper.

Richard is confused. I struggle through the veils of encroaching darkness.

"I want a kiss, then I want you to float me down the river."

He looks at me like I'm crazy, but Richard knows how stubborn I am. Knows how I can make my last moments a living hell for him if he doesn't grant these last wishes.

The first is easy. Richard kisses me deeply, a desperate embrace I can't return. His eyes scan mine. I try to smile. His determination alters.

"Right you are, Sliver." His nickname for me, one last time.

It's like a baptism. I can hear him stifling a sob, then once the current takes me, the sound of trickling water is all.

A blue sky with candyfloss clouds, gleaming sunlight through the willow fronds. The water isn't even cold, but then all sensations are slipping away.

Eventually, only buoyancy remains. This feels familiar, a return to the womb. The river embraces and supports me and sends me on my way…

Eyes in the Dark

I am not well-travelled, despite writing about places as far-flung as Indonesia and Svalbard. I'm an essayist and a novelist and when my now ex-wife asked me if I wouldn't rather hop on a plane than spend endless hours researching exotic places on the internet, I told her that's why God gave us imagination.

"But you don't believe in God," she said, mystified.

"That's right," I replied. "But I do believe in imagination. Lived experience is all very well but writing isn't just transcribing what we see, hear or feel."

In truth, I'm rather afraid of flying and I tend to get melancholy on holidays and trips abroad, particularly if I'm by myself. It's a love-hate relationship being an introvert. I'm both socially avoidant and morose when alone. Still, this gives me much to write about, solipsistic though my novels may be, as one critic recently pointed out.

When I was recently invited to Romania to visit and write about a newly discovered complex of karst caves containing prehistoric paintings which haven't seen the light of day for tens of thousands of years, I was both thrilled and filled with trepidation. My editor, too young and green to know any better, offered me this assignment because he'd read and loved my prehistoric thrillers, the Black Moon Trilogy. Apart from one visit to the caves of Lascaux, I'd done all my research for those bestsellers in the British Library, British Museum, and online science journals. But Adam didn't know that, and he imagined an all-expenses trip to the Carpathian Mountains might both excite and inspire me. As much to save Adam's face as my own, I decided on this occasion to swallow my fears and to counterfeit excitement for the upcoming trip.

My research assistant Lucia, who to be honest had done most of the work behind the Black Moon books, couldn't be persuaded to come with me, and nor could my daughter who, I'll admit, I'd not previously spoken to for three months.

"Dad, I only live an hour away by train. You can't even be bothered to make *that* trip and you want me to use a week of my annual leave to come with you to Romania, of all places?"

Her scorn was withering and frankly unwarranted. I've had it in mind to visit her these last few months and if deadlines didn't keep reliably coming around to scupper my plans, I would definitely have gone to Winchester.

"Jane, at least talk to David about it, will you? Remember when we went to the caves at Lascaux?"

"I remember it rained all day and we had to queue in a downpour for a guided tour in German because you hadn't booked in advance and the English one was full."

Jane sourly promised to talk to her husband, but I know she'd undersell the idea and I'd be travelling alone as usual. Two days later, Lucia put me on a mercifully brief flight with a ghastly budget provider flying out of Luton. I vowed that this would be my last overseas commission, regardless of it being the cover story in Humanity, the magazine I most frequently write for.

For the first forty minutes of the flight, Andrei, the Romanian businessman sitting next to me, bored me with how much he loved London and how he hoped to grow his business renting chalets in the Romanian Alps to hunting parties. I told him I thought killing wild animals for sport was indefensibly cruel and the strategy worked quite nicely. Apart from the odd polite intrusion, I had the rest of the flight to myself and spent it re-reading *The Brothers Karamazov*.

Following the flight, I took a train from Cluj-Napoca to Brasov, a much more arduous journey, although the scenery was pretty enough. Nine hours with two changes of train, however. Surely Lucia could have found a more direct route. When I finally stumbled into the four-star Excelsior Hotel in Brasov (it would be lucky to obtain three stars in London) I was thoroughly exhausted and elected to take a cold platter in my room rather than face a chattering restaurant. Tomorrow I'd meet Tatiana, the local cultural attaché, who'd be my guide to the caves. We'd be driving up there in her car and I confess I spent a restless night having oddly erotic fantasies involving my imagined sylph-like companion seducing me in the mountains.

In reality, Tatiana was pushing fifty, stout as a wrestler and clearly inclined more towards members of her own gender than mine. She had a very pleasing voice, however, and a smile of genuine warmth and professed herself a fan of my books. I felt we'd get on very well indeed. Her car turned out to be an old Rover TC2000, a vehicle not too dissimilar to one I'd owned in my youth. Tatiana was impressed that I recognised it, and we bonded over the pleasures and pains of owning a vintage motor car as we drove up winding 73 road towards the foothills of the Carpathians. The countryside was remarkably green and lush, with heavily forested regions interspersed with farmland and tiny villages. We passed a line of wagons, heavily laden with blue barrels of something or other, each vehicle drawn by two horses, dark-faced children scowling from the rear.

"Romanies," Tatiana explained needlessly. "They live like the nineteenth century."

What's wrong with that? I couldn't help but think but held my tongue.

"Do you like Bram Stoker?" said Tatiana, with a testing expression, like she was teasing me. A moment later, I realised why. We turned a corner and there on a rocky outcrop, surrounded by forest, was an impressive castle, its steep stone sides, and turreted roofs immediately familiar. With a flush of embarrassment, I realised this must be Bran Castle. Why hadn't I known it would be on our route?

"Of course. Count Dracula's supposed home. It rather lives up to the hype."

"Glad you like," said Tatiana, raising an eyebrow. "Was closed to tourists a couple of years ago. Too dangerous. Do you know why?"

I thought for a moment and shook my head.

"Family of brown bears moved in," she said. "You don't mess with bears."

I laughed a little uneasily, realising we were about to drive deep into the forest in a fifty-year-old car that had probably already had its fair share of breakdowns.

"How, er, far is our hotel?"

Tatiana laughed. "Hotel it is? Lodge is thirty-two miles into mountains. Hold onto your hat, Mr Buckhurst. May be a bumpy ride."

An astonishing two and a half hours later, as the sun was skimming the tops of the trees, we were still rollercoasting up and down narrow roads whose left-hand sides were pitted with massive potholes.

"Why are they ruined on one side?" I asked Tatiana.

"Logging," she replied, leaving me to work out the

implication. I guessed that full logging trucks roaring down the mountainside caused most of the damage, whilst the empty ones on our side were far less destructive. I felt rather pleased with myself, as my theory was proven by one of those monstrous eighteen wheelers roaring by at unconscionable speed as we swerved onto the verge to avoid a collision. The driver's air-horn blast either signified mania or some species of apology. Probably the former, since most Romanians, Tatiana included, seem to drive like maniacs.

We almost missed the turning, a tiny gravel track forking away from the main road alongside a rushing stream. Tatiana reversed at speed and righted her route, revealing that this was only the second time she'd come here, the first being to bring the team of archaeologists and palaeontologists who had spent a month here cataloguing, photographing, and measuring everything. Apparently, the site had been discovered when logging and weather erosion caused a landslide, opening up the mouth of a thirty-foot-long limestone cave, and a habitation not seen for perhaps fifty thousand years. The very thought of it sent a shiver down my spine. In spite of all my misgivings, I was looking forward to being only the tenth person to see the cave paintings since humans first explored the Eurasian continent.

It was too dark to see much by the time we arrived at the small, prefabricated shelter that Tatiana had termed a 'lodge'. That turned out to be a rather grandiose term for what was really a glorified bothy. It had a communal room and two bedrooms, each containing four bunk beds. Each room had a wood-fired stove for heating, a rudimentary shower, and a toilet. Laminated instructions in broken English revealed that you had to keep the stove going for half an hour in the main room before the water would be warm enough to shower. I decided to give this a miss until tomorrow.

The communal room boasted a range to cook upon, a pile of cut logs, plus cupboard space, tables, and chairs. The windows rattled in the growling wind and a sudden hailstorm gave us both a start as Tatiana fuelled and lit the fire. I had to admit that my guide was both resourceful and thoughtful. However, it was bitterly cold and draughty in the wooden shack. Fortunately, there were piles of clean blankets, so we helped ourselves to several each and after a reheated bowl of Tatiana's unspecified meat "stew", said our fatigued good nights and went to our respective bunk-rooms. It was scarcely nine pm, but I felt thoroughly drained by my journey. Late autumn had so far proven reasonably mild, but the weather could change suddenly at this time of year at high altitude, Tatiana informed me. I put an extra pair of socks on and read a few pages of Dostoyevsky by torchlight before giving in to my exhaustion.

That night, although I slept surprisingly soundly, I was troubled by a strange and ambiguous dream. I found myself in a forest clearing, for some reason attempting to replace the wheel on a logging truck (quite unlike me, if you knew anything about my level of vehicular expertise). Nevertheless, I had got the damaged wheel free and was about to roll a fresh one into place when a hunched, bedraggled figure burst into the clearing.

He was scarcely five feet in height and had the prognathous jaw, bulbous forehead, and flattened nose of some species of prehistoric humanoid, whether neanderthal or homo something-or-other, I couldn't say. He wore a loose-fitting loincloth of hide and his muscular body was thickly matted with dark hair, which was smeared in places with something darkly red, presumably blood. As I froze in place, half-hidden by the cab of the truck, the creature sniffed the air, seeming to search for the source of something. I held my breath, hoping that something wasn't me.

The creature suddenly met my gaze, turning his head to one side, like a dog does when he's trying to understand his master. I froze in fear as the humanoid hoisted a flint-pointed spear aloft and nimbly dashed across the gap between us. I flinched and threw up my arms but found myself frozen to the spot as the humanoid pulled one shoulder back, preparing to hurl the spear. I could almost anticipate the searing pain of that blade, imagining it tearing through my chest. My attacker unleashed a cry both animalistic and filled with inchoate rage.

I awoke sweating, entangled in my blankets, and lay in my top bunk, afraid to move for a moment until I remembered where I was. Hopefully, I had not cried out, as I sometimes do when dreaming. It would be a significant embarrassment to be discovered in my babyish fears by Tatiana. Eventually I was able to turn my head and see the empty, moonlit room, with just the dull red glow of the stove's embers to provide human warmth.

I did not sleep further that night, pacing the room to keep warm at first, then going into the adjoining main room to light the range for hot water. I impressed myself by accomplishing this within ten minutes using the remains of an old newspaper and several logs. By the time Tatiana appeared, I'd even managed to make a pot of coffee on the range. My guide's raised eyebrow revealed that I had exceeded her somewhat inadequate assessment of me.

Ninety minutes later, we were fed, showered, dressed, and picking our way up the winding trail hacked out by loggers who had gone to investigate the landslide, then further flattened by the scientists who had followed. It was a twenty-minute walk and involved much clambering over fallen trees and edging around precipitous slopes. Fortunately, I'd bought a new pair of hiking boots for the trip and they stood me in good stead. Nevertheless, I was rather out of breath and light-headed when we arrived at the cave mouth. Somewhat annoyingly, Tatiana seemed to be entirely untroubled by the exertion.

A long tangle of fallen trees, dirt and rocks had fallen away to reveal a vertical slash in the limestone bluff. Evidently a layer of rock had sheared off when the slope collapsed, since the exposed rock was free from lichen and vegetation. The cave mouth resembled an obscenely grimacing mouth turned on its side. The interior was utterly dark, in contrast to the grey-green limestone surrounding the entrance. We switched on our hand torches and crept into the gloom.

Before we turned our attention to the walls, Tatiana's mission was to locate the generator and working lights the scientists had left behind for future use. She accomplished this with ease and moments later a chugging oil-fired machine supplied enough electricity to light up four large klieg lights and throw the interior of the cave into sharp relief.

The space was bottle-shaped, the neck tapering off into the far side of the cave and ending in darkness. Tatiana had informed me that a second cave might lie that way, but the bottleneck had been filled in with rubble. Further explorations would ensue in the spring.

I stepped back away from the widest wall and felt my

heart rate rise as before me spread a canvas of ancient drama – a herd or bison-like animals, with smaller deer-like shapes, pursued by a small army of stick figures. Swirls and spirals of dots decorated the scene, and the colours were still remarkably vivid – a dark red like congealed blood, a yellowish ochre, and an ashen blue-grey. The stick figures and animals were outlined in black, probably with charcoal. The entire frieze was full of life and it was hard to grasp that it may have been painted tens of thousands of years before.

"Turn around," said Tatiana softly, "the artists left self-portraits."

I spun around and Tatiana had swivelled one of the lights to illuminate the knobbly, sloping opposite wall of the cave. Arcing all the way up from floor to ceiling was a zig-zagging pattern of interlocking handprints. They looked stencilled, the pigment outlining the hands smeared evenly and fading gently into the naked stone as if air-brushed.

"It's believed they blew the paint from their mouths," Tatiana says and suddenly I saw the scene. More specific-ally, I saw the creature from my dream leaning against the wall, mouth filled with berry juice, spraying liquid against his outstretched hand. The handprints were smaller than my own; I couldn't help but stretch out my left palm to place it over one of them, realising moments later that I perhaps should have asked for permission first.

"It's okay, everyone does it," Tatiana said, answering my unasked question.

The handprints were not all uniformly small, although they were all smaller than my own would be. There were some tinier outlines, near the floor, presumably the prints of children. The sight of these tiny, familiar shapes brought a lump to my throat and I quashed the memories that started to form. Jane lay asleep in my arms in the hospital still clutching my finger, even in sleep. I wasn't about to cry in front of the Romanian cultural attaché, so I pulled myself together and took off my backpack to retrieve my sketch book and pencils.

"I arrange for a couple of scientists to come and visit tomorrow but I want you to see it… pure," said Tatiana, reaching for the word. Uninflected, I thought, without offering the clarification.

I'm a reasonably accomplished sketch artist, and I wanted a record more personal and tactile than a mere photo, so I unfolded a canvas stool and sat down to draw the hunting scene. Within seconds, I became so engrossed I almost completely forgot that Tatiana was still there.

"I have some provisions to buy," she suddenly announced. "We will need more firewood too. I'll get in town. Are you okay if I leave you for an hour or so?"

I was a little disappointed that she wasn't intending to chop the logs herself with a mighty axe and could picture the scene vividly. Evidently middle-class conveniences had reached even rural Romania. I nodded and returned her smile, then went back to my drawing.

Shortly, I heard the distant wheeze and splutter that announced the Rover's engine starting, down in the valley below. I could see her car pull away from the lodge, which could just be made out through the thinning pines.

It was getting a little chilly as I munched on the packed-lunch I brought with me and drank coffee from the flask. The drawings would take some time. It felt important to capture the sense of fluid action in the scene before me. I wondered just where the tribesmen were herding the animals, and why. Was this an illustration of persistence hunting, whereby hunters wore down the fleet-footed animals until one or more of them dropped through exhaustion? I would ask this and other questions of the scientists I'd meet the following day.

I felt a little odd sitting with my back to the wall of handprints, almost as if hands might emerge from that strangely domestic frieze and grab me. I knew I was being fanciful, however, and shrugged away my fears. What I really wanted to do was light a fire. For one thing, it was getting rather cold, and the wind was building to fury again beyond the cave-mouth, howling drafts penetrating the interior to where I sat.

Secondly, I wanted to see these paintings the way their creators once had. I'd read that they really came alive and even seemed animated in the flickering flames of a hearth. Would it be so awfully bad to light a small fire here now? I guessed that I probably shouldn't, in case the smoke damaged the frescoes, but as soon as I had this thought it seemed ridiculous. These walls had been lit up by firelight and patinated by woodsmoke for centuries. There were actually the remains of a fire here in any case, presumably made by the loggers who first found the cave, as well as a pile of unburnt tangled branches and logs.

In the end, after who knows how long, the oil-fired generator made my decision for me, together with the gathering storm. Two things happened in quick succession. First, I realised it had grown quite dark beyond the vertical slash of the cave entrance. I glanced at my watch. It was almost 4pm. I'd been drawing for three hours. Oddly, I'd hardly felt the time pass, although my frozen knuckles and stiff legs testified to how long I'd been sitting for. I walked to the cave mouth and was buffeted by a gust of wet wind that scoured my face viciously. A full storm was raging outside, and I'd somehow been entirely oblivious!

The trail was already being eroded by rivulets of rainwater and I couldn't see any sign of Tatiana's car down in the valley below. If I'd had any phone signal, I'd have called her but surrounded by granite and limestone mountains on three sides, there wasn't so much as a flicker of reception on my outmoded Nokia.

I decided to try my luck with the trail, reckoning I'd be safer and more comfortable in the lodge than the cave. However, after one too many disastrous and painful slips, the last of them sending me toppling towards the lip of an abyss, I realised it was now too dark and dangerous to attempt the path, even with a torch. I returned to the cave to wait out the storm, or Tatiana's return.

The second calamity which befell me was that the generator, whose oil reservoir must have been perilously low when we arrived, began to splutter, the Klieg lights flickering decisively. I tilted the generator to encourage the remaining oil to flow into the combustion chamber, or whatever it was called, but I doubted I had more than a few minutes of electricity left. That realisation clinched it. I grabbed handfuls of twigs and dry bracken and began to build a fire in the blackened space in the centre of the cave, lifting the lights closer to the walls to give me space to work.

I decided to sacrifice a few of the remaining pages of my sketchbook and was glad to discover that I had pocketed the lighter I used to light the stove this morning. Just as the generator wheezed to a halt and the lights went out, I managed to get the paper to catch, and the smaller twigs followed suit. Within ten minutes, the cave was illuminated with the amber flickering of a roaring fire. I felt a sense of pride in my second act of fire-lighting that day, which momentarily overcame the primitive fears lurking at the back of my mind, somewhere in the basal ganglia where the nightmares lived.

I realised I was wet through and there seemed no reason to remain modest, given the circumstances, so I stripped off and hung my shirt, trousers, jersey, and coat over the light stands, so that they caught the fire's heat. They would be dry in no time and although everything would stink of woodsmoke, at least I wouldn't perish from pneumonia. I was conscious of my flabby belly as I stood up in my socks and walked to the cavemouth, edging along one wall to stay out of the rain as it slanted down. I could dimly make out the streetlamps and illuminated windows of a village on the opposite hillside and the taillights of a few vehicles winding their way around distant B-roads, but there was no sign of life from our valley. Something must have happened to Tatiana. An accident, a flooded track, or a mudslide, perhaps a tree fallen across the road. It could be any of these things. Perhaps the likeliest explanation was the Rover breaking down; I regretted having cooed over the ancient automobile quite so much.

I returned to the fireside and positioned my backpack to create a pillow, then spread out some of the dried bracken that littered the cave floor. I might just rest awhile, I thought. Perhaps a little lie down to recuperate from my ordeals. As I lay my head down, I looked up at the dancing, panic-stricken animals fleeing their hunters. The antelope seemed to be leaping over the little diamonds of flame that separated from the main mass of the conflagration. The crackle and scent of burning pine began to have something of a soporific effect. I wasn't planning to fall asleep, just rest my eyes awhile...

I woke with a start; the flames having died down considerably. I had the unmistakable sensation of being watched. Again, I felt the prickling along the arms and the back of the neck. I was afraid to turn, for I knew who would be there. I was an interloper in his domain. There was a strange sound, like something sniffing and I felt hot breath upon my neck. I could have turned round, and confirmed my terrors but I was surely fantasising, so instead I lay back down, closing my eyes firmly. My body curled in on itself, refusing to turn and confirm my trespass upon the creature's domain. Somehow, even though my eyes were firmly closed, out of the darkness of the cavern behind my own orbs rose a pair of startlingly intelligent blue eyes, pushing forward into pale illumination to reveal a high eyebrow ridge, matted hair and then a curl of jutting top lip that showed a cruelly curved incisor.

I woke again... this time for real, revealing my previous experience to have been a dream. I was almost naked and shivering, with the dull, pinkish embers of the fire revealing that I had been asleep for hours. My watch did not have an illuminated dial, but I guessed it read a little after 11pm. Disaster must have befallen Tatiana, and I was quite alone.

As I reached out for my shirt, I heard it. Something not quite human. A deep-throated grumbling sound. Something waking, something lying in the shadows of the bottleneck of the cavern. It raised its head and I made out thick black fur, a snout and, in the dim moonlight and reddish fire's afterglow, the incisors from my dream. But this was no imagined neanderthal. This was a very real brown bear. One that had no doubt also sought refuge from the storm in this warm cave, perhaps not even noticing my presence until now.

My heart was beating a crazed tattoo as I desperately tried to remember what advice Tatiana gave me about encountering a bear. I think it amounted to little more than "don't". Bears can run faster than a man, climb trees and swim rivers. If a bear wants to take you down, it probably will, was the general message I got from the cultural attaché.

I shrank back against the wall, willing my half-asleep legs into utility. I needed to get out of there, and fast. Without my clothes, if that what it would take. The animal gradually rose onto all fours, then pushed itself onto its hind legs, almost like a man arising from a sound slumber. If I had awoken this animal from the start of its winter hibernation, that didn't bode well for its congeniality.

I had the embers at my back and the bear in front of me. I slunk into the shadows of the wall and started to back away as the beast reared up to its full height and roared at me. The noise was terrifying, even without the cave's echoes magnifying it. I felt a gust of hot, moist breath engulf me as the bear lolloped out of its corner. I backed further away at speed, wondering if I should roar back, when I felt something hard and metallic collide with my back. One of the lighting stands toppled over, its lamp hitting the stone floor of the cavern, the bulb exploding. Glass showered my feet.

The bear roared again and swiped at me with one immense paw as I tried to scramble away. A sensation like a garden rake slamming into my chest spun me round, bouncing me off the wall and directly onto the still-hot embers of the fire. I screamed and scrabbled out of the ashes. The bear hesitated, uncertain whether to move in for the kill or let me escape. Then, as I scrambled out of the cinders, I felt, rather than saw it lurch forward again, and everything slowed to a crawl, as one might imagine one's last moments doing.

Turning my head and damaged chest away from my attacker I saw a pair of bright and intelligent eyes in the darkness of the cavemouth. Then a mouth opened, pink with tiny sharp teeth. A chest thick with matted hair, splattered red. I felt a shock of recognition as the newcomer first turned its head to one side, then placed a finger to its lips, in the universal sign for silence. I felt myself freeze, like I had in my dream. What would be, would be.

The thick lips pursed and blew, and an immense blast hit both me and the fire's embers. Flame leapt into being and the bear backed away in fear, whimpering. I had screwed my eyes shut but now opened them to see nothing before me but the open cavemouth. I grabbed my coat from the floor and ran out into the now-dwindling storm, pressing the bundled fabric against my torn chest as I slipped and scrambled down the trail and back to the lodge.

I have no idea how long I lay bleeding and half-delirious, wrapped in blankets on the floor of the main room. At some point a vehicle drew up and two men carried me out into a waiting Jeep. I believe Tatiana was with them but by this point I had lost a lot of blood and nothing cohered – neither my thoughts, my sense impressions, or my perception of time itself. I remember vaguely bumping down the gravel track and then a needle being applied to my forearm.

106

I remember the taillights of the Rover as our vehicle followed it down onto blessed tarmac once more.

My recovery was slow and filled with troublesome half-memories and nightmares. I could hardly tell fact from feverish fiction and was unable to separate the bear in the cave from my memory of the apparition who had apparently saved me. The bear's claws had raked me down to the ribs. When I awoke blood was seeping through my bandaged chest from hastily-applied stitches. Fortunately, after a couple of calls, Lucia and Tatiana arranged my convalescence and paid the necessary bribes for a private suite.

"How do you feel?" was the first sentence from Tatiana I felt able to process when I awoke on the fourth morning after my ordeal.

"Confused..." I replied, "and dehydrated."

Tatiana poured me water and listened to my chaotic, scarcely credible story. I described the bear in full detail but, for some reason, felt unable to mention the humanoid who had saved me from its clutches. Once Tatiana had listened to my recap, she very calmly explained what had happened to her and confirmed certain aspects of my own story.

"I broke down halfway up the gravel track. Could not get car started," she began. "I decide to walk back to the village to get help. But the storm was ferocious so I stay there, imagining you must have gone to lodge. I would send mechanic in morning to fix car and collect you. When storm started dying down, I met Yuri and Alexandr and we decided to take Jeep to check on you."

"Thank you. I might have..." I replied feebly. "Well, thanks. But... the bear?"

"We see droppings and footprints," she said. "Brown

bear prints… and… human ones."

I attempted a laugh, but it became a grimace of pain.

"I took off my wet clothes and my shoes."

"And socks too?"

"No, I was never barefoot."

Tatiana frowned slightly. "That's odd. Did you fall in the fire?"

She had not criticised me for building a fire and had in fact agreed that it was the right decision. People die from exposure in the Carpathians at this time of year.

"I did. Trying to get away from the bear. Fortunately, it had all but gone out."

"You will have big scar, I think," she said, looking more than a little apologetic. I suspect her bosses at the Department of Culture might have given her a dressing down for leaving me alone in a gathering storm. Strangely, I felt no animosity towards my guide. I had wanted to be alone with the elements and the ancient artworks. I had longed for solitude to ingest all that was ancient and un-knowable. I had got more than I'd bargained for. I vowed to write to Tatiana's superiors in support of her hospitality and quick thinking. I would certainly have perished on the mountainside had she not returned for me.

I called Jane from the hospital to let her know what was happening, since she had expected an update regarding my trip. At least, I'd assumed she'd expected a call. Her first words to me were "Dad? Two calls in one month. You're spoiling me." Jane changed her tone immediately when I told her about the cave, the storm, and the bear. I did not talk about the apparition.

I had all but decided that my neanderthal saviour was a full figment of my frenzied imagination, a being constructed from pure panic and adrenalin, when something happened that threw me back into incomprehension. It was on the seventh day of my recovery, when I came to remove my bandages in the local hospital's surgical ward, so that the duty doctor could examine my stitches. A full-length mirror was positioned in the curtained-off cubicle and I was left alone while a fresh bandage was sourced. I stood before the tall glass and examined my tortured body. I had three livid, diagonal slashes across my ribcage and a sequence of smudgy bruises testifying to the many falls I'd suffered scrambling down the trail.

But what most perplexed me was the red-black weal on the small of my back. Looked at from one angle, it could clearly be interpreted as the burnt imprint of coals from the fire. But viewed from my own vantage-point it resembled nothing more nor less than the outline of a di-minutive hand, placed there in support, or perhaps as a vivid warning against trespassing the incalculable ages.

Agonía

Some tasks are quickly and readily achieved, others take time, patience and cunning. Infiltrating a Mexican drugs cartel run by a ruthless tyrant whose men had murdered hundreds takes determination verging on the monomaniacal.

Luis Martinez had that kind of focus. An ex-petty-criminal turned confidential DEA informant, Luis evaded prison following his last bust (a trunk-load of cocaine he'd smuggled deep inside beef carcasses in a refrigerated truck), by coming up with a ludicrously clever plan to embed himself in the 2020s' most powerful organised crime enterprise. As a cover story, it made good business sense for lone wolf operator Luis to offer his service to the Rodrigo Lopes cartel. Unfortunately, they would never accept a stranger like Luis without references.

So, Luis concocted a plan to steal back a confiscated shipment of Lopes' product from the high-security police evidence facility in Albuquerque, then sell it back to Lopes, with the suggestion that Lopes take credit for the heist. It was exactly the kind of audacious move that would appeal to the druglord's ego – he saw himself as a latter-day Scarface, conveniently forgetting how that movie ended.

It would all be staged; the police putting up minimal resistance, everyone firing blanks. Luis would take the shipment and a bullet to the shoulder and Lopes would hire the brave young soldier who'd pulled off an incredible feat. Everything went according to plan, looking so convincing on CCTV footage leaked to local news channels that Lopes didn't suspect a thing.

Three days later, Luis' blindfold was removed, and he was pushed into a chair in front of Lopes himself. His bandage shoulder throbbed painfully. Lopes had had his incisors lengthened and filed to points to make himself look more ferocious As Luis found himself being fastened to the chair with cable ties, he wondered if Lopes planned to use those incisors on his neck.

"So…" Lopes drawled lazily. "You stole my shipment back from the DEA and now you want to sell it back to me? Are you out of your mind?"

Luis winced as one of Lopes men pushed down on his shoulder.

"You'd have to write it off otherwise," said Luis. "There's fifty million in that haul."

Lopes bent down for a closer look at Luis.

"Unless the police marked it."

Luis shook his head: "I checked."

"And what do you want for my cocaine?" said Lopes, humouring him.

"Five hundred thousand," offered Luis. "I'm not greedy."

Lopes laughed. "Señor Martinez, you confuse me," he began. "You have my product, and you are largely un-known. I might never have found you. Why didn't you go to one of my competitors?"

"Because you have eyes everywhere. I couldn't be sure you hadn't someone in the police, or even in my crew. You were the only one I could safely sell to."

And you feel safe now, do you? Tied to a chair, at an unknown address, alone?"

Luis gave a faint chuckle. "You don't know where the drugs are. I do."

Lopes stepped back, as if sizing Luis up (but for what?)

"I applaud your entrepreneurship. We'll talk business in a little while. I have a little welcome treat for you. Or rather, an initiation."

Lopes drew a small packet from his pocket – it contained a half dozen small blue pills.

"I'm getting out of cocaine. The heat is too great. I have something far better. A designer miracle, they're calling it. On the street, its name is Agonía. You're going to road-test it."

What was this? Luis had heard of "Agony". A drug more rumoured than evidenced, it supposedly acted as a polar opposite of MDMA, in that it caused every single pain-registering synapse in the brain to fire at once, for a split-second, the equally sudden removal of this pain leaving the taker in a blissful state of release, and also very suggestible. In other words, it could be used as a truth drug. Or so he'd heard.

Luis had recently received a text message from a shady friend. It consisted of a photo of a man who had died of a heart attack taking Agonía for sexual gratification. The victim had been found purple-faced, dangling from his trouser belt, his feet partly eaten by his Doberman. The caption his friend had appended was – 'hang on in there, buddy'.

Luis was gripped from behind, while one of Jose's people forced open his mouth. Luis knew better than to bite. He swallowed the pill and waited for the inevitable.

It came at him like a wall. A wall made of fire, knives, and acid. Luis's body spasmed. He went momentarily blind, the agony so intense that he lost all sense of time, space, or identity. He wasn't Luis anymore – he was the locus of all the pain in the world.

Then, just as suddenly, he felt nothing at all. Just an extraordinary floating sensation. Luis realised he had a big, dumb smile plastered on his face.

"Tell me, Mr Martinez," said Lopes, crouching down to look into Luis' wide, rolling eyes. "Who sent you? What do you really want?"

Even in his paradisiacal haze, Luis sensed that something was wrong. He should probably get out of this place. Rivers of adrenalin still flooded his system. The chair felt wobbly.

Luis chose his moment, using newfound strength to push off with the balls of his feet, launching himself and the chair into the air. He flew three feet and crashed down, wood splintering under him. Luis yanked both hands free, stumbled to his feet and pushed a shattered, pointed chair-leg under Jose's chin before anyone could react.

Jose waved his men's guns down.

"Remarkable, Mr Martinez. Now tell me what you want."

Same question, different tone.

Luis, higher than the clouds but stronger than the noonday sun, whispered in his captor's ear.

"I want in."

After a moment, Jose nodded, and a DEA legend's career was born.

Charity

Ex-LAPD detective Leroy Bixler had been in charge of security at the Vehicle Impound Yard for the Hollenbeck district for seven years.   One more year and he'd retire. He'd be sixty by then and his back, feet and eyes would thank him for some time off.

Over the seven years since he'd been gently encouraged to take a desk job, following the Crazy Lady Incident, he'd occasionally met an ex-colleague from the Robbery Homicide division, who would chat amiably enough but always with a slightly condescending air of 'poor you'.

He'd only done what many seasoned cops had talked about doing throughout his 28-year tenure on the street – he'd taken himself out of the line of fire, to look after his ailing father, his overworked paramedic wife and two young children. Leroy had experienced his share of out-there incidents.   He didn't need any more grief now he was approaching the big six-oh.

Therefore, he probably shouldn't have locked up the seventeen-year-old boy in the impounded school bus at the back of the yard.   It was for the kid's own good that Leroy had done this.   After all, who but a hopeless junkie would attempt to raid an LAPD impound yard?

Okay, the kid had waited until the Easter weekend, when security was less tight (and Leroy had let his young deputy Broderick White leave early), plus he'd managed to get himself a really good pair of metal-cutters and a balaclava, but he must surely have known there'd be someone on patrol and CCTV everywhere.   He clearly didn't care – without the balaclava, he'd had the gaunt and greasy-haired look of the hardened meth-head. When Leroy had heard the gates clang shut, he'd been on the other side of the yard patrolling. It had been a little after 3am, and he'd found the boy, trying to jimmy open a Maserati belonging to a local drug-dealer.

Leroy, a former alcoholic whose condition had worsened after the Crazy Lady Incident, could recognise the all-consuming desperation in the boy's eyes so he'd elected to use the taser rather than the gun to take him down. There were no witnesses to see Leroy fail to announce his presence or ask the thief to put his hands on his head or kneel down or follow any of the other protocols. Leroy had simply crept up to him and deployed the taser.

He had plans other than arresting this boy and sending him on his first steps into a spiral of incarceration, unemployment, addiction, and petty theft followed by further arrest, and so forth. The judicial system would not be kind to this individual. However, Leroy held out some hope that the boy might still be green enough to save.

Once he had the kid unconscious, Leroy dragged him over to the school bus, which had just one door, prised it open and flung him inside, with some blankets, the fried chicken sandwiches his wife Leticia had prepared for his mid-shift snack, and a thermos of cold water. If he could just keep the boy here for three days, he'd probably lose the worst of the chemical dependency and might be open to some tough love and persuasion.

Leroy had made a secret vow seven years ago not to arrest any addicts and he meant to stick to it.

Right now, that might prove challenging. The boy had come to about twenty minutes ago and was trying to break the bus's windscreen with the thermos, which was already badly dented. Leroy had tried to explain that the bus had two layers of toughened glass in case of accidents and was pretty impregnable. He had wrapped a thick chain around the door handles, trying them shut. He'd also backed the bus up against a wall so the emergency exit at the rear wasn't accessible. The kid wasn't getting out any time soon.

"Let me the fuck outa here!" the boy shouted, a look of desperation in his eyes. Leroy wondered when he had last scored. If it was more than two days' prior, that might well give Leroy a head start.

"I mean it man. I'll fuckin' shank ya!"

Nothing seemed less likely. Leroy weighted two hundred and eighty pounds and stood six feet four on his flat, size fourteen feet. The kid probably weighed less than a female figure skater.

The last time someone had screamed at Leroy like that, it had been a woman so raddled and confused by her addiction that she was practically speaking in tongues. In a fugue of disorientation, she had walked into the middle of the Macy's thanksgiving parade, swinging an eight-inch knife at the startled musicians and baton-throwers who filtered around her.

She could have been anywhere between twenty-five and fifty. She had only half her own teeth and was clutching something foul-smelling in a plastic bag and screeching about "my baby, my precious one."

Whether it was the drugs, her distress, or the chaos all around her, it had been clear to Leroy, the first officer on the scene, that this wouldn't end well. He'd done right thing, halting the parade, and approaching the woman with weapon drawn but pointed at the ground.

When he was about twelve feet away, she raised the

knife to her shoulder and came at him, screaming. He'd gone for a shoulder shot but had misjudged it and blown half her head off. Children and adults alike were screaming in fear and horror around him.

In a daze of bewilderment, he'd forgotten all procedures at that point, and had approached the woman's body, disentangling the plastic bag from her claw-like fingers, ignoring his stomach's instinctive recoil at the unmistakable smell of rot, and looking inside to see what she'd been screaming about. It was the body of a baby boy barely less than a month old, but probably dead for at least a week. He couldn't rid his nostrils of the smell of shameful, obscene rot for days.

"Kid, I'm keeping you here until Monday", Leroy shouted. "I know why you're here and what you really want but it 'aint' too late to turn it around."

The kid tossed Leroy the bird and spat on the glass.

Well, thought Leroy, charity had to start somewhere.

The Fundamentals of Susan

Susan Callander watched two ducks – drake and female – spiralling around one another in the reedy pond. She wondered what on earth their peculiar dance signified. A single-wheeled hoverboard whizzed by, its rider missing her shoulder by inches, disturbing her reverie. Susan considered hurling some abuse his way… but didn't.

Susan had arranged to meet her friend Jess at 4pm. She still had the best part of an hour to kill in the sunlit park on what was becoming an especially fine June afternoon. She had a lot on her mind; perhaps a wander among the rose beds and past the fountains would help soothe away her anxieties.

Before she had left the house, Susan had assessed herself in the hall mirror, a regular little ritual, not so much to boost her confidence but more to get a sense of proportion. What exactly am I dealing with? she asked herself, as she had done a thousand times before.

Reflected in the oval frame, Susan saw a thirty-four-year-old, slightly plump, ruddy-cheeked woman with fair-to-brown hair, green eyes, freckled skin, and a silken blouse that was a little too tight around her ample bosom. So much so that the shirt gaped a little between buttons, revealing glimpses of pale belly and a black, underwired bra.

Damn it, thought Susan, I'm sure this fitted last time I wore it. She must have put on a few pounds over the spring – all that partying, no doubt. Works events she felt obliged to intend, birthday parties. From now on, she'd leave off the beer and wine and move back to spirits. This is what comes of trying to keep up with the boys, she thought.

Susan checked her jeans pockets for the essentials – keys, bank card, mobile, tissues – and pulled the door to her flat carefully shut, to avoid any more paint flaking from the jamb.

The park was as bright and lively as she'd hoped. The little West-London oasis was always busy, with plenty to see. She tried to maintain a contemplative frame of mind, inevitably interrupted by huffing joggers, skateboarders attempting something foolish with a bench or a scattering of toy dogs under the ineffectual control of an absurdly fur-coated old dear. Regardless, Susan remained happy to stroll through the rose garden and mull over the events of the preceding week, plus her plans for the week ahead.

Susan made it through the zig-zag path with the livid purple rhododendrons (quick stop for an Instagram post) and was considering pausing at the café for an ice lolly when she first caught sight of The Triplets. She paused to sit on a park bench and watch them from the periphery of her vision, intrigued and almost a little afraid, for reasons she couldn't wholly justify.

There they were, standing shoulder to shoulder, like foot-ballers facing a penalty. Three little men, each no more than five feet tall, clad in identical sky-blue trousers and tunics. Tunics… in this day and age? Susan could see silver buttons gleaming on their chests and although the men were diminutive (though not dwarves) their trousers failed to conceal an inch of hairy shin and two inches of white sock. They all work Birkenstocks, unapologetically. They had near-identical scrubbed, shiny faces, like windfallen apples. All three had the same haircut – side-partings plastered across their foreheads like miniature Hitlers. They had uniform toothy smiles, which Susan was alarmed to see were directed her way. Susan smiled feebly back. These men were perhaps on day release from some care home for the mentally different and she didn't want to appear un-friendly. She did kind of want to Instagram them though.

Susan turned her attention to her chipped fingernails and stubby fingers. Why couldn't she have elegant hands, like Jess? She couldn't imagine these doughy digits scam-pering along piano keys like Jess's frequently did at her din-ner parties. Colin, Susan's boyfriend, once said her fingers were like 'cute little chipolatas'. Then he'd kissed each one, making Susan smile and forget the swell of her belly over the turquoise lingerie he'd bought. Of course, he'd spoilt it by uttering that terrible old cliché about small hands making his willy look bigger. Colin could be crude sometimes. Still, he seemed to love her, and for that she could muster gratitude.

The triplets were standing right beside her bench, al-though Susan hadn't seen them move, still in a line as if joined at the shoulder. Susan looked up in panic; what if they were conjoined triplets? Was such a thing possible? With relief, she saw sunlight gleaming between two of the men. She mustered another weak smile, knowing that con-tact was imminent.

"Hi there. Lovely day," she said.

The Triplets smiled broadened.

We've found Susan. We are happy.

Startlingly, they spoke in perfect unison, their voices flat and comical, pitched about a semitone apart, creating a weirdly boring harmony.

"Sorry?" was all Susan could muster in response.

We have found her. Susan is an excellent friend.

Susan wasn't sure whether to laugh, or edge away, so she did both.

"How do you know my name?"

The Triplets giggled.

We know all about Susan. We are the Fundamentals. The Fundamentals of Susan. Susan is a brilliant cook but mostly dines alone.

"Who put you up to this?" Susan demanded.

The Triplets looked blankly benevolent.

"One of the guys in the office, wasn't it? Was it Dave Arcott? I'll bet it was – it's just his style."

We don't know about Dave. We know about Susan. Susan loves animals, especially otters and baby seals.

"How did you...? Was it Alan Moulder? Or Kris Zymanski? It's a bit surreal for Billy but he does have the IKEA account, so maybe..."

Susan has a lot of friends, but they seldom call. Susan is surrounded by love.

"Come on guys, give me a break."

Susan has excellent teeth and no fillings. Susan has a wonderful sense of humour and shares her laughter with others.

Susan did laugh then, but the laugh quickly faded. They were just so... attentive.

"Guys, I'm beginning to lose it. Was Maxine involved in this? Tell her it's not my birthday until next month and a card would have done."

Susan takes lovely long, hot baths. Often Susan masturbates under the soapy suds.

"Right! That's frigging enough!"

She got up and began to walk away. Susan got the alarming notion that the Triplets were following her. However, when she turned, after a heart-poundingly fast stride to the closest gate, they had vanished. Back to the day-release centre, she hoped.

Jess was in good spirits. She'd just secured her millionth follower for her cosmetics vlog and had won a freelance commission to write a piece on male grooming in the 21st century. Jess began filling the café table with a peculiar haul provided by the editors.

"Susie, I had absolutely no idea! Deep-cleansing facewash with aloe and provitamin B5 – for men! Foot cream. And look at this – it's a cucumber and sage face pack, for Christ's sake. What is the world coming to? Dan will be borrowing my epilator next!"

Normally Susan would have enjoyed joining in this diatribe. Or rather, she'd have countered it with some anecdote of Colin's bewilderment in the face of burgeoning toiletries, just to reassure her friend that some men were still inept in all the right ways. But something was disturbing her, something at the edge of her peripheral vision, something sky-blue. With three heads. Something she didn't want to acknowledge was there at all.

"Hey, Suze, look. Some sort of street theatre behind you."

Susan leaned across the table towards her friend.

"Jess, please don't…"

But it was too late. The triple headed blue blob swung into vision, inane gleaming faces preparing identical smiles. They sidled round, blocking out the late afternoon sunshine.

Susan has exquisite taste when it comes to restaurants, both al fresco and indoors.

"Susan, do you know these people?" Jess asked in wonder.

"No, I do not. It's some dumb joke the boys in the office are playing on me. Ignore them and I'm sure they'll go away."

Susan chooses her friends wisely.

"Why thanks," Jess replied. "Loving the tunics."

"Jess! Don't encourage them."

The Fundamentals seemed content to stand and gleam at them both, as waiters dodged around them with mounting irritation. Eventually a manager appeared.

"Excuse me miss, but your friends are going to have to sit down."

"They're not my friends. In fact, they're bothering me. Can you make them leave please?"

The manager contrived to look relieved and irritated at the same time.

"I'm sorry sirs, the lady would like you to leave."

Susan is outgoing but never outstays her welcome.

"That's very salutary but if you could just…"

The manager opened his arms and walked towards the Fundamentals. For normal men, the approach of an unfamiliar male body would cause an instinctive backing away. Not so these peculiar little men. The manager found a head lodged under each armpit, but the Fundamentals didn't give an inch. Back-up arrived in the form of a tall, blonde waiter but the tripartite chorus of admiration wouldn't shift. It was only when the manager lost his temper and began manhandling the interlopers that they stopped grinning, bowed to Susan (who cringed behind her hands while Jess

124

stifled laughter) and left.

Susan fills her days with meaningful tasks but always finds time for friends, they murmured plaintively as they trotted off down the pavement like autistic poodles, scattering pedestrians in their wake.

She'd give them hell on Monday. Susan didn't know quite what she'd do when she found out which of her colleagues set up the surreal stunt, but she knew her revenge must be equally cunning and unexpected. The experiences she'd had today had really shaken and embarrassed her. The random things those little fiends had said had got Susan thinking unprofitably about herself. Were they making it up as they went along or reciting some sarcastic little list Billy or Kris or Maxine or whoever had concocted with her in mind? Susan could only assume the intention was ironic; she felt it hard to believe anyone would like her enough to hire circus freaks to extol her virtues. What had they called themselves? Her Fundamentals? What the hell did that even mean?

She was still musing on the possible origins of the tripartite apparition when she went to turn the key in her front door and found it was already unlocked. That could only mean one thing – Colin was here. Susan had cut him a key midway through their second blissful month together and now she was beginning to wonder if it had been such a good idea. Surely, she should feel something other than mild dread that her boyfriend was home and possibly planning to cook for her or at least massage her feet? Indifference couldn't be a good sign six months into a relationship.

"Howdy love," grinned Colin, appearing in the doorway wearing over gloves and leaning in for a cursory kiss.

"Some of your friends are here. They've been waiting half an hour."

He lowered his voice.

"They're a bit odd."

With a sickening lurch in her stomach Susan realised who these "friends" must be.

Susan is punctual to a fault and always scrupulously clean.

"Hello boys! Make yourself at home," Susan said, trying a new tack.

The Fundamentals were sitting bolt upright on the sofa, with identical cups of tea untouched on their laps. Colin wandered in behind Susan with a plate of fresh, fragrant cinnamon biscuits. I'm such an ungrateful bitch, Susan thought. Colin tended to bake if left to his own devices, one of his more unique and endearing qualities.

"They won't tell me which one they're in," said Colin mysteriously.

"Which what?"

"Commercial. Is it Oculus Rift?"

The penny dropped. Colin was onto something. The Fundamentals were part of some elaborate transmedia ad campaign that one of the junior teams at Susan's agency had contrived. They were evidently road-testing it on Susan. She ought to feel honoured, she supposed.

Yet there was something simperingly strange about the ferocity with which the Fundamentals stayed in character. Nothing seemed to faze them.

Susan is intelligent and an excellent problem-solver.

"Not at all," Susan said. "Colin figured it out. Tell me boys – are you on deferred pay? If so, you won't see a penny of it. There's no budget for speculative pitches or test commercials."

They didn't flinch.

Susan knows the value of money and balances generosity with prudence. Susan has wonderful taste in men who bake wonderful biscuits.

Colin beamed.

"I kinda like them. I'd buy the product, whatever it is."

It wasn't an ad campaign after all. Susan found that out when, halfway through her crushingly embarrassing Monday morning, Mr Hagerty himself trotted down the spiral stairs into the gleaming glass and polished wood lobby and ambled over to her brushed steel desk.

Susan is attentive and polite and defers to powerful men with ease.

"Keep it down will you," Susan hissed.

Mr Hagerty, an ever-youthful figure in open-necked burgundy shirt and well-laundered slacks, smiled as he laid a jiffy bag in front of Susan. Blushing already, Susan tried to ignore the trinity of little blue men sitting in the waiting area behind her. Hagerty, not one to be fazed by the outlandish, registered their presence with the momentary raising of a single eyebrow.

"Susan. I know it's a bore, but could you make sure UPS collects this by three. I'd send it via the post room but it's so important, I'd rather leave it in your capable hands."

Hagerty smiled winningly. The lines on his lightly freckled face only added to his dashing yet boyish charm, Susan couldn't help but notice.

Susan is enamoured of older men, especially those of a creative bent.

"What?" Laughed Hagerty. He wheeled round to face the Fundamentals.

Susan turned an even deeper shade of pink , if that were possible.

"You don't know which team is behind this do you, Mr Hagerty?" Susan blurted. "Only they won't leave me alone."

"No idea. I doubt it's one of ours. I'd have heard of this for sure."

Susan is easily embarrassed in front of men she sexually contemplates.

Susan groaned involuntarily, startling Hagerty.

"Are you all right Susan?" he asked gently.

"I was until I had a freakish fan club, Mr Hagerty."

"Oh, do call me Tom."

"Okay then, er, Tom. Any chance you might find out who's behind this and make them go away?"

Tom Hagerty winked.

"I'll see what I can do."

Half an hour later, security had the Fundamentals ejected, Hagerty's groupwide email having solicited no answers. Now everyone in the agency knows about my fan club, thought Susan. Frigging heck.

Susan decided to thwart her Fundamentals by jogging home along the canal towpath. It was a route she'd run regularly about a year ago but after Christmas, New Year and all those Spring parties, her exercise regime had lapsed.

Susan dug out the tracksuit from her bottom drawer, got changed in the disabled loo, packed her regular clothes into her backpack and set off, red in the face with exertion after just five minutes.

Rounding a corner onto the towpath, Susan instinctively knew what awaited her. There they were, sitting buttock to buttock on a bench, feeding the ducks with bits of muffin from three identical paper bags. She grinned at the Fundamentals as she swept past.

"So long boys, eat my dust."

But ludicrously, thirty seconds later, they dropped their bags and started after her, struggling to kept abreast of one another on the narrow path, but seemingly undeterred by the physical effort.

Susan is health conscious and takes regular cardiovascular exercise, they shouted.

Susan leads by example.

Susan won't let incipient middle-age spoil her elegant figure.

You little blue bastards, thought Susan. If that's the way you want it, let's see what you're made of. She picked up the pace, trying her best to ignore the beginnings of a stitch under the left side of her ribcage.

"Not exactly dressed for jogging, are you?" Susan sneered at her pursuers, trying to quash a sneaking suspicion that they were somehow gaining on her.

An elderly male cyclist passed Susan, who attempted a smile. There followed a frantic tinkle of bell ringing, and Susan turned in time to see the cyclist half-topple into a thorny bush, then turn and throw half-hearted curses at the madly grinning, unperturbed Fundamentals.

Susan makes up for lost time.

Susan will be home in time for a nutritious evening meal.

Susan needs the embrace of a strong, nurturing male.

You're not wrong there, Susan thought, as if answering an inner voice.

When Colin turned up an hour later, in response to her frantic call, he found her sitting in the hallway outside her flat while giant raindrops splashed on the tarmac outside. Her Fundamentals were nowhere to be seen. The run home had almost killed her, and they had kept pace with her every agonising step of the way.

"Suze, where..?"

"I don't know. They just up and left ten minutes ago. They were driving me insane. I threatened to call the police after I called you and I was actually dialling 999 when I noticed they'd gone."

Colin helped Susan to her feet, the run and subsequent bout with her trinity of flatterers having left her devoid of impetus. He unlocked the door to her flat, inquiring as gently as possible as to the whereabouts of her keys. She forgot them regularly; it was one of the reasons he'd asked her to cut him a duplicate set.

"I think they must have fallen out of my jacket. Yes, here they are," said Susan, retrieving the keys from the arm of the sofa.

She slumped down and let Colin pour her a glass of orange juice, which she downed in one.

"Got anything stronger?" she gasped. Colin squinted at her, ascertaining whether she was serious or not. Evidently, she wasn't.

He pulled off her trainers and socks and knelt between her feet, massaging her toes.

"Colin is an attentive boyfriend," Susan murmured.

He laughed gently, working his thumbs into the balls of her feet. She sighed.

"Colin is good and kind and doesn't mind Susan's smelly feet."

"Colin is tired and hungry," he added, playing along.

"Colin would like to order a takeaway."

"Colin is full of excellent suggestions," Susan replied, kissing him, and leaving him with a taste of orange juice and stale perspiration.

Neither of them heard the voices murmuring in soft, mournful accompaniment from behind the open window.

Colin and Susan enjoyed a night of surprisingly good sex, both of them giving and taking their pleasure with an easy equilibrium. For once, Susan felt herself willing to provide her boyfriend with what he needed, as well as taking what he was eager to give her. As a result of their exertions, Colin slept in the following morning and dashed out the door frantically at half past eight, vowing to return that evening.

Susan had asked him to take the day off, to phone in sick. In a way she was testing him, but she knew playing truant was something Colin could never do. He said it was going to be an especially busy week at the recruitment consultants where he worked, and he'd only feel guilty and wouldn't enjoy the day off.

"Even if you spent it with me?" Susan asked coyly.

"Especially then," he replied ruefully, entirely missing the point.

Susan had no such qualms, phoning in and talking to Marie, who helped out on reception three days a week – fortunately, Tuesday was one of those days. Marie didn't mind covering. Susan claimed PMT and a migraine and that seemed to satisfy her colleague.

She lay back and basked in the rays of light sneaking in between the gap in the curtains. In a moment, she'd get up and fix herself some muesli. First, she wanted to see what kind of day she was stealing. She got up and stretched.

Walking towards the window, which was open behind the gently billowing cloth. Colin always thought her central heating was turned up too high. His own stayed off from May through September, probably his Scottish genes at play. Strange man, she thought fondly. Were her feelings towards him changing again? Would she always be this ambivalent, blown from one feeling to another like a dandelion seed on the breeze?

She threw open the curtains.

Susan is in a lazy, contemplative mood.

Susan should be at work but deserves a day off.

Susan's nightgown is translucent in the morning light.

She slammed the curtains shut on the three grinning heads and dialled 999.

"I'm sorry Madam. If they haven't actually threatened you, and they leave when you tell them to…"

"But I don't want them here. They're bothering me."

"What exactly is it in their behaviour that bothers you?"

"It's what they're saying."

"Can you give me an example? Are they using bad language? Calling you names? Would you describe it as a hate crime?"

"No, nothing like that. They say… nice things about me, mostly."

There was silence at the other end of the line.

"Hello?" Said Susan, wondering if DC Dunlevy had hung up.

"I'm still here. Did I hear you right? They say nice things?"

"Yes. They're very complimentary. Insanely so."

"I see. And they've not touched or threatened you in any way?"

"Well, no. But it's very off-putting and embarrassing, frankly."

"Miss Callander, I'm afraid there's nothing we can do then."

"What? You're going to let them keep at it?" Susan said incredulously.

"There's no law against compliments, I'm afraid," he said, with the hint of a smirk in is voice.

"Officer, are you taking me seriously?" Susan said, trying to control herself.

Dunlevy cleared his throat, and his voice regained its professional sheen.

"Absolutely, Miss Callander. I want you to keep us informed. We do take this sort of thing very seriously so you must let us know the moment it escalates."

"The moment it what?"

"Escalates. If they try to give you anything, offer you gifts, or make friends with your friends. That sort of thing."

His voice was reassuring but Susan got the sense that he was making it up as he went along, humouring her.

"Thanks DC Dunlevy. I will."

They caught up with her in the frozen food section of her local supermarket as she examined frozen pizzas with Colin. He's insisted on coming with her. In fact, he'd been practically living with her for a fortnight, fending off the Fundamentals by whisking her into cars, taxis, and cinemas (her favourite choice as the management could be relied upon to eject Susan's persecutors within minutes).

But Colin was now as omnipresent as the little blue pests had been. Coming food shopping with her was simply too much. Her once-weekly trawl around Sainsbury's was one of the contemplative highlights of Susan's week and she resented sharing it with anyone. Colin had denied her the second tub of Haagen-Dazs. He'd scoffed at the £8 bottle of shampoo she'd bought, opting for a basic brand for his own thinning locks. And the ten minutes he'd spent poring over the deli counter she usually whizzed straight past were ten minutes of her life she'd never get back, mixed olives and feta cheese notwithstanding.

Now, as Susan weighed up the pros and cons of various macrobiotic yoghurts and Colin threw in his tuppence worth about organic options, there the Fundamentals were. Susan almost felt relieved.

Susan's weekly shop is spontaneous and unplanned.
Susan's basket is filled with healthy provender.
Susan likes the good things in life and frets not for her hips.

"Come on chaps," Colin began, amiably enough but scanning the store for a security person. Susan began to seethe, head down over the trolley and shuttling down the aisle, as the Fundamentals scuttled after them.

Susan is not afraid to shop until she drops.
Susan efficiently visits every aisle, selecting wisely.
Susan is a perfectionist.

Susan exploded.

"I'm NOT! I'm not a bloody perfectionist!"

She rounded on the triumvirate of followers.

Susan seldom gets angry.

"Really? Watch me."

Colin told her to wait there. He headed off looking

decisive but failing to locate a nearby member of staff.

Susan is a loving girlfriend, who heeds her boyfriend's well-intentioned advice.

Susan is kind and giving.

"No, I'm not! I'm frigging well not!"

Susan, with gritted teeth, caught the little man in the middle of the trio unawares, grabbing the collar of his tunic and pushing him up against a freezer cabinet.

"For the last fucking time, I'm not kind or giving, or a perfectionist. I'm not efficient or wise. I don't choose sensibly. Sometimes I feel like I don't choose anything at all! Things and people find me, like you found me. Like Colin found me."

Though she had only one Fundamental gripped in her quaking fists, all three were backed up against the frozen pizza display in sympathy with one another. Susan's rant continued, unabated.

"Go find Colin. He's the perfect one. The selfless bloody do-gooder. Always there for me, always right. If you want a subject for your total adulation, choose him. Mr Perfect. Here he comes now, with two man-mountains to throw your scrawny little arses out into the street!"

Which was exactly what happened.

Susan didn't see her fan club at all for nearly a month. She also didn't see Colin after that shopping excursion. He'd helped her home with the bags and was in the middle of putting away the groceries when she'd taken a jar of beetroot from his hands and told him she needed a little time to herself.

"But what about them?" He asked plaintively.

"Let me handle them," she replied.

In the event, she didn't have to. They disappeared. Susan didn't ask why. Instead, she enjoyed 27 blissful days of silence and solitude.

And then came the call.

"Susie, Suze... listen!"

"Col, I told you I need some time to think. I've had a really restful few weeks and it's put things into perspective..."

"No, I mean, literally listen."

And the line went dead. Except it didn't. Susan clamped her right hand over her ear, pressing the iPhone to her head, stepping off Oxford Street and down a flight of urine-smelling stairs onto a Soho backstreet. She could hear something at last.

The sound she heard was like a rising lament. A chorale in tripartite unison.

Colin mournfully awaits Susan's decision.
Colin is strong but alone, alone but strong.
Colin is a man who loves very deeply, as an ocean swells.

Despite her better instincts, Susan had to laugh. She kept on laughing for longer than was entirely reasonable.

Wheatfield with Crows

Yesterday I burned three paintings in the yard at the Auberge. The acrid smell as the oil paint blackened and curled away from the browning canvas satisfied me deeply. It gave me as much pleasure as cooking sausages over a campfire had when I was a boy.

Dr Gachet cycled by and threw his bicycle down, rushing up the lane to stop me. The pain in his eyes was almost comical.

"Vincent! What are you doing?" he said, coughing in a curl of blue smoke.

I held him from the flames with an outstretched hand, as I dropped the last work into the brazier. He tried to grab the edge of a frame, just as its varnish caught the flames. The old fool would set fire to his beard if he weren't careful.

"Removing ugliness from the world," I explained. I couldn't help feeling a sliver of sadistic pleasure as my old friend struggled to comprehend what he considered an atrocity.

I don't know where he gets his boundless sentimentality – those works were inferior, inauthentic, wrong. I tried to explain but he just kept bleating – "at least keep the frames and paint over the canvases!" It cheered me up – watching him blow on his burnt fingertips and do a little dance of fury in the garden.

"Old friend," I told him. "You mustn't worry so. It will damage your health."

We both laughed, since we are already ruined and I am convinced the good doctor will perish first, despite his homeopathic remedies, which I am sure are simply water blessed by naïve optimism.

It's a great pity the farmer and his boys will come with their scythes soon. In a matter of days, the wheatfields will be razed to a stubble shorter than my own. I paint with diagonal dabs and slashes that are filled with urgency. Midsummer will be upon us, then just as quickly autumn with its scatterings, before winter throws a shroud over the Val d'Oise.

Each season races by with a terrifying acceleration. I paint like a man frenzied by the scythes coming up behind him. In just three years I will be forty! What have I achieved? Nothing! Everything! I oscillate between these conclusions.

I long for Theo and Johanna's next visit. Someone sane should remind me that what I do each day is worth doing. They departed, last week, my infinitely patient brother, his wife, and their little boy. They've named him Vincent. I wept when they told me.

The field is like a stretched canvas, like a pair of open palms. A steady wind slants the sheaves to the right, causes the crows to wheel drunkenly on its turbulence. I try to capture this motion against a darkening azure sky. I'm tempted to look at my pocket-watch – a present from Dr Gachet. I refuse to do it. What need have I of clocks? I can tell by the shadows and the deepening blue that I have an hour and a half of sensible daylight. It is enough. I pull my coat tight around my neck and force the cap down over my ears. I really ought to obtain a scarf.

Honey, cocoa, and asparagus. The colours of the field make me momentarily hungry, but the thought passes with a shot of absinthe from the flask in my inside pocket. It's astringent bite never fail to warm me. Perhaps I will eat in the tavern on my way home if the landlady extends my credit. The money Theo left me has all but flown.

I fill a flat, medium-sized brush will a daub of burnt umber, to delineate the pathway cutting between the fields and zigzagging out of sight over the hill. It is rutted by the wheels of carts and the hooves of horses, red-brown dirt alternating with stripes of green grass where the wheels cannot reach. I've haven't yet walked that path; I don't know where it leads.

I'm glad I chose this wide canvas and came out today, instead of painting in the Auberge. The mistress doesn't like it when I splatter her floorboards. But it's good that I am not cooped up in the Yellow House with lesser painters sneering at my furniture and complaining of cockroaches.

The sun is behind me and I can feel its dying warmth on my neck. I'm glad I don't have to squint. Looking into the sun all day gives me headaches and fills me with fury and frustration.

It's time to do justice to the clouds. They are usually magnificent in early July but today there are just two blobs of blue-white cumulous, rolled like napkins on a restaurant table. Once I have layered them in, to my satisfaction, I'll concentrate on the crows. This painting is really about them, as they wheel and dance, daring one another to dive for worms or nibble at fallen seeds. They resemble the blades of scythes. I dash off several dozen, exaggerating their number, because I want them to merge into the sky. In fact, I'll darken the sky at its fringes, and they can emerge from that unfathomable space above. A murder. That's what the English say, and they know what they are talking about.

I don't feel melancholy today. I rarely do when I'm working. There's just too much to think about when I fill up my mind with colours and textures and shapes. Damnable art critics say my work lacks depth and form and precision, as if truth could be attained by making art like you might take a Daguerreotype, freezing reality onto a plate! As if there's any truth in the bourgeois depiction of lords and ladies and prancing horses and spoilt ruddy-cheeked children! Give me a weathered farmer, crooked as a hawthorn, tilling his field, or a red-nosed postman drinking away his wages. That's my kind of truth.

But worse than ignorance is the greatest sin of all – pity. I see it in Theo's eyes constantly. And sometimes in the eyes of Dr Gachet, although fleetingly these days because I mostly just frustrate him. I see it in some of the kinder townspeople, wet-eyed and slack-jawed in incomprehension. Why must he stand out in the cold for hours, why must he live on bread, cheese, wine, and stolen apples?

Because I must. That's the only answer I'll give them and if it makes no sense then damn them all! There is always the revolver, and the wine. There is always the lovely light just before sunset, the wheatfield before the scythes come, the cackling of crows and the rich red earth under my boots.

10 Social Isolation Games

1. CURVE: Take an item of household furniture and saw it into pieces approximately 12 inches by 8 inches square. Whittle or carve these pieces into rounded, flat, chevron shapes. After carving each piece, take it into the garden (open a window if you live in a city). Hurl each piece into the sky, imparting a rapid spin. Some of the objects may return, after describing a giant curve; others will not. Teeth may be lost, windows endangered. In the interests of charity, you may wish to write encouraging messages upon each missile: *take heart, hope springs eternal, help is coming.*

2. ANATOMY: Label each part of your body with its function with a black marker pen. Give each part a mark out of ten depending on how much you like and need it. Make sure your assessment is honest and accurate. This will help when playing game 7. It may help to remember some of the uses you previously put these body parts to. Arms were once used for hugging, hands for stroking the hair of others. Feet once walked along beaches or climbed rugged hillsides. Do you really need more than one hand? What is your penis actually for?

3. POETRY: Find all the rhymes for coronavirus, glad you named your first child Cyrus. Should we all work until they fire us? What if no one else will

hire us? All these strictures serve to tire us, reprogram us, restart, rewire us. Will our future kids admire us if we let the thick mud mire us? If of hope you are desirous, in the grey matter 'tween each gyrus, lurks a thought that might inspire us. Write it quickly on papyrus! Alas, this battle may require us to trample down the purple iris, on the road to meet Osiris.

4. CONSPIRACY: Find as many people to blame as humanly possible for the situation you find yourself in. This game is best played by one player alone. It will help if you are the President of the United States and a massive narcissist forced by the weight of the entire world's suffering to realise both your innate inadequacy and fundamental inconsequentiality, along with the fact that you have been handed the most poisoned of chalices and required to drink. Sup deep, sociopath! Feel the frothy poison calcify in your fat-deadened arteries. This is not fake news, this is ineluctable truth.

5. AFTERLIFE: List all the things you plan to do when the strictures are finally lifted. Visit the Great Wall of China, play badminton with your cousin Adam, finally talk to the pretty girl in the coffee shop, start running again, wear livelier and more colourful clothes, call your parents at least once a week, shop for presents for all the friends you missed desperately during the Lockdown Year. Plaster the garden wall. Take up windsurfing.

Learn mandarin.   Climb Mount Kilimanjaro.
Dance with a real live Brazilian.   Drink absinthe.
Will you finally learn to play the piano?   You will
not.

6. BLOODTHIRSTY: You have long been aware that
    black pudding is basically just oatmeal, and con-
    gealed pig's blood.   There is an awful lot of oat-
    meal sitting in that high cupboard berating you for
    not being able to like porridge.   There is a surpris-
    ing amount of blood in the human body.   YouTube
    can supply a How-To video for almost anything –
    why not self-cannulation?   As a vegetarian, you
    can't have a moral objection to consuming your
    own blood, can you?   Is there really any need to
    inform the other members of your family what
    they are eating? I don't think so.

7. DISMEMBERMENT: Just hangs there, being
    pretty redundant, and by that, I mean not at all
    pretty.   It's just a fleshy tube, really.   You hardly
    even bother getting it 'excited' anymore.   If it wer-
    en't there, you would still be able to pee, and your
    trousers would fit better.   You might even be able
    to wear Speedos without embarrassment.   Hell, you
    could even wear your wife's bikini bottoms at a
    pinch.   It's not as if you were going to have any
    more kids, anyway.   Hair straighteners could be
    repurposed as a cauterising device.   I wonder what
    it would taste like, sautéed?

8. CONTINENTAL: Declare part of your home is another continent and set up a toll. You needn't collect money for passing through the checkpoint. Any item of worth, special favour or shameful enactment might suffice. This way, you can ensure social distancing, whilst shoring up your own reserves of toilet paper, flour, and entertaining memories of the self-abasement of those you love. However, unless you can recruit other family members to work shifts with you, you may find border encroachments become rife. There is only one punishment for such foolhardiness, isn't there? and you know just what must be done.

9. SENTINEL: Stand in the middle of your street at night, with face upturned. Let the stars bear witness as you declare: I am the sentinel and I watch the road. I am the sentinel, and none shall pass. I am the sentinel; I bear witness, to the end of days at last. I am the sentinel, on my shoulders, rests the weight of future days, I am the sentinel, growing older, burnished by the summer's blaze. I am the sentinel, ceremonial, to the ghosts who pass away. I am the sentinel, testimonial, for other ghosts who came to stay.

10. GUEST: Go to the house of another and look in his windows. Hold up a placard: *give me shelter; I am homeless.* You will be allowed into the home of this good Samaritan. Take off your clothes and hand your host a piece of chalk. Tell them to draw a

pentagram and ask for five candles. Write sacred symbols inside each of the five points. Lie down in the centre of the pentagram, light the candles, and turn off all the lights. Offer the blade handle first. If your host blanches, you may have to do the bloodletting yourself.

◄

Saving Face

Flashes blaze as the cameras freeze the tears upon my cheeks. I thank colleagues, family, and God and am led off-stage by the young woman with the earpiece. Before I slip behind the velvet curtain, I catch the eyes of a tiny grinning, bald man who stands by the stage, quite alone.

After the ceremony, he accosts me, as I sashay in the Oscar de la Renta frock towards a waiting limo. Red rope in one hand, a small wooden box in the other, he whispers.

"I have your face," still grinning. "In this box." Public and paparazzi start screaming.

Allies in the Deep

Enfolded in blankets on the top shelf of the walk-in wardrobe, Kathi heard the sound of her family being eviscerated. The horrific memory replayed itself over and over in her mind. She shook and wept and forced her fingers into her ears and rocked herself into a kind of numb stupor, until the screaming stopped.

When she unplugged her ears, some hours later, having not been discovered, even though the metallic tentacles did penetrate the wardrobe and tear up the clothes beneath her perch, all was silence.

She'd been holding onto her pee for hours now, not wanting the liquid to run out of the wardrobe and give her presence away. Now she ran to the adjoining bathroom and voided her bladder. They physical relief engendered a feeling of guilt and shame. Terrified, Kathi crept barefoot to the cabin door and eased it open an inch. Nothing moved but the gangway was awash with blood and a pair of lifeless legs protruded from the next-door berth.

When, several hours before, the sycamore seedlike shape descended from the whirl of clouds above the main deck, the cruise guests had gathered in shocked silence to watch an alien ship land on the helipad. Kathi, just three days shy of her thirteenth birthday, had done what her father had sternly demanded and raced back to the cabin to hide.

She'd paused halfway to turn and look back, something she would eternally regret. A horde of spider-like aliens descended from their ship, surrounded the assembled guests and crew, and began blasting them apart with dark red lasers. Kathi, emerging from behind a bulkhead, sprinted barefoot for the lower decks.

It seemed likely that, in the hours she's been hiding, the creatures from another world had scuttled on their many legs around the ship's cabins and dragged every last human from their quarters. As she peeked out into the gangway, Kathi could hear a shrieking sound that resembled a circular saw struggling to cut sheet metal. In fact, there were several different tonalities. Voices. Somehow these sounds constituted an alien language.

Kathi shrank away from the gap in the door as three or four of the invaders scuttled by, dragging heavy bags of something across the bloody gangway. Sneaking back to the door, Kathi caught a glimpse of what was inside the semi-translucent fabric of the sacking... the glistening, squirmy shapes of human organs. Kathi felt her bile rise. She gulped the nausea down and began to formulate a plan.

Her unusual mind shut off the horrific certainty that her family was dead – father Karl, mother Solveig and brother Marten – all gone.

Kathi had only two choices. Continue to hide and hope that the aliens would leave without finding her or emerge from the cabin and attempt to escape. Given the freezing temperatures of the Norwegian Sea, escape would not normally be an option. Sure, she could try to release a lifeboat, but the chances of doing so without being caught seemed slim. However, since Kathi's parents were keen scuba divers, and had enrolled their kids in the sport, there was another possibility open to her.

Kathi pulled her small suitcase from under the bed, glad to discover the aliens had not ripped it apart. Inside was her folded wetsuit and flippers. She quickly pulled on the suit and folded her matted hair into a ponytail.

Kathi was a strong swimmer, but the aliens had descended from the storm clouds when the ship was halfway between Alesund and Molde. Land was probably 500m distant, either the mainland to the port side or Otrøya to the starboard. Could she make it? The wetsuit was a midweight one, suitable for cold seas but not for the deep channels the cruise ships travelled. It didn't matter – what choice did she have?

The family had planned to rent oxygen cylinders from the resort at Molde. However, Kathi had packed a tiny 500ml tank she could strap across her chest. It would give her twenty minutes to swim under the waves and she could use her flippers and maybe even move faster. Having seen the lethal power of the alien's devices, she couldn't risk swimming on the surface.

Kathi tested the airflow, and a reassuring hiss came from the mouthpiece. She put on her goggles and double-checked everything. Then she flopped as quietly as the flippers would allow to the door and listened. She could hear nothing but the lapping of the waves, the wind, and the occasional squawk of seagulls.

Taking deep breaths, Kathi opened the door, trotted to one of the lifeboats and clambered over the handrail, letting herself down the ladder built into the ship's hull. She descended past the lifeboats to a few feet above the frothing grey-blue waves. The sky was ominously dark, and Kathi knew she had half an hour at best before the sun went down.

Taking one final breath of fresh air, Kathi jumped off the ladder and dropped feet first into the waves, as above her a cacophony of shrieks sounded.

As she plunged under the surface, hot blasts of lasers cut through the water, creating columns of bubbles around her. Kathi kicked out and dolphined her way down into the dark water. Soon she could feel the pressure increasing, but the red glow of the lasers couldn't reach her here.

As she was struggling to get her bearings, a dark form to Kathi's left emerged from the murk – something huge and silent. Another ship? No – something more remarkable. A tailfin sliced the water, and a barnacled behemoth hove into view – a mink whale.

It seemed to be swimming directly towards the ship. Kathi kicked out in a perpendicular direction as behind her a massive, dull clang suggested the whale had hit the vessel. Several other impacts followed, and Kathi could feel currents from the rocking liner rippling along her body.

After forty minutes of swimming, Kathi's legs were aching with a fiery pain and she was taking ever-deeper gulps to power her onwards. She had no idea if she were swimming in the right direction and her oxygen wouldn't last for more than a few more minutes.

Before long, she reluctantly stopped using her legs, forced off the flippers and began to swim breaststroke through the water. Her arms were far weaker than her legs and quickly lost their strength. Should she rise to the surface?

The dark shadow appeared once more. This time the cetacean was beneath her. Kathi felt a welling up of panic as the oxygen ran out and she gasped convulsively, swallowing brine.

Simultaneously, the huge whale rose, and she felt its bulk under her as it lifted her and breached the surface. Somewhere beyond her, a blowhole blasted a jet of water into the air and Kathi rolled onto her side, astonished to realise she was lying on the back of the whale as it swam slowly around a jutting promontory of rocky cliffs.

She sat up, amazed and thrilled, then realised with a strange mixture of joy and pain that the liner was listing to one side, a pod of whales buffeting and attacking it while lasers cut into them.

The animals were indomitable, redoubling their efforts, despite the blood darkening the waves around them. With a grinding sound of tortured metal, the liner began to sink, taking on water. Moments later, the lasers cut out, and the ship slowly flipped upside down. A faint shrieking of many alien voices could be heard as the cliffs of the islet obscured Kathi's view.

She turned and saw a crescent of sand. Behind it lay grassy fields and a cluster of stone houses. Arrayed on the shore was a small group of people, waving and shouting. The whale suddenly descended, leaving Kathi floundering in the dark waves as a rowboat made its way out towards her.

Kathi Sveinsson caught one final glimpse of her saviour's tailfin clapping the water into spray before it sank out of sight, a dark silhouette in the despairing depths.

Needlework

There were days when Ilse Muller told time by the colour of the light falling across her desk. She'd become so entranced by her work that she wouldn't even turn her head to look at the clock. As she completed her miniskirts, the hammering of the Singer sewing machine and the Christopher Street traffic generated a hypnotic rhythm. A seamstress in the Garment District for twenty years, Ilse was finally working for herself. It made all the difference.

She was creating a collection to sell in a downtown boutique. Ilse would intermittently take in repairs and alterations to augment her income. Next month she turned fifty, and she felt that if she didn't focus upon her business now, it would soon be too late. She'd neither married nor had children, although she was godmother to two teenage girls, the twin daughters of her best friend Maggie.

On the 17th of May 1984, Ilse received a visitor who shattered the trance of her flashing needle. The doorbell sounded and she trotted downstairs to greet a portly man, tall and well-dressed, who stood silhouetted in the mid-morning light. He has a suit-bag over one arm and looked out of breath. Behind him, a sleek Mercedes gleamed, its engine still running, a driver at the wheel.

"Madame Muller," he said, removing his hat, "I believe you do repairs?"

Direct and to the point, Ilse thought. Did she also detect an accent similar to her own, a clipped Germanic tone that turned the 'v' of 'believe' into an 'f'?

"I do," she said, mimicking his business-like manner. "Have you seen my prices?"

"I'm sure they are perfectly adequate," her visitor said. "I need a dress suit taken out and promptly."

She nodded and led him upstairs, wondering why she felt flustered by his presence. He was a big man, practically bouncing off the walls as he huffed up the narrow staircase to the attic. In her sunlit workroom, a sunbeam caught his fleshy features. Isle felt the first flicker of recognition.

She gestured to a clear worksurface and the man, a little older than her and well-groomed with unfashionable sideburns that belonged to a previous decade, unzipped the bag, and laid it out. Ilse reached in and retrieved a three-piece suit, extremely formal, with tails and outmoded, wide lapels. She glanced at the label. Volkmar Arnulf. There was also a white dress shirt in the bag, its lapels equally wing-like.

"I'm Joseph Weber, perhaps you recognise me?" he said as Ilse's heart began to hammer with all the force of a sewing machine at full tilt. She whirled; her eyes wide as he handed her a playbill. Carnegie Hall; a programme of Schoenberg and Wagner. The Berlin Philharmonic, conductor: J Weber.

"Do you enjoy classical music?"

Ilse turned away, so as not to betray herself, since he didn't seem to know who she was. Why should he, after all? Her surname had changed in 1942, exchanging Rosen for Hellmann. Roses for mustard; it had seemed a shoddy bargain. They had been children back then. Of course Joseph wouldn't remember her, he'd almost certainly forgotten her as soon as his callous deed had been done.

It had been the summer of 1942. Ilse lived with her parents, a piano teacher, and an industrial chemist, in the quiet, lower middle-class Munich district of Schwabing.

Their apartment had been situated above a dressmaker, where Ilse had first become fascinated with the flashing needles.

The family's unspoken secret, which became more vital to conceal with every passing year, was that Ilse's mother Gertrude has been born Levisson, raised in a largely secular household, but still technically a Jew. Since they never attended church or synagogue, carefully observed Christmas and Easter, and Gertrude's blonde hair didn't immediately betray her Semitic origins, the Rosen family passed as gentile and felt in little danger when the goose-stepping morons took over.

Until, that is, an over-inquisitive 10-year-old piano student took to rummaging through closets and found the menorah that Gertrude had been gifted by her grandmother, plus a tattered Torah.

A devious boy, Joseph did nothing for ten days, until one rainy afternoon when, frustrated by his lack of progress with Schubert, Gertrude's scolding and Ilse's gentle teasing, Joseph had run out into the street, approached a passing SS officer, and screamed one fateful word.

"Juden!"

His stubby finger pointed back at the window behind which Gertrude hid, peering out through lace curtains. With a mother's instinct for the preservation of her child, Gertrude had shut the curtains as the officer approached their front steps.

"Run, Ilse, Run!" her mother had commanded, the terror in her eyes inspiring Ilse to do exactly that, clambering out the rear window, dropping to the small yard and running, without coat, without papers, without any idea where she would end up.

She was recognised on Theresienstrasse by Inge Hellmann, a young ex-student of Ilse's mother and taken into hiding, although she begged for days to be allowed to return to her home. Inge's boyfriend Mikael covertly visited the Rosen family flat and found it ransacked. A couple of small suitcases and some clothes were missing, as were the menorah and holy book. There was no note, no sign of Ilse's parents. She never saw them again. Twelve years later, in 1954, Ilse discovered their names on a list of those who had died at Auschwitz, murdered by the Nazis.

In 1943, the Hellmanns emigrated to the United States, sneaking through Austria and Switzerland, under the guise of business travel. They settled in Staten Island, and Ilse had a new home, new guardians, and a new life.

Ilse managed to hold herself together, even as these dark memories resurfaced. She nodded and listened to Joseph's instructions about how to modify the suit and shirt. He had evidently piled on weight during his European tour, a roaring success.

"Those Italians know how to feed a fellow," he guffawed, quite ignorant of the effect he was having on Ilse. He offered a clammy handshake and Ilse informed him that the suit would be ready by five the following evening, in plenty of time for his American debut. Joseph seemed satisfied and left her to her work. Ilse heard his Mercedes pull out into New York traffic, horn blaring, scattering students on their way to lectures at NYU and delivery men collecting boxes of bagels from the deli below.

She had thirty hours. Would that be enough time? An idea had formed in the back of Ilse's mind. A childish act of cruelty had consigned her parents to the gas chambers, a callous and careless thing that deserved an equally juvenile retribution. Ilse was willing to believe that Joseph was merely an oafish celebrity now, perhaps an accomplished conductor and musician, maybe even a beloved father and husband. He might not be the very epitome of evil she'd always imagined. However, his actions had orphaned Ilse, and some sins could not simply be forgotten.

She worked more intently than she ever had, abandoning her collection and the piecework that was due for the Catholic school in Queens. Joseph's suit would have to be deconstructed and rebuilt. She would have to complete every modification to an exactingly high standard. There would be no time for sleep. Fortunately, Ilse was accustomed to working late in her studio, even spending the night there on occasion. She would get by on strong coffee and deli sandwiches. This job would be her masterpiece, her virtuoso performance.

The following afternoon, an exhausted Ilse realised the suit would not be ready by 5pm. She called Carnegie Hall box office and, after some argument, was put through to Mr Weber himself.

"What on earth?" Joseph demanded. "We have a sound check to do, Frau Muller. Where is my suit?"

She explained that it was almost finished, but she had noticed some of the buttons were loose and she wanted to tighten them, so would it be okay if she brought the dinner jacket to stage door in around an hour's time? Joseph wasn't best-pleased but concurred with blustery exasperation.

Two hours later, Ilse donned her finest frock (self-made), scooped her hair into a passably neat bun, and grabbed a yellow cab to the legendary concert venue. She pushed through a gaggle of autograph hunters waiting outside stage door. Joseph was nowhere to be seen. He'd no doubt be smoking a cigar in his dressing room, or doing stretching exercises, or whatever conductors did to warm up.

Ilse dropped off the suit, insisting that it be taken to the conductor post-haste. She told security she couldn't wait around, hoping that Joseph would be so self-absorbed that he'd entirely forget about paying for her handiwork.

Ilse's next task was challenging, but she managed, after a few frustrating encounters, to flirt with a ticket tout and obtain a balcony seat for twenty bucks, way more than she'd wanted to pay. It would be worth every cent.

When the doors opened, Ilse climbed carpeted stairs under glimmering chandeliers, her heart racing with an excitement she felt certain Joseph shared, though for entirely different reasons. A young man held the door open for her on the uppermost level and she returned his smile. He turned out to be sitting next to her, way up in 'the gods' as theatre-goers say.

Her view was partly obscured by a pillar, and she had to lean towards Hector, her new concert friend, to see the stage. Fortunately, the conductor's dais was situated right in front of the orchestra, and he couldn't be missed as he strode out, resplendent in his evening wear, adjusting the cuffs of the Italian shirt as he tapped his baton on the music stand and silenced the tuning-up musicians. There had to be at least sixty of them arrayed before him, plus a crescent of choir, all hanging on their conductor's every move. She felt a momentary flicker of guilt that died the second it was born.

"Do you enjoy Wagner?" whispered a voice to Ilse's left. Hector, a gold fang gleaming in an array of brilliantly white teeth. Spanish accent; perhaps Cuban?

"Can't stand him," hissed Ilse conspiratorially, watching a frown cloud her would-be suitor's features.

A hush fell as the musicians took up their instruments, straightened their backs and waited intently. Joseph swept into motion and the opening notes of the Tannhauser Overture washed warmly over the appreciative throng, the cream of New York society arrayed to see the legendary orchestra and its mercurial conductor. Despite her protestations, Ilse couldn't help but be moved by the gentle washes of orchestral colour, although the melody's melancholy tone felt like a memorial for all Germany had given away — its honour, its pride, its people.

The piece passed without incident, even as Joseph's shoulders began to jerk with the descending string pulses, which he marshalled with vivid sweeps of his baton and delicate touches of his free hand. Despite her loathing of him, she had to admit Joseph was wringing every nuance out of the sentimental soup of Wagner's tale of competing medieval minstrels.

Wait — was that a glimmer of white appearing at Joseph's shoulder? A thin pale line that nobody but her would fixate upon. She leaned forwards eagerly, then felt a tapping at her shoulder, as the music began to swell to an energetic crescendo.

"Miss, would you like to borrow…"

Hector was offering her a pair of brass opera glasses. Eagerly, Ilse thanked him and squinted through the lenses, turning a small wheel to bring her victim into sharp focus.

There he was, hunched beneath the dark serge, which

she'd made tighter than Joseph would have liked, but not so snug that he'd cast it aside for an alternative. Now he was on tiptoes, a lock of lank hair dancing over his collar as he jerked along with the bee-swarm of violas. Brass blasted out a cacophony of funereal notes while strings skittered, and timpani rolled to a portentous conclusion.

Unseen by others, Ilse saw daylight between sleeve and shoulder, as her sabotaged stitching began to give way. When the overture ended, and the audience erupted into applause, Joseph turned to acknowledge the adulation. He looked grimly delighted, but perhaps just a little uncomfortable? She watched him wriggle his shoulders and tug at his left sleeve, as a cuff slid down over his baton hand.

There was nothing to be done – a sixty-piece orchestra and hundred-strong chorus awaited his initiation. Joseph turned back to his music, the audience got their coughing out of the way and silence fell once more. The Tannhauser Bacchanale was next on the program, a delirium of circling bows and blaring horns. Joseph gave it his all, and Ilse felt her spirits soar as his left sleeve suddenly tore free from his suit and began to slide down his arm, at the same time as his right lapel fell away and flopped over the music stand.

Ilse had found an ancient roll of fifty weight cotton thread mouldering away at the back of the dresser. Far too fragile to put through the Singer, Ilse had stitched Joseph's suit back together by hand. Ninety thousand stitches in total. She'd had to distress some of the key joints with a nailfile to make sure the stitches gave way when warm and wet.

The conductor gamely soldiered on, swapping his baton to his right hand so he could furiously hurl his errant left sleeve onto the floor, as gasps and giggles began to break out. The music whirled like a dervish as Ilse, not familiar with the piece, wondered if she'd even know whether Joseph was losing control. She needn't have worried.

Moments after doubt entered her mind, the seat of Joseph's pants began to slide down his hips, the leg fabric tearing away from the waistband. Joseph was wearing pink boxer shorts. Audible laughter broke out as the maestro lost his struggle, the musicians fell out of step, the chorus wavered, and the orchestra slithered into silence. Joseph swore violently in German, threw down his baton, pulled up his raggedy trousers and hobbled, red-faced from the stage to the accompaniment of confused murmurs and scattered applause.

Ilse handed the opera glasses back to the aghast Hector, who couldn't understand why she was grinning from ear to ear.

"I take it back," she remarked merrily. "I rather like Wagner, after all."

Then she rose, took her leave, and floated out into the warm New York evening air. The denizens of the city, strolling from restaurant to bar to taxi rank, seemed imbued with hope and love. The world was in balance and Ilse had no intention of returning to her attic room, or her Alphabet City apartment. There was a dive bar on Bleeker Street calling her and an ice-cold Lowenbrau to celebrate. If her Jewish ancestors were wrong, and there was a heaven after all, Ilse only hoped her parents were up there, in 'the gods', looking down, and laughing uncontrollably.

Far from the Beaufort Sea

Security guard at the zoo is a job title that sounds like the punchline of a joke. Given the kinds of anecdotes Ian Klemmer had at his disposal, that wasn't far from the truth. Take last weekend, for instance.

Ian and two of his colleagues had been called to eject a naked young man who had climbed into the sealion enclosure on a dare. He'd tried to tell the arsehole, who was busy being fêted by his companions, even as he struggled to put his clothes back on and shivered uncontrollably, that sealions are hugely dangerous. Adult males can weigh up to 1100 kilos and have been known to attack humans who stray too far into their domain. The idiot, apparently on a stag weekend, had been unimpressed. Ian realised he was only fuelling the young man's notoriety, so he took his photo and added it to the admin office's wall of lifetime bans.

Then there was the time a woman strayed too close to the fence of the lion enclosure, leaning back against the diamond-patterned mesh to take yet another selfie. Her long, flowing blonde hair may, Ian surmised, have been mistaken for the mane of a rival male. Whatever had been the case, the King of their jungle, dubbed Hercules, had launched himself at the woman and swiped a full clawful of her hair out from the roots. The victim's screams had caused panic in the aviary on the other side of the park. Ian could only imagine what her selfie looked like.

Today's anecdote in waiting had left Ian shaken to the core and quite possibly would end his career. As a fourteen stone, six foot two former marine and Afghan veteran, Ian didn't scare easily, but today's calamity had been a misadventure too far.

For weeks, the same kid had turned up at the zoo, having evidently been bought an annual pass by a well-meaning teacher. He had the wan expression, long jet-black hair, and faux-military fatigues of the kind of young person Ian instinctively despised. Yet Ian had warmed to this strange figure, permanently listening to angry-sounding metal music through wireless earphones as he haunted the primate zone or sat sunken-eyed in the reptile house. Their first encounter had not been a promising one. Ian had tapped the boy on the shoulder, since the kid had failed to hear Ian's throat clearing. The young man whipped round as if electrocuted.

"S....sorry?" said the boy, wiping something away from his eye. Surely not tears?

"I said, would you turn the music down? You'll scare the snakes."

"Aren't they, like, behind an inch of plate glass?" the kid suggested, before doing as he was told. Ian was gratified to note that from then on, the boy had his music loud when outdoors but took it down a notch or two whenever he went in to look at the reptiles, scorpions, or giant crabs. The kid, who he nicknamed Overkill, after the T-shirt he frequently wore under his ripped and patched field jacket, was always alone and looked habitually depressed.

One Sunday afternoon while doing a round in his electric buggy, Ian saw Overkill by the polar bear enclosure. The steep-sided pit contained a deep pool of chilled water and artificial snow was regularly blasted in from overhead pipes. Sometimes, when the sole adult male resident was fed, live fish were released under the water so that Ernie the polar bear could do his thing, in part for the crowds, mostly

166

to give him some semblance of normality. It didn't convince Ian.

Although Ian dutifully told anyone who asked that the bear was much better off safe and well looked after in the zoo than facing environmental destruction, trophy hunters and starvation in the Arctic, Ian wasn't sure he believed his own shtick.

Ernie was doing his "dance" as the little kids often called it. The bear was shuffling in a semi-circle around the top of the faux-iceberg, then doubling-back on himself and returning to his starting point, before repeating the moves. It looked like he was caught in a tedious loop of time. Ernie would sometimes do this for up to two hours a day, generally before his afternoon feed. Ian couldn't help but admit that Ernie looked miserable when he wasn't tearing into prepared slices of seal or hunting trout.

Overkill was on tiptoes, peering over the wall, staring at Ernie as he paced his imaginary cell. Ian stopped the buggy behind the kid, presuming the near-silent engine wouldn't draw attention to him.

"He's depressed," said the kid, without turning. Overkill's hearing evidently hadn't yet been impaired by all the insane screaming he listened to for pleasure. Ian jumped down from the buggy and strolled over.

"Keeper says he's just exercising. Polar bears travel up to 30 kilometres a day, normally."

Overkill snorted. "Then why doesn't he walk around on the main bit. There's more room."

Ian had to admit, the kid had a point. Overkill returned his gaze to the loping off-white beast.

"I'll bet he's lonely. Plus, he remembers when he had thousands of miles of wilderness to explore. Now he just

167

has fibreglass and fake snow."

Ian felt he should leave the kid to his depressive musings, but something troubled him and made him linger.

"Keepers tried to introduce a mate a couple of years ago. He attacked her, bit her in the neck. Kids were screaming. It was a scene. They had to take him down with four darts."

When he'd started the story, Ian had thought he was telling a joke. Yet somehow it had come out as a depressing memory of failure. He should be getting on. Hanging around Overkill would make anyone miserable.

"He does look lonely," was all the kid said as Ian got back into his cart and drove off around the enclosure wall, past a wall of pampas grass, in the direction of the giraffes. He only got a few hundred yards along the main path when he heard screams and cries from behind him. Ian pulled a U-turn over the lawn and raced back to the polar enclosure. He half-expected what he saw.

Overkill had evidently jumped the wall and slid down the side of the tank. Another swimmer, thought Ian, although this time clothed.

"Hey! Stay where you are! Stay very still!"

Twenty or so people were craning over the lip of the enclosure, trying to see the kid, who was now breast-stroking out across the dark water towards Ernie's iceberg. There were indentations built into its side so the keepers could climb it and hose the top down whilst their charge was safely caged. Overkill was making straight for that ladder.

"Do not go near him! Come back this way and grab the rope."

Ian uncoiled the rope ladder he kept in the back of

the buggy for just this reason and tossed it over the wall, after clearing away the spectators with an angry sweep of his muscular arms. Overkill ignored him, of course. He was a young man with a mission, evidently a suicide one.

While everyone gawped and Ian radioed for assistance, Overkill now began to climb the berg. Ian remembered he'd not packed the dart gun today – he only took it when he was helping one of the keepers. Or in case of emergency, like this one. Shit.

Ernie hadn't seemingly noticed Overkill at all, so far. This changed when the boy poked his dripping head over the edge of the berg. Ernie stopped in his tracks, giving a low warning growl. Water pouring off him, Overkill climbed up onto the stained white fibreglass. The kid looked strangely calm, which worried Ian, who was still shouting almost incoherent instructions that Overkill was roundly ignoring.

"Stay away from him – he'll attack!"

Overkill sank to his knees, eyes closed, arms out as if inviting an embrace. The kid's insane, Ian thought. Then something remarkable happened. Ernie closed his mouth, loped over towards the boy, and sniffed his hair. He even licked the kid's face with his huge pink, sandpaper tongue. Surely Overkill would bolt? He didn't.

Instead, he put his arms around the bear's neck and hugged him. It would have been a touching sight, had it held for more than a few seconds. And had it not involved a 450-kilo polar bear. It might have made another amusing anecdote if the kid had just jumped off the berg into the water and swum to safety.

But he didn't, and now Ernie pulled away, reared back, roared, and swiped the boy, with one huge claw, across the

169

back and shoulders, cuffing him off the concrete and fibre-glass berg like a straw doll. Overkill's body spun and flailed down into the icy water.

All hell broke loose. Screaming, terrified shouts. Ian had to pull back two men who were about to jump into the enclosure to rescue Overkill, who floated face down in the water, his back horribly torn. Moment later, dart guns blasted out and a second body slumped from the berg into the oily, dark, fake ocean.

To their credit, Ian and his colleagues had the boy out within minutes. As soon as Ernie fell, Ian jumped in, followed by three others. Overkill was still breathing, just, although he was barely conscious and severely injured. They carried him into the veterinary suite and called the paramedics. Overkill would probably live, and he'd have some fearsome scars to remember his misadventure by.

Ian was baffled as he thought about it in the car on the way home that evening. Why had the kid done it? He supposed he had to take Overkill at his word. Before the morphine silenced him, the boy had been muttering deliriously, saying something over and over. Eight barely audible words that Ian only figured out later.

He looked like he just needed a hug.

Stardust at the Beehive

It was ten thirty on a Saturday night and the joint was jumping. The joint in question was the Beehive Club, a 133rd street basement speakeasy 200 yards from the Cotton Club and the Savoy. Although integrated like all the best places, it lacked some of the glamour of those more celebrated venues.

The Beehive's clientele was a little shadier, but it was a cooler and more intimate dive. Owner and host was mob boss Slim Hernandez. Nobody really knew where Slim was from – some said Cuba, others Puerto Rica, but he had cornered the local prostitution and protection rackets. The Beehive was his pet project: a bid for legitimacy, a money-spinning melting pot and a hothouse for the coolest swing and big band music around.

At a booth near the stage sat two men and one woman. The men were black, the woman mixed race, but on the pale side. She was a young journalist called Cindy Bruford, who mingled in circles as varied as meat-packing mobsters and midtown grandees. A jazz fanatic, she was keen to catch ex-pianist turned cornet player Billy Fleming's comeback.

The older man was sports talent scout Lennie Hampton, and the younger of the two was star baseball player Fred "Lefty" Capshaw, just signed to the Dodgers, whom Cindy was profiling. Fred had brought Lennie to his frequent hangout as a thank-you. Cindy was a happy tag-along.

The band were playing a single set, as support for The Nighthawks Big Band, since Fleming was making his bandleading debut and they had only begun rehearsals a couple of weeks' prior. Slim Hernandez himself jumped onstage to introduce them – a rare honour.

"Ladies and gentlemen, do we have a treat for you tonight. A brand-new five-piece with a familiar face at the helm, our old-friend Billy 'Knuckles' Fleming."

Cindy, eagle-eyed as ever, saw Fred wince at Slim's sardonic use of the nickname 'knuckles'. She sensed a story and leaned over to get it. Fred looked around before replying. Nobody was paying them the slightest attention – all eyes were on the band as Slim introduced each member.

"It's one hell of a tale," Fred began. "Billy was a great accompanist for small groups and signers, including none other than Maeve Sharp, before she had her hits, when she was Slim's main squeeze. Only Billy had his eye on her too and had the bright idea of spiriting her away to Kansas City."

Cindy got her pad out under the table. She'd learned the useful skill of scribbling shorthand notes out of sight. Lennie, a taciturn soul, leaned in too, as eager for the gossip as anyone.

"Towards the end of the night, Billy overplays his hand, blows Maeve a kiss onstage. It's just showbiz schtick but Slim sees it different, storms over and slams the piano lid down. Shatters both of Billy's paws. He only regained use of one of them completely."

Cindy winced but Lennie laughed, as if hearing an urban legend. She'd canvas his opinion later.

The first number had begun, drummer, pianist and bassist working the intro up before sax-player Willie Jackson stated the melody. Take the A-Train, played at lightning speed, as if it might derail at any second. Dancers were already crowding the floor.

Cindy was aware of something shimmering nearby, sequins reflecting the light. She turned and there was a curvaceous young black woman, who looked like she'd been poured into her golden tasselled dress, slashed up to the thigh on one side. The newcomer was sashaying to the music. Cindy overheard Lennie whispering to Fred:

"That who I think it is?"

Fred nodded and Cindy twigged. Maeve Sharp, transfixed by her erstwhile accompanist's grand return.

Then came a piercing, keening note, which floated over the dancers like a flight of migrating birds. All heads turned to the stage, where Billy held the cornet in his one good hand, other thrust deep into his jacket pocket. Billy held that first note as long as he could before falling back into step alongside Jackson. Together they rattled through the verse before Billy took his first solo, a cascade of barely controlled notes in an excitingly raw tone that reminded Cindy of Bix Beiderbecke. Clearly, Billy was a man for whom music was a vital force that had to come out. If not with ten fingers on a keyboard, then with three on a horn.

The first song ended, dancers and drinkers alike exploding into applause. Slim beamed from the side of the stage, holding his trademark highball. Cindy, whose journalistic eye was always straying away from centre stage, saw Slim's smile change to a scowl. He had spotted Maeve, who, it had to be said, was hard to miss. The singer shimmied between tables towards the dancefloor. Billy saw her and beckoned to his pianist, who unhitched his vocal mike and tossed it over. Billy tapped it, ensuring he could be heard.

"Folks, we got an extra special surprise for our next

173

number. None other than Miss Maeve Sharp!"

Slim's eyes threw daggers at the man he'd sadistically mauled, looking like he might bite off the remaining good hand. Billy ignored him. Maeve took the mike and, lifting her sequins with one hand, gingerly ascended to the stage.

"Thanks everyone," she said, lowering her head with false modesty, before announcing the song with a single word: "Stardust".

A hush fell over the crowd. Fred turned to whisper to Cindy.

"That's what they were playing when Slim... you know."

Hoagy Carmichael's classic oozed magnificently into the room, with Billy and Willie trading licks on the snaky melody before Maeve began to sing:

Sometimes I wonder how I spend the lonely night, dreaming of a song.

Billy raised his horn and the rhythm section hushed, allowing a duet of horn and human voice to burnish the song to a bright sheen. Billy gazed lovingly at the singer; Maeve flicked little glances at the cornetist. Nobody in that room, least of all Slim, was in any doubt that this was a declaration of love – real love, not the sugary, sentimental kind that Tin Pan Alley traded in.

For the final chorus, the whole band took up the melody and wringed it of every emotional droplet. Once again, the crowd erupted. Slim strode along the front of the stage while Maeve coiled the mike cable and made to return it to the pianist. Slim grabbed her arm, aggressively.

Abruptly Billy took his gnarled, ruined right hand from his jacket. This time, the metal that flashed between his knuckles wasn't a horn. There was a bang, a flash of light and Slim clutched his chest, falling back from the stage, dancers parting as he hit the deck. Maeve and Billy, hand in hand, exited stage left while chaos ensued.

Cindy was later interviewed by the police. She told them that Billy had fired in self-defence. Slim would have killed the cornet player if he'd not shot first. Of that, she was sure. It didn't matter – there was more at stake than crime and culpability.

There was music and love and revenge. And, it went without saying, there was Cindy's first front page.

A Sign from Above

Fate is generally subtler than it was on the afternoon when Felix Steinberg met Melissa Hamilton. He was browsing in his favourite thrift store, a tiny place in downtown New York whose wares spilled out into a weed-choked yard. His cramped apartment was already full of peculiar knick-knacks and "characterful" old furniture, so he should have known better. When you're an inveterate rummager amongst the discarded and the forgotten, it's a lifelong curse.

Felix was on his way out of the store, having successfully avoided the temptation to purchase a stuffed squirrel, when his attention was drawn by a large metal object descending rapidly towards his jugular. He half-stepped, half-slipped aside as the octagonal metal sign glanced off his shoulder and came to rest in a stack of old literary magazines. Felix landed on his knees, looking up at a young woman on a ladder, arms outstretched before a suspiciously empty stretch of wall.

"Oh my God, I'm so sorry! Did I hurt you?" Her pale dress, dotted with violets and celandines, rippled as she raced down to ensure her customer hadn't been bisected.

Her oval face was framed by a curtain of reddish-brown hair. She had long pre-Raphaelite nose and Cupid's bow lips. Her face was practically an art history lesson, chiefly centring upon the Romantics.

"I'm Melissa, can I help you up?"

Felix stammered something as he rose, staring at the bright red "STOP" sign that had nearly killed him with irony. He fought for a sensible reaction.

177

"I slipped on these old Macsweeny's, just in time to foil your assassination attempt."

Melissa laughed. "Is there anything I can do for you?"

What Felix said next was hugely uncharacteristic and seemed to escape from his lips without the usual filtration processes of sensible discourse.

"You can buy me a coffee."

Remarkably, she said yes, closed up the shop and they went on their first date, sitting outside a little Bleeker Street café in the amber haze of a July evening. Felix was conscious that he'd basically thrown on a random assortment of items in lieu of clothing that morning, and was overdue a shave and a haircut, but Melissa didn't seem to mind.

She was funny, engaging, and well-versed in music, art, architecture, science, political history, all the things that fascinated him. Within an hour he was imagining yoking her name to his own, her life to his, their futures together.

Twelve years later they were both approaching their forties, having lived together in a Williamsburg apartment for most of a decade. He wrote his novels, and she ran her ever-expanding empire of extraordinary curios, and life was... fine... but Felix began to wonder if it had all been a romantic construct. Was their marriage just a collision that his love of narrative had fashioned? A happenstance? A joke awaiting a punchline? They had wanted a family, but Felix was unable to provide the necessary elixir (as he put it). Now their relationship was falling apart in a series of increasing rancorous arguments about everything and nothing.

"You didn't hang the washing up!"

"You didn't ask me to," he would reply.

"I shouldn't have to ask." Her frown imputed a degree of carelessness Felix considered a huge exaggeration. He had a lot on his mind.

"I am never on your mind," she said as anger gave way to tears.

The inevitable occurred and Felix hired a self-drive truck and began packing books, records, old typewriters, broken Hasselblads, Japanese calligraphy brushes, Turkish lanterns, Tales from Topographic Oceans and his 1962 Mickey Mouse alarm clock. Melissa had gone to her sister's place in Long Island for a weekend. Felix hoped he could finish the move in three trips. He didn't count on the power of iconography.

STOP.

The sign, the only item of his left in their apartment, offered its stark rebuke. Felix glared up at it, pugnaciously. "What? he said. "You stop! It's a bit late to be smug now." He weighed up the pros and cons of taking the sign with him, a permanent reminder of a moment when hope had triumphed over reason and experience. No, Felix concluded, I'll leave it there. He'd already driven two loads of his possessions to Greenpoint, where he'd found another bijou apartment. This would be his final journey north and out of Melissa's life.

Felix carried the last box downstairs and inserted it into the three-dimension Tetris game of his U-Haul truck. Then he trudged back upstairs to the third floor to double-check he hadn't missed anything.

STOP.

There it was, reminding him of the moment when he'd first seen the woman who would absorb his thirties.

Melissa would fill his days and sweeten his nights and obsess him like a puzzle he felt determined to solve. Was fixing this an impossible task? Felix sat down in what had been his favourite chair and stared at the red warning. For over an hour he sat, keys dangling from one finger, waiting for clarity, waiting for certainty, waiting for validation.

"Oh... you're still here," Melissa's half-hurt, half-surprised voice woke Felix from his slumber.

"Sorry, Mel," he said, rising awkwardly. "I fell asleep, looking at that thing."

He pointed at the sign. It scowled back.

"Aren't you taking it? If not, can you just toss it in the trash? It'll make me cry."

Felix looked at his wife as she placed her keys in the glass ornament by the door. They had found it together in a flea-market in Hoboken. She seemed exhausted.

Felix leaned up to unhook the sign from the wall. He put it under one arm, walked over to her and brushed his cheek against his wife's in farewell.

"Is it really too late?" he asked, as she pulled away to check for insincerity. Melissa shook her head, Felix walked towards the door, as slowly as he could, waiting for the one word he wanted to hear above all others.

"Stop."

Frozen Rain

Branston's world was simple, even simpler than the existences of most of his fellow citizens. He'd receive an instruction packet, jump in his buggy, and go neutralise the threat, wherever it lay. He did this quietly, efficiently and with the minimum of fuss. Branston was a man of preparation and precision, a loner who didn't so much love his own company as have an extremely high tolerance to it.

On one particularly balmy summer evening he heard the vacuum tube clunk in the corner of his pod and the siren sounded. Branston strolled over to collect the instructions. The roll of paper inside the tube gave precise coordinates, the name of the tribe, the individual recipient and disposal instructions. It all seemed quite straightforward. He finished his evening meal, switched off the screens and began to pack.

The only unusual aspect of this particular assignment was that it was the first time he'd be visiting the Federation's northernmost tribe, the Inuit. Named after the indigenous people of the ancient northern regions, the Inuit were secretive, even more isolationist than most tribes and rumoured to be prone to melancholia and early suicide.

Must be all that endless night, Branston thought, as his buggy shimmered up into the night sky on its four props and began to convey him towards the selected coordinates. His Octo told him it'd be twelve hours and nineteen minutes until arrival, so Branston decided to get an early night, unrolling his sleeping back and snuggling up in the foetal position that was all the one-person bug would allow. Branston asked his Octo to play some gentle oceanic sounds and slipped easily into a deep sleep.

When he awoke, the northern sun was already up, or perhaps he should say it was still up, since at this time of year, his Octo informed him, it never truly set. His own tribe, the Southern Caucasians, were used to a lot of diurnal and seasonal variation, living so close to the Earth's equator, in New Scotland, the mountainous archipelago left behind when the oceans flooded the United Kingdom, almost four hundred years ago. He wondered what it must be like to endure whole seasons of light or darkness. He'd heard the rain sometimes froze this far north too, although he couldn't quite imagine that – it must be like dodging bullets.

Branston slurped down a protein shake from the bug's food processor and asked Octo to fill him in on what to expect from the Inuit. Within minutes, his mind filled with a whirl of facts, sensations, even historic old memories which he could experience as if they were his own (the flashing icon at the periphery of his vision served to remind him that none of these things had ever happened to him). Branston had certainly never butchered a bull seal, sawed a hole in the ice for fishing or brewed tea from stringy vegetation in thawed-out ice-water. Christ these people were primitive, he thought, before reprimanding himself and recalling the Federation's motto (the 3RDs): reserve judgment, respect difference, remain distant. Still… fishing through a hole in the sea ice! Come on.

An hour later, the bug descended quietly behind a copse of stunted trees adjacent to the target house. Branston checked his pulse weapon and clicked on his Feed, so that everything he experienced would be sent directly to Home. A small wooden shack was half concealed by the pinewoods, at the edge of a field whose rutted mud was frosted over. It was hard to imagine anyone living so far off-grid, although of course nobody was truly off-grid these days, since Home, the AI overseeing Earth's people, was all-seeing and all-knowing. Home had known that this man, Kallik, had somehow managed to switch off his Octopus, the cranial implant that all humans have fitted at birth to enable meta-consciousness. This was an illegal act, although it was also possible it had been accidental. Branston was there to find out.

He knocked loudly on the well-weathered door of the shack.

"Federation Inspectorate! I have a warrant."

He heard nothing in response apart from, after a moment or two, a pattering percussive sound. Footsteps?

A figure emerged on the far side of the house, making off across the field. Damn! His target was running. It happened sometimes. He fired off his pulse gun a couple of times – it would usually connect, even with a turned-off Octo, and cause temporary paralysis in its wearer. Unfortunately, nothing seemed to be happening and the small, stocky man in the heavy hooded coat was making surprising speed as he bolted for the trees on the far side of the field. Branston could go back for the bug but then he'd lose sight of his target and with the subject's Octo entirely dead, tracking his target could prove tricky.

He began to run after the receding Inuit, shouting for him to halt. Hurling his authority status after the running Tribesman seemed futile and absurd, so Branston shut up and concentrated on not tripping over the frozen solid, rutted earth. He'd never seen mud do this – the Arctic permafrost had receded to a little over ten thousand square hectares and temperatures in Branston's world hadn't been subzero for three hundred years. He shivered under the electro-heated suit and felt a numbness in his extremities that he guessed might be dangerous. His breath clouded around him as he ran, another weird phenomenon he'd been warned about but hadn't expected to be so surprised by.

The target, a man supposedly in his sixties, was making surprisingly good speed but Branston was thirty-four and ran five times a week for fitness and within a few minutes, he'd caught up with his quarry.

"Wait! I don't want to use force!"

He really didn't want to grapple a pensioner to the ground, but it looked like he didn't have to. A few hundred yards from the treeline, Kallik stopped, bent over, hands on his knees, breathing heavily.

"Kallik Kilmartin?"

The man waved a cursory hand, still catching his breath.

"What do you want?" he said, without looking up.

"You turned your Octo off," said Branston, getting out his reactivation kit. "I'm required to reinstate it and issue you with a warning."

The man, remarkably, was laughing. Most people blanched, knowing that the reactivation process was invasive, painful and had legal ramifications.

"Look here," said the man, his accent peculiar.

Branston moved closer. Kallik had taken his hood down and his wizened sun-bronzed skull shone in the light as if polished. All along the side of his head, round the back and along the opposite side was a jagged scar, the flesh recently stitched back together. There was still crusted blood along the seam in places. Branston felt like vomiting. This man had had radical and amateur surgery performed upon him.

"You took it out," said Branston, unnecessarily, an edge of wonder in his voice.

Kallik nodded. "You want to arrest me now?"

Branston wasn't a law enforcement officer, as such, but he should call this in, report this man so that he could be taken in by the appropriate forces. That's what I should do, he thought. But I don't want to. Without asking himself why, he clicked off his Communication Feed. He could say it had malfunctioned.

"Why?" he asked, almost plaintively, "why would you do that?"

"Why?" asked Kallik, as if this was a really dumb question. "Same reason I came up here, became Inuit. For some fucken' peace and quiet, that's all. Look around you." Branston did, hearing nothing but very distant birdsong. His Octo, as if perturbed by the lack of data, began to feed him statistics about the region. Branston cast the feed to the periphery.

"Beautiful silence," said Kallik. "No need to be connected with gadgets and squids. I'm as connected as I need to be already. See those trees?"

Branston looked towards the forest fringe.

"Can you name them?" Kallik asked. "Without asking your squid."

Squid was the derogatory name for the Octo, used by those who rebelled against Home and its far-reaching tentacles. Branston shook his head. "I have no idea. What's your point?"

Kallik grinned smugly, waving a pointing finger along the trees like a conductor. "Spruce, Douglas Fir, Scots Pine. Used to be too cold, ice too thick for trees up here.

185

These are youngsters, less than two hundred years old. I know all this from experience, not because I downloaded it."

Branston sighed. There was so much wrong with what the old Inuit was saying that he didn't know where to start. Octos weren't implanted to replace experiential learning, just to augment it. He was about to begin to explain why he ought to report Kallik to Home, when he felt something peculiar on the side of his face. It felt like moisture but also like a feather. He felt another one touch his eyelash, looked up and saw strange white pieces of something spiralling down.

Snow. As ever, Octo supplied the word but even experiencing it, Branston scarcely believed what was happening. It was as if the sky had been torn into confetti and thrown down. This was the frozen rain he'd heard about, not falling as bullets, but drifting, swirling, collecting on the ground in crystals. Kallik was looking at him quizzically.

"I've never seen snow," Branston explained, knowing now that he would stay a while, watching the snow fall, then get back into his bug and fly away. He'd tell Home that the old man had suffered a coronary and died before Branston could serve his warrant.

"Beautiful isn't it?" said Kallik. A lump had formed in Branston's throat and he couldn't speak, so he simply nodded and gazed up into the drifting white chaos all around him. It wasn't like using your Octo to draw on the MemoryBank and pull up an recording of snow – immersive as Home claimed its memories to be, that second-hand experience felt like a crude sketch of snow compared to this.

"Would you like some tea, warm you up before you

go?" said Kallik.

Branston smiled. "Can we watch the snow for a bit?"

"You can see it from inside. I'll make a fire," offered Kallik.

A fire. For primary warmth, rather than simply decoration. What more wonders awaited?

Kallik patted him on the shoulder in passing and began to trudge back towards his house. The snow had formed a paper-thin layer that nevertheless felt crunchy beneath Branston's feet as he followed the old Inuit back towards the shack. As he did so, he took out his pulse weapon and switched it to its lowest setting, the one that would knock out an Octo for up to twenty minutes, before it rebooted. When he reached the house, he'd apply it to the back of his own head.

It would be nice to enjoy a bit of peace and quiet for a change.

In Too Deep

The noise that told Jennifer Allbright that she might die down here, thirty feet under the Sea of Marmara, was the sound of the winch unwinding. As if it could no longer be held in tension. As if there was no-one there to hold it.

The cage was six feet square, made of rigid steel struts welded securely together. On its floor and ceiling was an additional layer of strong wire mesh. There were four flotation devices on the roof which could be inflated remotely if the winch failed. The bars were nine inches apart, too small for the intrusion of a tiger or bull or hammerhead or indeed any of the forty-three other species of shark to be found in the Mediterranean. Large enough for Jennifer's camera lens, however. Large enough for her hand if she was brave, or stupid enough, to risk contact.

Just twenty-four years old, Jennifer was an inveterate thrill-seeker. She had bungee-jumped off a viaduct in Italy, skied black runs in Austria and cracked a bullwhip at a lion in an unrepentant animal circus in Romania. These activities were indulged by her father, who had won a local lottery and retired to a vineyard in the Yarra Valley. His millions had meant that his two children, Jennifer and Roger, could travel the world, indulging adventurous whims. The siblings were inseparable on their adventures, so much so that people often assumed they were a couple, a source of constant embarrassment.

Roger, unfortunately, had eaten some bad seafood the previous evening and had been up all night throwing up. He'd had to cry off today's Swimming with Sharks extravaganza, so that he could recover in bed and FaceTime his boyfriend Bruno, back in Sydney.

Roger had bribed the ship's captain, Hakki, to make Jennifer's special birthday experience a private one – just Hakki and them. Usually, Jennifer wouldn't have been allowed in the cage alone, but Roger had offered the captain a supplement of two thousand lira and Hakki had five children to feed.

As she gulped oxygen through her aqualung, holding her underwater camera at the ready, Jennifer was momentarily startled by a blush of red amidst the blue. Hakki must have thrown in a handful of chum to attract the sharks. He had boasted that a great white shark could dismember a man, or a woman, with a single bite. "Like you would a stick of celery," he'd added, unnecessarily.

In the first 20 minutes Jennifer had photographed a feeding-frenzy of fearsome looking fish, including a half dozen blue sharks, a comical-looking hammerhead, and a tiger shark. Only the latter had paid her any attention at all, primarily because the others had devoured all the chum. The tiger had flickered swiftly into the periphery of her vision, then swum underneath, to rise before her like an apparition. Despite her bravery, Jennifer backed away, as the shark nosed between the bars, as if smelling her. Jennifer wondered if the shark could tell she had finished her period yesterday.

Five minutes of the allotted time remained, and Jennifer had seen nothing since the tiger shark apart from glittering shoals of fish. Then something slid sinisterly out of the murk directly ahead of her. Jennifer's heart throbbed. It wasn't the familiar white underbelly, or the immense size of the thing (six metres from snout to tail) that told her the shark was a great white. It was its grimace and the calm, cold appraisal in its eyes. The creature in front of her wanted nothing more than to chew her into pieces and devour her.

Jennifer was too terrified to move, having lost all desire to touch the monster, even when it turned tail and swam quickly away. The encounter lasted less than a minute, but Jennifer had its deathly visage imprinted on her mind. Those teeth – so many of them – the morsels of torn up flesh between them. The great white was a messy eater.

The time came for Jennifer to be hoist to the surface and she felt the winch engage with relief. When the cage stopped moments later, ten feet from the surface, her relief dissolved. Fearfully, she jerked on the safety line – twice, as she'd been instructed. Nothing… what was Hakki up to? She guessed the winch was stuck. Why had he not inflated the emergency floats? She laid the camera down and tried the safety line again.

Ten minutes later, with her oxygen indicator in the red, the truth dawned. Something had happened to Hakki. She'd have to free herself.

A shadow passed overhead – a barracuda, thankfully. Jennifer remembered what Hakki had told her about the explosive bolts that would jettison the roof. She had to twist the lever to vertical, push the red button and stand back. Jennifer did a 360, saw nothing. She crouched at the base of the cage, and pushed the button. Only then did she remember to look down. There was the great white, waiting.

The top of the cage blasted free, and the base dropped, causing the shark to duck out of the way. Fighting impossibly slowly through currents like treacle, Jennifer kicked out. She couldn't see the shark, only the sunlight sparkling down from overhead as she kicked hard…

Jennifer broke the surface of the water, a shadow circling beneath her as the adrenalin dragged her up the ladder, still wearing the heavy oxygen tanks. She flopped gratefully onto the deck, sobbing with relief. Inches away, was the sun-tanned body of Hakki, sprawled onto the floor. She checked his pulse, found it absent, and raced into the cabin to locate the radio.

Two hours later, she was rescued by the local lifeguard, checked over at hospital and released in a taxi. Hakki had suffered a coronary. He'd probably been dead for at least twenty minutes when Jennifer found him. She'd spent at least that much time alternating between the CPR she'd learned at college, and the boat's defibrillator the coastguard instructed her how to use, while she waited for their rescue. Jennifer's attempts had been futile, and she'd found herself sobbing over the lifeless body of a man she hadn't known.

Now, two hours later, Jennifer staggered into the hotel room, where Roger was snoring loudly. Outside, a glorious sunset blossomed over the Bosporus.

All Jennifer, retired adrenalin junkie, would see in her dreams that night were those endless rows of teeth, those implacable eyes, and that terrible smile.

Curfew

The echoes of the sirens still resounded in the empty streets as Bill and Emily reached the only house with its porch light still on. 24 Wilberforce Way. Emily imagined the Entity wrapping invisible tendrils around them both as Bill hammered on the front door, ignoring the buzzer. There was no time for niceties. They had perhaps two minutes to gain access before things became really dangerous. Emily leaned against a pillar, struggling to catch her breath.

"Come on!" Bill muttered between gritted teeth.

"Why don't they answer?" Emily asked. "Everyone knows the rules, don't they?"

"Hell knows," said Bill, looking behind them for signs of other stragglers. The pervasive silence, broken only by the tinkling of a distant piano, revealed that they were the only ones still out. They couldn't be taking these risks forever. One day the Entity would catch up with them, as it always did. Either that or the Nightwatch patrols would slap a caution on them, and they'd be confined to one specified domicile, with strict controls over their movements. That would make their business, and thus their lives, impossible.

Emily felt a strange chill fall upon her neck and shoulders, together with a tightness in her throat. Here it was, right on cue.

"In the name of God, will you open up?" Bill shouted through the letterbox, trying to sound more plaintive than angry.

It worked. There was a click, and the door catch released. Emily felt a glutinous tug attempting to pull her back from the doorstep, but Bill grabbed her arm and

193

yanked her into the hallway, where they sprawled on expensive parquet flooring. Bill kicked the door shut with his foot.

Nobody was to be seen. Bill scrambled to his feet, cosh at the ready.

"Hey! Cutting it fine, weren't you?" he yelled.

Bill was short-tempered by nature. Emily found her fear and frustration quickly gave way to gratitude and relief once she'd found a Haven for the night. She didn't hold onto things for long; it wasn't wise in the late twenty-fifties to be quick to anger and slow to forgive, but Bill was almost sixty and had been born before the coming of the Entity. He held a grudge that burnt like a red-hot coal; easy to fan into vivid flame.

Nobody answered Bill, so they walked along the well-decorated corridor, past the stairs, alongside a series of doors. Emily and Bill tried each one – all locked. An open doorway lay at the end of the hall.

"They have cameras," Emily noted, spotting the tiny dimples above each door. "Old school."

The tech did look very retrograde, but this might still be a remote Haven, its door triggered from afar by someone. Everyone loved a remote Haven – you didn't have to do any of the awkward chit-chat.

"Jiminy," asked Bill, "any nanos or heat signatures?"

Apparently, Bill had named his own nano after a character in an ancient cartoon. When Emily got hers, she followed suit; Emily's was called Tinkerbell.

No nanos but I'm detecting a heat signature from the attic, said Jiminy, floating just above and to the right of Bill's head.

"Shall we go say hello?" Emily asked brightly. She was the extrovert of the two, and actually liked meeting new people. For Bill, these random encounters were an occupational hazard.

"I don't think they want to meet us, sweetie. Remote trigger, remember?"

They passed through the open door at the end of the hall into a sumptuously furnished lounge – dark wood antique furniture, with the occasional twentieth century classic. An Eames chair in the corner, in front of a small writing desk, illuminated by an arcing floor lamp with a round copper shade. A Persian rug defined a central seating area, with several ottomans and a large wrought iron and glass coffee table, on which lay a neatly ordered pile of tasteful magazines and art books. Kokoshka, Klimt, Sonia Delauney. A relatively convincing faux-log fire blazed under an old marble fireplace. By the door through which they had entered, a grandfather clock ticked away the seconds. Whoever lived here had money and was painfully tasteful in spending it.

Also on the coffee table was a laminated A4 card. Helvetica, 36pt. Raising an eyebrow, Bill picked it up and read from it.

Dear Visitors, I am sorry I am not here to welcome you. I have Asperger's and find it difficult to meet new people. I hope you do not mind if I decline to come downstairs this evening. Make yourselves at home. There are two bedrooms unlocked for you on the first floor and a bathroom opposite. The kitchen is accessible by the door to the right of the bookcase. Feel free to eat or drink anything you find. I'm sorry but I have no screens; you are welcome to read my books. I only ask that you leave this Haven in the condition you found it. All rooms are monitored 24/7. Have a good evening, Monika.

No screens! Emily had felt a sense of something missing but hadn't twigged that it was the lack of videowalls.

Nothing but paint and wallpaper.

"Tinks, are there any audiofeeds available?" Emily asked, looking around for her nano, which seemed to have found itself a perch on top of the mantelpiece.

This Haven is not feed-enabled, Tinks replied.

"I guess we'll be missing the evening report," said Bill, slumping down on an ottoman and letting his backpack slide onto the floor. "Any chance of a quick shoulder rub?"

Emily didn't mind missing the daily rundown of casualties of the Entity and its current drift pattern. It was usually just depressing. The missing persons, the vegetative, the suicides, the imprisoned and the insane. Bill had once told her there was a dark-web book running on the daily numbers. Emily couldn't imagine anything more callous. She half-suspected Bill enjoyed a flutter now and again.

Bill lay flat on the ottoman and kicked off his shoes. Emily knelt on the rug beside him and rubbed his tensely knotted shoulders and neck. Maybe she shouldn't be so critical of her partner. His cynicism and lack of sentimentality had saved both their lives on more than one occasion.

"No telly either. What are we going to do, play board games?" Bill said.

You could make love to me, Emily thought, quickly quashing the notion. They'd tried that a couple of times and although it had been fun, broadly speaking, neither of them had been fully into it. They were very definitely better as friends and colleagues than lovers. Bill was still obsessed with his wife, taken and incarcerated for her own safety. He couldn't love another woman while Suzanna still lived. Plus, he was too old and tired and desolate for Emily, who hadn't yet had her thirtieth birthday. She still hoped to have a child one day. Bill had laughed when she'd told him that.

"I wouldn't mind reading for a bit and maybe getting an early night," Emily said, finishing off the massage with a deep dig between the shoulder blades that made Bill yelp (as she'd known it would).

"All right, brainbox," he said. "You read and I'll try and fix those screeners."

Instinctively, Emily put her finger to her lips to shush Bill. It was illegal to screen Visitors, but Emily and Bill made their living selling tiny devices you could hammer into your front door to record whoever came knocking. The way Bill saw it, they allowed people to screen out those victims who still possessed the wherewithal and cunning to knock on doors when the sirens sounded. There had been dozens of assaults, rapes and murders committed by victims (colloquially, the Taken) of the Entity who were mistaken for ordinary citizens. Bill had explained to Emily that they would actually be helping the Nightwatch patrols as well as protecting the inhabitants of Havens, by selling their illicit devices. Emily hadn't bought this entirely, but it helped her overcome her squeamishness about breaking the law.

Bill took out his box of second-hand screeners extracted from the front doors of customers who had died, moved on, or upgraded. He would reset them and sometimes physically straighten them out so they could be reused. Sometimes he'd replace the tiny lenses on the diamond-tipped heads. Emily liked watching him work; he was a craftsman in his own limited way. Bill had told her that he once used to repair antique clocks and his dexterity underlined the truth of that assertion.

A shelving unit spanned the wall where a screen would normally be, so Emily perused the books. Twain, Eliot, Borges, Woolf, Murdoch, Golding, Calvino, Auster – the inhabitant of 24 Wilberforce Way had an appropriately tasteful collection of literature. Nothing too outlandish – no satanic texts, no pornography. This too was reassuring. Emily picked up a collection of short stories by someone called Barthelme she'd not heard or and was about to choose a comfy chair when she saw a floor-level shelf containing a set of photo albums. Would it be wrong to take a peek?

Before she consciously answered her own question, Emily had reached for a volume at random and opened it. It did not contain the antique family photographs she anticipated. Instead, its pages contained small, square photographs showing people sleeping, taken in a greenish light, eerie and also strangely touching. Elderly people, children, teenagers, middle-aged men, all in different, vulnerable attitudes of somnolence. Some tangled in their sheets, others stretched out like cadavers. How peculiar. She replaced the album.

Emily felt a tug of disquiet but shook it aside and settled down with her book. Later she got up to explore the kitchen, finding the ingredients for a mushroom omelette and, to Bill's delight, some bottled cider. They ate voraciously, and Bill drank a little more than Emily thought wise, though she didn't criticise. By eleven o'clock they had both run out of reasons to remain awake and the evening had proved unusually peaceful. no Screamers, no spot checks by the Nightwatch, and, as promised, no appearance by the mysterious Monika.

As Bill washed up, doing the plates and cutlery by hand as there was no dishwasher, Emily found herself talking to their mysterious host, as she climbed the stairs to the bedrooms. Tinkerbell glowed softly, providing enough illumination to see by, without having to look for switches (the lighting was just as antique as the rest of the house).

"It's a shame you won't come down to meet us. You have a lovely home and we're very grateful to you for letting us stay. Well, I mean, I know you have to, but you've been so hospitable. And your library is fantastic. I've never seen so many books in one place. Tinks, is that the biggest library we've come across?"

Tinks took a microsecond to reply. *That is the fourth largest collection of paper books I have encountered.* Jeez – Emily really ought to program in some personality for Tinkerbell. She was such a buzzkill.

"Anyway, it's a lovely home and don't worry, we'll be out of your hair first thing in the morning. If you do want to say hi, we're going to bed soon, so now would be a good time."

Emily paused on the first-floor landing, listening for a sound from upstairs, but there was nothing, save the usual creaks and whispers of an old house settling. Monika, true to her word, would not be drawn.

Emily opened the first bedroom door, locating a switch to her left and flicking it on. The room was simply, but prettily furnished, with a large brass-framed bed and two fluffy towels on the bedspread. The window was shuttered, and a small radiator oozed enough warmth to make the room cosy but not stifling. One detail caught Emily's eye – in front of the window hung a child's mobile with a series of balsa wood planes gently rotating in the convection currents from the radiator.

"Such a sweet room. I hardly feel I need to check the other one."

Of course, she did, hearing Bill clumping heavily up

the stairs behind him. Emily felt momentarily irritated that he hadn't taken his shoes off. The second bedroom was larger, but a little colder and more spartan. She knew immediately that it would appeal to Bill. He appeared behind her, his hands on her shoulders. Bill got tactile when he was tipsy.

"Do you want this one?" Emily offered. Bill edged past her, looking around the white-walled room with its twin beds, tall oak wardrobe, and heavy drapes. Bill yawned, then cracked a rare smile.

"I thought we might share tonight," he said, almost shyly. "If that's cool with you."

Emily hadn't expected that. Perhaps this would be another of their nights of comforting but inconsequential sex. Frankly, she couldn't be bothered.

"Sure, that'd be nice. I am really sleepy though."

Bill laughed. "Don't worry, I'll keep my hands off you. Too many cameras, anyway."

It was true. Although most Havens were heavily monitored, ones like this, with very visible camera points, made Visitors a lot more self-conscious. When you couldn't see the lenses, it was easy to forget they were there.

"Probably disappoint the mysterious Monika," Bill murmured.

"Don't be mean," Emily chided. "Come and see the other room. It's cuter."

Emily was pleased that Bill agreed they'd sleep in the smaller room and they both unselfconsciously stripped off to their underwear and went about their nocturnal routines. Bill even went back downstairs to fetch glasses of water for them both (unfiltered, but fine in a pinch). Who was he trying to impress?

Before Emily switched off the bedside lamp, Bill raised his water glass to the camera-dimple above the door.

"Here's to Monika, best hostess ever!"

They had both almost entirely forgotten the horrors of the last week.

Somewhere in the small hours, a key turned cautiously in a lock on the second floor. A petite, barefooted figure tiptoed down from the steep flight of wooden stairs leading up to the attic safe room.

With feline grace, Monika walked along the hallway, placing her feet carefully, like a dancer. Even carrying the bulky bag against her side, she remained balanced and silent. This was a journey she had made many times, in near or utter darkness. Her feet knew which boards to avoid, and which steps to skip as she minimised the many creaks the ancient wood sounded. It paid to live in the same house for sixty-seven years.

In the kitchen, Monika was gratified to note that four of the eggs had gone, as well as a quarter of the milk. They hadn't spotted the tiny perforations in the shells or the slight sourness the drug imparted. Good. She looked at her wristwatch. Almost quarter to four. Perfect.

Monika adjusted the bag on her shoulder, feeling the dull ache of sciatica. Perhaps her project would be completed this year. She was no longer quite so fond of her nocturnal life, creeping about in a sinister fashion. The immorality of her actions now began to trouble her in particularly reflective moments. It had seemed like a reasonable thing to begin with, a little over five years ago, when the Entity arrived, and the world went to hell. A safe Haven to all comers, in exchange for a secret gift, an addition to her library. Now, even her Asperger's-straitened mind knew that there was something unseemly about it. Still, if there was one thing Monika had learned, after all these years of solitude, it was the importance of finishing what you'd started.

In the middle of a very strange dream, Emily heard the whirr of a moth close to her ear, and a ratcheting mechanical sound. She felt herself stirring towards consciousness and half-saw, half-sensed a presence in the room. Her eyes struggled to open.

She'd been dreaming of a tiny, wizened lady with long, white hair and the gait of a dancer, light-footing it across the floor with some sort of mechanism in her hands. As she struggled to consciousness, Emily began to wonder if this had been real. She heard the unmistakable click of a door closing somewhere, and managed to prise heavy-lidded eyes open enough to notice an indentation in the bedspread – had someone been kneeling there?

Emily rubbed her eyes and swivelled her legs out of the bed. Bill was snoring at her side, deeply unconscious in a way Emily could never comprehend. It was if he had forgotten the world's terrors entirely. She padded over to the door and opened it. Her head felt woozy, and her senses remained indistinct. She listened. Was that a creak from upstairs? A noise of diminishing footsteps?

"Monika?"

No reply, no chance of one really. She must have imagined it. Emily went back to bed and pulled the bedclothes up under her chin. Bill half-groaned and rolled onto his side, facing her. Still asleep, but somehow vigilant. Fortunately, sleep came quickly for Emily too and she had no more visions of nocturnal visitation.

As promised, the following morning, they made an early start. By seven thirty, they had both quickly showered and eaten some breakfast (toast for Emily, while Bill fried himself an egg). There was even coffee, a rare and expensive commodity these days. They planned to hit some of the rich homes on Chestnut Grove – somebody there would be looking to upgrade their surveillance. It paid to get to the clients before they set off to their various workplaces, in their air-conditioned luxury AVs (autonomous vehicles).

Emily found a pen and wrote a note for their mystery host. It read:

Dear Monika

Thank you so much for hosting us this evening. Your generosity and your lovely home will stay with us forever. E & B.

Excessive perhaps? Bill couldn't hide a slight wince when he read the sentiments she'd handwritten. Emily didn't care. It was nice to be nice. Then, on the doorstep, Emily had another thought. She stopped Bill from closing the door.

"One moment. Something I need to check," she said. "Just give me a second."

Emily edged back into the house and marched straight through to the lounge, crouching to take out the photo album she'd looked through the previous evening. She made as much noise as she liked – she wanted Monika to know she was still there, even if their mystery hostess wasn't looking at her videofeeds.

Emily's heart began to pound as she turned to the last-completed page of the album and found a new photo inserted into the blank page opposite. Bill and Emily, of course, asleep in the 'spoons' position they sometimes fell into, unaware of the spectator taking the photo with whatever archaic device produced these shiny images.

Emily peeled the photo out of the diagonal slits holding it in place. It was sort of beautiful, she thought. She could take it with her; perhaps she even should. Emily instead fitted the Polaroid image carefully back in place and folded the album away, slotting it back onto the low shelf. She should probably mark Monika's front door with an invisible chemical cross that could be seen in blacklight only, warning off other travellers. But she didn't do that either. She just took one final look up at the camera dimple above the living room door and nodded, a tacit acknowledgement of a debt paid.

A simple transaction – a stolen image for a safe and restful night's sleep. They had both given a lot more of themselves to imperfect strangers.

Thermals

Hector had begun to hate Dr Susan Gleeson of the Pan-American Society of Surveyors, thirty minutes into the flight. Firstly, she talked even more than he did, and if there was one thing Hector Zambrano liked to hear more than the propellers on his 1962 Cessna Skylark, it was the sound of his own voice bellowing over them.

Secondly, her opinions on Ecuador were widely off-beam at best and borderline racist at worst. What did a thirty-two-year-old Scottish woman get off calling Quito a "poor man's Cordoba?" The Ecuadorian capital was far preferable to that dusty relic of fallen empires. Cordoba could boast Moorish palaces and mosques, but Quito had that in spades, plus ancient Incan remnants *and* it was nearly 3000 metres above sea-level. You didn't boil in the winter, but got plenty of sun to top-up the tan on your lovely long legs…

Damn it! There he went again, objectifying a woman, like the counsellor had warned him he mustn't. What a degenerate he was.

"So… Hector…" Doctor Gleeson shouted, as they began to circle the south side of Mount Chimborazo, "how long have you been a pilot?"

At last, an opening.

"Thirty-two years. Could fly before I could walk, my father said. Used to sit me on his knee and let me operate the controls as a little baby."

Susie, as she'd insisted he call her, was squinting from under her headscarf at the snow-capped peak. He'd warned her not to wear expensive sunglasses, as the wind on Chimborazo would yank them clear off your face. Good cheekbones she had, mind you, and honey-blonde hair, escaping from the scarf in exuberant strands. Shit! He was doing it again. He reminded himself how irritating his client was and that his separation from Luisa shouldn't prove permanent.

"Why do you want to put an observatory down there?" he asked. The winters will freeze you solid."

"We don't really want to put it here, Hector," she replied. "But your government offered such tempting subsidies; the backers couldn't refuse. Only problem is the lack of infrastructure."

Another little dig at his home country.

The plane bounced, as if it were bobbing on the currents of a stormy sea. Susie Gleeson gave an involuntary squeak, which made Hector smile.

"Turbulence," he informed her unnecessarily. "The thermals can be pretty rough up here. We shouldn't get any closer."

"I need to get closer, Hector. I have to identify whatever bits of this volcano are in any sense flat."

That was a laugh. The 20,000ft Chimborazo was limpet-shaped, rocky, and inhospitable. Its last eruption had been 2000 years ago, but many locals felt another was about due. It had already claimed one plane, a Vickers Viscount which disappeared in its shadow in 1976. The crashed plane and bodies of its 55 passengers were only discovered in 2003.

"Nothing flat here," Hector shouted. "Even the goats don't want to climb that thing. Haven't you got a zoom?"

Doctor Gleeson had taken out her Nikon, as they passed from the sunlit side of the mountain into its shadow.

The air itself seemed to take a deep breath, and the plane dropped like a stone, until Hector levelled it out. The good doctor looked a little nauseous. That would teach her to badmouth his hometown.

"Get closer, won't you? We're miles away!", she yelled.

So, she wants to get closer, thought Hector impetuously. Okay.

He twisted the steering column and the Cessna looped into a steep descent towards the mountain. Hector knew what he was doing – he could safely ignore the hazard lights indicating they were getting too close. He often pulled this stunt to scare the rookie pilots back at the flying school in Quito.

Doctor Gleeson, surprisingly, seemed unfazed. She was taking photos with a determination he had previously only seen in his wife when she really wanted to win an argument.

But you couldn't argue with a mountain, as Hector was suddenly reminded. Without warning, the tail flaps jammed, and the wind dropped away again in the lee of Chimborazo. The granite mountainside reared up before them, and Doctor Gleeson grabbed the sides of the cockpit, gasping in terror.

Hector wrestled the controls, calculating the trajectories on nothing but instinct. They were assuredly going to crash; it was only a matter of where. They had a fractionally better chance of surviving in snow than impacting into rock at 280km an hour. With enough lift under the wings, he could hopefully use them to skate along the crusted snow.

"Susie," he yelled. "Get down. We're gonna crash!"
She did as she was told and moments later, Hector slammed

his twenty-thousand-dollar plane into the biggest drift he could find. The lights went out, the world became an avalanche, and the Cessna folded itself around them like the wings of a giant bird.

He came too when a beam of sunlight threw warmth across his snow-scoured cheek. Hector had a headache worse than any whiskey-sodden hangover and was in pain in at least five different places. He couldn't move at all, his torso trapped in a mess of fuselage and snow. There was congealed blood on the side of his face.

From somewhere above him he heard a grunting of effort and he glanced up to see a face appear in the hole in the snowbank.

"Hector! You're alive, then?" Gleeson said. "You've got to be the worst pilot in Quito. Now sit still, I'm coming."

She began to dig frantically, with something Hector recognised as one of the ailerons. My poor Cessna, he thought dimly, before fainting again.

Seventeen hours later, relaying their adventure, and miraculous survival to a bar full of agog locals, Hector was again silenced by Doctor Gleeson, the irritating scientist who had used a shard of broken wing to dig them out of their showy tomb, then that self-same bit of fuselage to reflect light into the eyes of the helicopter pilot who rescued them; that Rosie Gleeson slammed a bottle of Aguardiente (literally firewater) down and said:

"You owe me a drink. Or rather, I owe you several. You found me the site of our observatory. You have to christen it with me – its only l…logical."

Evidently several sheets to the wind, Rosie's hair blew away from the line of stiches just behind her ear. She didn't seem to blame Hector for anything. I have underestimated her, he thought, procuring two shot glasses. He filled them with fiery rum and chinked his glass against hers.

"Salud!" he cried. Susie downed her shot and slammed the glass down on the counter. "See you around," she said, and ambled out of the bar.

Hector stroked his naked ring-finger. Maybe he wouldn't be putting that ring back on anytime soon.

Flotsam and Jetsam

At the third attempt, I land the hook into the exposed mid-riff of the floater, a middle-aged woman, we guess, although it's hard to tell from the bloating. The gnarled silhouette of Jackson nods against the lurid backdrop of a fading sun as he guns the engine. I tie the rope to the gunwale and the small skiff begins to tow the unfortunate through the reeds towards the shore. We'll leave the body by the roadside for the authorities to identify, assuming they can. Assuming there are still authorities. Jackson and I have taken this task upon ourselves. Nobody asked us to do anything more than survive.

When the tsunami came, the seawalls shattered, and mass evacuation took place. Jackson, I and perhaps a dozen other villagers stayed behind. Our lowland realm had long been on the verge of giving itself fully to the sea and we were too exhausted to run. The names of the villages on the north Norfolk salt marshes quaintly hint at an amphibious nature – Wells-next-the-Sea, Cley-next-the-Sea.

Now those places are fully and finally *in* the sea and a relationship has been consummated. The old granary at Wells remains a rare protrusion on the coast (its top floor and gantry our current home). The sea washes inland as far as Norwich as a few of us cling on in our boats and dinghies, breaking into the six-storey granary to take ownership of the designer flats the wealthy second-homers fled.

Jackson and I are friends, but people assume we're a couple. I'm fifty-seven and Jackson refuses to state his age but the lines on his sea-weathered face place him squarely in his seventies. He was always alone; I lost my husband in the catastrophe. Jackson is a charismatic former seaman turned painter who owns – owned – a small gallery on the Wells shorefront. I'd been on holiday with my husband Steven, living in the Albatros, an eighteenth-century Dutch schooner turned floating bar with tourist berths. When the tsunami hit, the Albatros' owner struck out to sea to better weather the storm and did not return.

I was sitting in a restaurant with Steven when the wave shattered the windows, and all became chaos. Jackson rescued me in his outboard-powered skiff as I shivered on the Granary roof, wondering what the hell to do next.

I don't know for certain that Steven is dead and am dreading the day we find him floating face down in the green pools of the New Lagoon. That's probably why I always insist on turning the floaters over. After this many weeks, you can hardly tell the men from the women; everyone bloats the same. So, we haven't found Steven; a shred of hope persists.

Once we heave the mystery man onshore and plant a stake and rag of white cloth to mark the spot, we putter round the coast in the direction of King's Lynn, where a couple of church spires mark the square quarter mile or so of the town that remains above the waterline.

Near the shore, a row of beech trees that must have clung onto some fertile ridge amongst the dunes, now lies horizontal on the water, branches still lividly green on the upper boughs. As we glide around the raised fans of muddy roots, an inflatable dinghy noses out from cover, its engine spluttering into life. A man in his early twenties kneels at the prow, levelling a shotgun at us.

"Toss over whatever you got," he commands, all pleasantries and empathy gone in his gaunt search for sustenance. Jackson kills the engine as we drift alongside, the skiff swivelling so that we sit prow to stern with our attacker's boat. I can see Jackson reach down for something out of sight and I know what it is. He nods slowly with one eye closed, our secret sign – a call for desperate measures. We have just one bag of food left, mostly canned goods, and we can't just give it up. I grab the back of tins and wait until the young man starts to turn my way.

I hurl the bag into his chest and duck as two things happen at once. A shotgun blast illuminates the sky above our boats as Jackson stabs the young man with the darts that he plucked from the dartboard I found earlier, floating over the marbled surf. We both know this brutality is essential – the young man would not have let us live. You learn to recognise a certain look.

Our attacker drops his gun and grabs at his neck, as blood gouts between his fingers. He gurgles something indistinct while I retrieve our food, along with a knapsack I find in the bottom of the boat and the shotgun. I fire the remaining barrel into the inflatable skirt of the dinghy, shredding it. It slumps and begins taking on water.

The young man claws our gunwales with slippery fingers. Taking pity, I toss him a t-shirt.

"Tie it round your neck."

It's more to give our attacker the reprieve of hope than to offer any real solution to his incipient death. I think Jackson hit an artery. The young man will bleed out in minutes. As we motor away, I look back to see our victim, neck duly wrapped, clambering onto a trunk as his dinghy sinks.

"Fuck, Jackson, that was intense!" I mutter.

"Didn't have any other option," he says quietly, "he would have shot us both."

He sounds like he's trying to convince himself more than me. I nod, finding a tear running down my cheek, which I wipe away. It's been a while since either of us wept in the face of death. Our world has been devastated by storm after storm, heatwave after heatwave, the failure of the crops, the dissolution of Europe and the second American Civil War.

Everyone's a survivor now. Nobody quite knows why any of us are clinging on to the fringes of civilisation, but survival is a hard habit to break.

And there's a chance, just a chance, that we'll find something of value floating amongst the detritus of our unexamined lives. Thus, we live in hope, for what else is there?

Import Export

Once again Macauley and Sykes were out on a dank and foggy night, surreptitiously hauling cargo onto a hovertruck destined for the nearest Starbase, using old-fashioned man-power instead of big-data linked robot lifts (which would report their activities back to a logistics supernode some-where in China). They had bribed the usual security guards to let them have half an hour to replace some of the cli-mate-controlled pods, with their own near-identical ones.

Import-Export wasn't what it used to be – what had once been an adventurous racket for devil-may-care types, was now a strange and unpredictable blend of high-tech and old school. They swapped custom-built isopods for their own low-tech cryogenics. Trillionaires in the former pods whose off-world visas were pre-approved were ex-changed for pre-frozen ordinary middle-class folk in the latter. Their clients had greased the right palms and spoken to the right shady go-betweens (this is where Macauley and Sykes came in) to buy illegal passage for the sum total of their entire earthly worth.

The price of transit was always simple – everything you had. After all, rather like dying, you couldn't take it with you. Customers' assets were liquidated and poured through a network of cybercurrency exchanges until they were scrubbed clean. Some of the flow, a few thousand Quarks, trickled down to the lowly fixers who actually ran the show.

It really wasn't enough for the risks they were taking. If they were caught, Macauley and Sykes would undergo personality erasure, their synaptic structures harvested and put to use in the WideWorld Web, a hive construct of enmeshed human minds. Capital punishment had been outlawed four hundred years previously, when some bits of the world were still inhabitable for more than a couple of months a year. If anything, personality erasure was worse. You lived on, in theory, as part of the very system you had spent your adult life battling.

Macauley, a birth-male currently spending time as a woman, and Sykes, a herma-female, slammed shut the warehouse door and palmed value into the outstretched hands of the two security-guards, both normative birth-females (most security personnel were, due to their superior peripheral vision). Macauley jumped up into the cab and programmed the pilot for Starbase ED-19, deep in the heart of the Pentland Hills south of Edinburgh.

Sykes phased out and began to recharge heris batteries, from the truck's own fusion reserve. Charging was a new alternative to sleep. MacCauley was still creeped out by how a Chargee could answer simple questions and even look at you with eyes open, whilst deep in this uncanny slumber-substitute. Sykes, a herma of few words, neither opened heris eyes nor spoke; s/he might as well be asleep.

Half an hour later, they cleared security at ED-19 and proceeded to chaperone their charges, namely ninety-eight legitimate evacuees and two smuggled ones, into the Stringship Hawking-09. Tomorrow it would shimmer off for the Pleiades wormhole, and their transactions would be ratified – Quarks would flow into their accounts. Just one more of these runs and Macauley would have saved enough to have sa-himself illicitly transferred off-world to join sa-his wife and kids.

The Earth's two million inhabitants lived a nomadic

existence following a habitable band around the planet's circumference, living and working this month in Scotland, next month in Norway, then Russia for six months, then off to Canada for three and finally a deliciously cool spell in Greenland before stopping off in Scotland again. The average daytime temperature was a shade under 45 degrees. Beyond the band it soared towards boiling point, and the seas were permanently swirling with hot mist.

Once they'd clocked-off (another one of those perplexing pre-catastrophic turns of phrase), Macauley turned to Sykes and suggested:

"Drink? There's a place in Auld Reekie still has a few bottles of 2035 Macallan?"

Sa-he knew it was futile. As well as being a herma of few words, Sykes was also an aesthete. S/he neither ate organic foodstuffs nor drank anything but filtered water. Gel and water… what a mad way to live.

"I'll pass," murmured Sykes. "See you next time."

Neither of them knew when that would be. They'd simply receive a skin-message telling them a client wanted to talk. They'd go and seal the deal in one of the blind-spot alleys in the Old Town (the bit built in the 1700s, not the old-old town, which predated it).

Sa-he liked working with Sykes. S/he was fun in heris peculiar way, possessing a very dry sense of humour without babbling endlessly the way the malfunctioning cyborg who'd preceded he/r had. Nevertheless, without enough Quarks for an entanglement chat with his wife and kids, Sykes was at something of a loose end.

Sa-he had an idea – there was still a drop or two in Sa-his hipflask, the oldest and most valuable thing Sa-he owned, although its contents ran close, at 40 quarks a fluid ounce. Enough to get Sa-him up the crags to get a look into Arthur's seat. The former tourist draw had been walled-off recently, due to the occasional rumble and gout of magma, but, as ever, Macauley knew a security guard to bribe.

Fortunately, Sticks Murphy was working Queen's Park security detail tonight, and gladly led Macauley through in exchange for a wee dram and a captive audience for her latest assault on the drumkit she kept at the back of the booth. A few appreciative head nods from Macauley later, Murphy palmed the pad on the wall and the force-field melted away for ten seconds, letting Macauley slip through.

Macauley began to climb with sa-his ears still ringing, forcing sa-his way through a hot and filthy rain that had sprung up from nowhere, clicking sa-his VisionAid onto heat-mode for the full lightshow as sa-he ascended the curving path leading up the side of the slanted slab of rock that constituted the crags. From its top, sa-he would be able to look across into the smoking cone that was Arthur's seat. A reawakened chasm, an angry wound in a planet that was fast disintegrating.

Sa-he'd look down at all that violent, raw, red power, an ancient force that revealed how inhospitable the planet Earth could really become, and sa-he'd dream of all that Martian greenery and fantasise about smelling the rasp-berry-scented roses and diving into the cool crystal lakes, and making love to Alison (as a woman, for the first time!), and cradling Angus and Maddie in sa-his arms.

Sa-he'd look into the fire and dream of ice. Sa-he'd never seen ice; at least, not proper ice. Cryo didn't count.

Rockabye Baby

"Push the self-rocking cradle."

The instruction from Darren's manager at the Orpington KidsWorld filled Darren with dread. In a fit of ill-informed enthusiasm, Mr Sanchez had ordered fifty of the ridiculous creations and the supplier did not do sale or return. If the cradle was self-rocking, Darren wanted to ask, why on earth did he need to push it? But witticisms didn't go down very well with Sanchez, who had no discernible sense of humour.

Darren had worked in retail since his recovery from a rare blood disease which left him partially incapacitated. He suffered from troughs of deep fatigue which meant he had to rest from time to time. So far, he'd gotten away with so doing. On a wet Tuesday morning, he was having one of these brief sit downs, when a young woman came in. She was olive complexioned, had raven-black hair and was quite heavily pregnant. She was also undeniably lovely.

However, Darren held as an absolute moral axiom that you didn't mess with another man's wife. The wedding ring on the customer's right hand was practically gleaming out a warning.

Darren, it had to be said, had a bit of a 'thing' for pregnant women, not an uncommon fetish, as the lonelier reaches of the internet might testify. However, as he ambled over, half-hoping another member of staff would get there first, Darren was determined to remain on his best behaviour.

"Can I help you?" he asked. The customer was actually looking at the self-rocking cradle with evident interest.

She laughed as she straightened up, with some effort.

"Is this a ridiculous gimmick or what?" She had a slight accent and Darren guessed that she might be Greek and wondered if he should ask her name. He'd read that if you could get a customer's name, you were 43% more likely to sell to them.

"It's unusual, I'll give you that. It has five standard speeds and its even got a setting that starts a gentle rocking if it senses your baby is restless during the night. Plus, you can start it remotely, say, for example, if you're using a video baby monitor. We've got a sale on monitors at the moment, actually."

Darren tended to blurt when he felt self-conscious and the lovely Elena (as he imagined she was called) was making him quite hot under the collar.

"So… What's the cost of this amazing gadget?"

Was that sarcasm or just a foreign intonation?

"Retails at £299 but with the sale on, it's marked down to £250."

Elena whistled her surprise.

"I'm all for labour-saving devices," she said. "No pun intended. But I can rock a cradle myself."

"When are you due?" Darren said, for the lack of anything better to say.

"Well," she said, with a widening of her lovely brown eyes. "Any time soon. Actually… I know this is a bit weird, but I've been on my feet for a couple of hours, and I would kill for a sit down…"

"Of course!" Darren exclaimed. "I can do better than that. Come with me."

He led Elena round to the special niche he'd found, the little blind spot where the mock-up of the 'tweens bedroom was. It included a double bunkbed, out of sight of the sales desk, the manager's office, and the CCTV cameras. Darren sometimes grabbed a quick power nap towards the end of a quiet day. He confessed as much to Elena, who gladly sat on the bed and swivelled her legs up onto the Harry Potter duvet.

"I won't tell if you don't," she said with a conspiratorial wink, one that melted his heart and gave him an inner flush of unadulterated lust. Jesus, what was wrong with him!

"Oh my god, being pregnant makes lying down the best thing ever," Elena said, gratefully.

They sat in silence for a while, Elena with her back against a pile of cushions and her legs up, shoes kicked off onto the rainbow-patterned vinyl. Darren sat in a small chair opposite her.

"Maybe I could use a self-rocking cradle," Elena mused, eyes still shut. "I mean, I'm going to have to do everything else myself."

Darren frowned and Elena, who had opened her eyes, noticed. She gestured to her ring finger.

"Hubby never wanted kids. He ran off as soon as we had our little… miscalculation."

Darren definitely shouldn't ask.

"Why do you still...?"

"Wear it?" she said. "Force of habit. Plus, it keeps the perverts away. You'd be surprised how many men have a thing for pregnant women."

Darren truly hoped he was not blushing.

"I can offer you a 40% discount," Darren blurted. This was not entirely true. He would have to use his staff discount code to ring that through. But Mr Sanchez did say

– push the cradle.

"You're wearing me down," said Elena, swivelling to a sitting position. "Let's have another look."

As he led Elena back over to the cribs, Darren caught Mr Sanchez' eye gave him a surreptitious thumbs up. He'd bloody better make the sale now.

Darren picked up the remote and put the Little Rocker™ through its paces.

"One setting for degree of rotation and one for speed." Darren passed over the control to Elena, who adjusted the parameters to maximum. At full rock, the cradle resembled a fairground ride.

"Is it safe?" said Elena, seemingly seriously. Was he actually going to sell her this thing?

"Absolutely," he said, nodding with vigour. "Passes all the British safety standards. They're very rigorous."

"Do you have kids?" Elena asked, seemingly out of the blue. Darren, at thirty-five, was used to making excuses for his singledom and non-parenthood.

"No, but I'd like to," he simply said. "I'm Darren. Shake hands and I'll ring up that discretionary discount."
A bit weird but he really wanted to know her name.

"I'm Helena. You drive a hard bargain."

She put her soft hand into his and shook it firmly.

And that's how your mother and stepfather met.

Going Down

Coming back from his run, Brian McDonald saw a familiar figure on the stoop outside his Alphabet City apartment building. Manny Rodriguez was smoking but the smell that wafted towards Brian as he exhaustedly grabbed hold of the railings, wasn't tobacco. Did Manny want to get fired?

"Hi there!" said Brian, with forced warmth. As a recent settler, he'd learned a breezy greeting was the American way. A taciturn Scot, this hadn't come easily to Brian. He'd taken some persuading that when bodega owners encouraged him to 'have a nice day', they meant it. How steeped in cynicism and irony his home country must seem to the average American, even in this era of 'Fake News' and presidential idiocy.

Manny returned Brian's greeting with a half-hearted wave, taking a draw. He squinted into the early morning sunlight and offered the roach to Brian.

"Don't know if Mary Jane kills the virus, but it's gotta be worth a shot," Manny said wryly.

Brian laughed awkwardly and declined.

"Can hardly breathe as it is. Six point eight miles today."

Manny nodded with the minimum of acknowledgement. "Good, man".

Was that an edge of sarcasm? What was up with Manny?

"You okay?" Brian said, stretching out his calves.

Manny shook his head. "They sent me home. I'm out of a job."

"What? Why?"

Manny was part of the social glue that held this fifteen-storey apartment block together. When Brian first moved to Manhattan, taking up a friend's offer to apartment-sit while Jackson sailed the Eastern Seaboard, writing another adventure travel book, Brian had thought that the notion of an elevator attendant was an embarrassing anachronism.

Manny pushed the button to take you to your floor, held the doors, helped with luggage, previewed the weather, and shared his seasonal expectations for the Knicks or the Mets. He was always immaculate, in the livery of the Solomon Turley Apartment Complex (nicknamed "the stack") and didn't expect a daily tip. Fellow residents had clarified the complex etiquette around Manny's birthday (October 9th), when a bottle of fine bourbon or pack of Cubans would make the elevator man extremely happy.

Manny sighed, stubbing out his roach.

"Have a look. Fuckin' Coronavirus."

Manny never swore. This was serious. Brian wished he'd brought some cash with him but somehow, giving money to a man sitting jacketless on the stoop felt a little shabby, compared with letting a uniformed lift attendant palm a five spot. Brian settled for a shoulder squeeze and a well-intentioned "I'll come back," although he wasn't sure he would. Was it up to Brian to cheer up a depressed Puerto Rican?

As Brian entered the air-conditioned lobby, his skin began to goosebump. There was Karl, the Slovenian (Slovakian?) concierge, who job-shared with Luisa, the petite, curvy Mexican on whom Brian had a crush. Karl was wearing a surgical mask. What was going on?

"What's up with Manny?" Brian said, approaching the

desk. He'd left his keys with Luisa as he always did before a morning run. He was a little disappointed to see she'd finished her shift already. "And what's with the mask? You look like a Japanese commuter."

Brian couldn't tell whether his possibly xenophobic joke made Karl smile or not, since he could only see the concierge's eyes. Karl's smile seldom reached that far north. "New measures. Cuomo reckons it's pretty bad. New rules on the lift too. They had to let Manny go."

Shit. Brian had heard about the virus ravaging China and Italy but there had only been a few cases in the States. Was it really so bad?

Karl reached into Brian's pigeonhole. He was wearing latex gloves. Brian might have laughed but didn't want to appear rude. He would turn on CNN as soon as he got upstairs. Emily was going to cancel their date. He could feel it. On her profile she'd described herself as a 'total germophobe'. There was no way she was going to have a blind date with a random Scotsman with a killer virus roaming the city. Another strike to his broke bachelor status, Brian thought glumly.

He glanced through the mail. Atlantic magazine – that was Bill's, a circular from a cleaning company, a postcard from someone called Shelley, in Verona. Whoever Shelley was, Brian hoped she'd checked her flight home. Italy was locking down fast.

The Turley developers had skimped on lifts – there was only one per block and, although it could supposedly contain eight occupants, only if they were as skinny as gymnasts and didn't mind a spot of frottage. A note Scotch-taped to the wall read "ONE HOUSEHOLD AT A TIME". Perhaps he should take the stairs? Sixteen flights

— forget it.

Brian jabbed the 8, imagining tiny microbes crawling up his fingers and invading his skin. This was ridiculous. It was basically a bad dose of flu, wasn't it?

At the seventh floor, the doors slid open, revealing an elderly woman with two toy dogs. She backed away as if Brian were contaminated.

"It's okay," Brian stammered as the doors closed. "I'm only going one…"

Inside his apartment, Brian had two conflicting desires. He felt grimy and cold and really wanted a shower. The heating had been off all night, the air-con accidentally left on. The large open-plan space felt like an industrial refrigerator.

Brian also wanted to give something to Manny. He had a book of vouchers for Dean and Deluca that came with a case of wine. That and twenty dollars would do. Manny didn't look like he'd be going anywhere in a hurry. Brian decided to get clean and warm first.

Seven minutes later, surely a record, Brian bounced down the stairs in a hoodie and tracksuit bottoms. Surely this was the quickest he'd ever showered and changed? Nevertheless, when he got back out onto the steps, now flooded in early spring sunlight, the Puerto Rican had gone. Just the stub of Manny's joint remained, plus the grey-black smear where he'd extinguished it, a blot on the pristine grey.

Paragon of Pulchritude

When the Great Gandolfi stooped to present a handker-chief he'd supposedly produced from inside a raw egg, Susanna was tempted to boot him into the crowd. His plentiful rump was a tempting target and the uncomfortable heeled booties he made her wear, despite her protestations that they cut her heels and toes to ribbons, would have launched him pleasingly into the front row.

The only thing that stopped Susanna from ending her career in that moment was the realisation that she might hurt some of the young women who stretched up to beg the bigoted fraud's favour. It wasn't their fault Gandolfi had a reputation as a fiery Latin lover, when in reality he was an Irish bruiser from Spokane. The newspapers and playbills all portrayed him in glowing phrases like 'magnificent magician' and 'flamboyant conjurer.'

Susanna knew him to be a small-town fraudster who'd bought his act wholesale from an ailing blind prestidigitator who could no longer tour, and who had sold Gandolfi a warehouse of equipment and a few hand-written books of tricks for fifty dollars.

Susanna had encountered Paddy Byrne when he was developing his act on the lower reaches of the vaudeville circuit. She'd been a seventeen-year-old throwing cartwheels in a park in Pine Bluff, Arkansas and he'd admired her from the shade of a nearby oak and introduced himself with typical grandiloquence:

"My dear, you have a rare grace and elegance. Have you ever considered a career on the stage?"

Of course, Susanna had been flattered. Life didn't

promise her much more than working in her father's grocery when she left school at the start of that summer. She'd dreaded telling dad she was leaving but Byrne had come cap in hand to beg her father to release his daughter to the magician's care.

Susanna had been slicing ham behind the counter while her father and Byrne chatted outside the store and she'd noticed how obsequious her would-be boss seemed. This surprised her, since her father had the darkest skin of any shopkeeper on the street and Byrne seemed to be treating him as an equal. It was this reversal of the norm that impressed her more than anything. When her father came back into the store, he shook his head fondly, looked at his expectantly waiting daughter and said:

"Go on then, Suzy. I'll finish up the ham."

Suzanna had raced out into the street to shake Byrne's hand and start her new life in showbiz.

Of course, it was too good to be true. When Susanna turned up at the warehouse two days later, expecting to start learning the art of conjuring, Byrne had grabbed her shoulders, pushed her back out into the sunlight and appraised her like a piece of meat.

"Goddamit, you're so pale-skinned I'd never have took you for a mulatto."

It wasn't the welcome she had hoped for. Her boss's attitude to her seemed to fluctuate daily, depending on whether he'd had a skinful or not. That said, Byrne did teach her the ropes with a minimum of verbal abuse. He even sent her to a local seamstress to be fitted with a fancy costume, all sequins, and feathers. Just fourteen nights later, they pulled up in Kirksville, Missouri on the afternoon train, to prepare for their first show.

"Boy! Here's a quarter. Go get a trolley for our boxes," said Byrne to a negro lad who jumped up from talking to his friends at a shoeshine stand. Soon a teetering circus of boxes and trolleys was wobbling its way towards the Opera Theatre, five shoeshine porters in tow, paid-for with shiny quarters.

For the next six months, The Great Gandolfi and his Paragon of Pulchritude would perform twice-nightly fifteen-minute vaudeville sets, featuring a dozen tricks ranging from the mundane (doves from flattened top hats, interlinked metal rings) to more elaborate (Susanna disappearing into a large cloth bag and reappearing from the wings).

The high point of the set was the 'Zig-Zag Girl' routine. Susanna would step gracefully into a tall box painted with oriental dragons. The box had gaps for her left toe and right hand to protrude, concealed behind little doors. Rectangular blades would be inserted into slits in the box's sides and then Gandolfi would slide the centre section fully sideways, seemingly slicing Susanna into three sections.

Of course, it was all a cunning illusion, a mixture of Gandolfi's substituting solid blades for flexible ones, as well as the design of the box itself. The trick used a combination of optical illusion and a 45-degree mirror flipping out to create a triangular space for Susanna to slide her slim torso into, whilst reflecting a red curtain to the right of the stage as if it were the red backdrop.

It was a clever variation on a common trick and generally wowed audiences, bar the odd drunk who would heckle until the management intervened.

Tonight, the forty-third night of the tour, they had reached New Orleans, and Susanna was entranced by the

French Quarter, with its voodoo vibe and lively nightlife, with jazz seemingly spilling from every other doorway. She felt immediately at home, even though her skin tone was so light she was often mistaken for a Mexican or even a white.

Byrne was in a foul mood. His fees had been reduced when audiences booed the more familiar tricks in his repertoire and the reviews so far had been mixed at best. In truth, he was a lousy conjuror, often dropping cards or fumbling his tricks. Furthermore, a vindictive theatre owner, who turned out to be a grand wizard with the local Klan, took one look at Susanna and cancelled their appearance, then called the other seven theatres he owned and closed those shows too.

"That's what I get for hiring a negress," Byrne grumbled, drunk on whiskey, and smoking one of his customary foul-smelling cigars, as he roughly adjusted the blonde wig he'd bought Susanna to disguise her mixed origins.

Things came to a head at the second French Quarter show. It was a segregated theatre, so they were playing a matinee for the black crowd and an evening show for the whites. During prep for the evening show, a black stagehand took a shine to Susanna and politely asked if she'd like to step out with him to a jazz club after the show. Although Susanna only offered a shrug in response, she thought that perhaps she would let Antony show her the sights later on.

As she finished helping Gandolfi with the Golden Rings, Susanna heard a scuffle from the back of the theatre. The house lights flickered on briefly and she saw Antony being frogmarched out of a sea of disapproving white faces.

He'd been watching from the back of the stalls, a big no-no in this segregated auditorium. Gandolfi continued his routine as if nothing had happened but, as he shut Susanna inside the box, her employer leaned in with his whiskey breath and murmured "looks like your boyfriend's been canned."

Then Gandolfi closed the upper door and Suzanna was alone in the musty, muffled darkness. She turned her head and noticed the drunkard had left a half-empty quarter bottle of liquor on the hidden shelf in the box. What a joker! Susanna decided this would be her last show for the Irish drunk. He hadn't even appreciated her clever innovation, a diagonally striped dress that emphasised her curves and made her look subtly bigger, reinforcing the impact of the illusion. He'd said it made her look fat.

As she stewed in the hollowness that was both her life and her immediate environment, Susanna heard the fake blades slide roughly into the slots by her left hip and shoulder. Then there was a hollow rumble of laughter – one of Gandolfi's corny jokes had hit home. The temperature in the box rose and the heavy wig made Susanna's scalp itch. The old buffoon was milking the crowd. Suzanna should have been emerging triumphantly to wild applause by now, but he hadn't even knocked on the box to signal the next vital part of the trick. Susannah waited and then…

She suddenly felt a brutal yank of the middle part of the box, then laughter. Gandolfi was pretending the mechanism had jammed. This wasn't in the routine, and it hurt! Susanna quickly twisted into position and pushed out the mirror so she could edge into a sitting position on the shelf. There! The mid-section of the box shuddered out and there was an audible gasp. Susanna just managed to get her foot and hand into the relevant spots to wiggle at the audience as Gandolfi opened the relevant flaps.

"It's not real! Her foot's not real!"

The wiseacre's heckle received a volley of support. Then Gandolfi did something that pushed Susanna's idle thoughts of rebellion into full focus. He deliberately trod on her toe!

Suzanna yelped and the audience roared with laughter. Gandolfi opened the door in front of her face and Susanna scowled into the hot stage lights, inspiring another volley of laughter. Gandolfi was sucking on one of his big fat cigars, clearly in no hurry to slide the box back into its vertical alignment so she could relax from her contorted pose.

"Goodnight, sweetie," Gandolfi cooed drunkenly, blowing smoke in Susanna's face as he shut the door. She began to feel fury swell within her; a hot, liquid fury that wanted vengeance. Susanna turned to the whiskey bottle and thought of the act preceding hers, and the lessons she'd learned that morning, just for fun, from Fernando the Fire-Eater.

When Gandolfi finally let Susanna out of the box, she was in considerable pain, and the magician presumably thought her puffed out cheeks were symptomatic of discomfort. As he took a mighty draw on his cigar, Susanna blasted a mouthful of liquor into the charlatan's face. His glowing cigar tip lit the cloud of grain alcohol and Gandolfi's tonic-slicked hair caught fire, sending him rushing to the side of the stage to dip his head into a bucket filled with chewing tobacco, sand, saliva and the stubs of a hundred cigarettes.

Gasps and laughter ensued as Susanna raced backstage

and exited by the stage door into the lurid light of a New Orleans evening. Anthony, remarkably, was sitting on the stoop, holding a trumpet in one hand and a rose in the other. Taking his arm, Susanna tore off her uncomfortable boots, threw down her wig, then sashayed barefoot out into the balmy summer night.

Keepsakes

There are only so many ways you can reorder your record collection, Adam Harper realised. Once you've tried alphabetical, rainbow patterned, random, chronological, then painstakingly rearranged your vinyl by genre, that's pretty much it. Harper would need another distraction strategy when the cravings came, as they inevitably would.

He had been abstinent for four months, unemployed for two and single for three weeks. Only the first of those abandonments provided relief. Covid-19 had rendered him jobless, once the government furlough scheme came ended and his employer, a publisher of sheet music, 'restructured its workforce'.

Joanna had tried to stick with Adam through these life transitions – kicking the booze and experiencing the joys of Universal Credit and shopping at discount stores. But she loved her Cabernets and Martinis just a little bit more than she loved Adam. And adhering to any sort of compromise between his abject poverty and her barrister's salary proved unworkable. Adam was too proud to let her pay for everything and Joanna didn't see why her social life had to be brutally curtailed. In the end, their differences in temperament became more and more apparent. They split with fragile good graces. Neither had wanted kids; there were no third parties to consider – separation was painful, without proving catastrophic.

Three weeks into his renewed bachelorhood, Adam was battling the urge to drink almost daily. With so little else going on in his life, it was proving difficult not to give in to the temptation to self-medicate with alcohol. Instead, he took his anti-depressants, went for long runs, and began reading the pile of books on his bedside table. When he found his mind racing and refusing to settle, like a butterfly unable to decide which weed to settle upon, he would rummage through old cardboard boxes containing the detritus of his past.

Old gig tickets, comics he drew in his teens, bad poems written for girls and discarded and disassembled stamp collections. Occasionally something seemingly inconsequential would ambush him with associated memories, such as a dried-up piece of orange peel that he was given by an ex-girlfriend (in the form of an actual orange), the day she left him. So many leave-takings.

Here were a couple of marbles Adam had won in a game with a schoolfriend when he was about eight years old; here was a photo of Adam and his sister, with faces painted as sad clowns; here was a photo of his parents, impossibly youthful, taken from their courting days – how had that slipped in there? At Adam's age, his parents had two teenage children. Adam had rootlessness and regret.

Ah – there it was – an inevitable discovery his subconscious must have known he would make. The miniature whisky bottle from his friend Tom's wedding. *Bunnahabhain* – nearly twenty years old now. Could he? He really ought not to and yet he wanted so much to savour that crisp peaty, burning sharpness on his tongue. Adam lifted the bottle out of the box and headed to the kitchen, where he found a small, stubby glass. He dropped the miniature, unopened, in the glass and rolled it around, contemplating all that he might lose if he were to crack open the seal.

With an effort of will, he managed to put the glass down on the counter and return to the box of memories.

He'd pour the whisky down the sink later.

Back amongst the relics, Adam found a small Ziplock bag containing a half-dozen old coins. Nothing too ancient – the earliest an 1868 penny, rubbed almost down into a smooth disc but still recognisably bearing the head of Queen Victoria. Actually, some of these coins, although almost black with dirt, looked in rather good condition.

There was a threepenny bit too, a twelve-sided brass coin he was sure the millennials who lived in the flat next door would not believe had ever existed. A quick Google search revealed some of these coins selling on eBay for up to four hundred pounds! He might have a couple of thousand quid's worth here, provided he could clean them up.

Back in the kitchen he opened the fridge to find that he was out of HP sauce, a classic coin cleaning agent. Needless to say, he had no vinegar either. He could pop to the corner shop for a bottle of Coca Cola but that would necessitate wearing more than his bathrobe and would result in his possessing the makings of a whisky and coke, and that could never end well. There was only one safe and fitting solution. Adam poured the coins into the glass, unscrewed the cap of the *Bunnahabhain* and hesitated. Just a sniff to remind himself, perhaps a sip?

He poured the amber restorative over the old coins, drew up a chair and for the next half hour Adam watched the whisky eat away at the grime of ages. It was both heavily symbolic and resonant with a kind of irony as the alcohol returned something aged to the condition of its immaculate youth. There was no way he was going to swig back the turgid contents of the glass once the coins within were renewed. Adam could only guess how many fingers those pennies and halfpennies had passed through.

Merchants, mothers, urchins, gamblers, gentlemen, ladies of the night... all had touched these pieces of alloy, now gleaming perfectly amongst a grimy suspension.

Adam poured the whisky down the sink and rinsed the coins off with soapy water, drying them with a hand towel. They looked beautiful – pristine and near-perfect. He wasn't sure now whether he'd sell them. Perhaps the two threepenny bits would make interesting cufflinks, should he ever need cufflinks again.

More importantly, he had faced down the venomous enemy and he had not been bitten. Pocketing one of the pennies for good luck, Adam decided to drop in on the Monday night AA meeting in his local church. It would be nice to have some good news to relay for once.

Things We Hold On To

Madeleine Fosse, forensic archaeologist wasn't used to emergency early morning callouts. Her profession wasn't a field where time was generally of the essence. Her last job had been determining the cause of death of some pygmy Neanderthals on an Indonesian Island (most likely drowning, she'd decided.) Her subject's loved ones had generally died at least five hundred years ago, and sometimes as much as 150,000 – nobody was on tenterhooks for her input.

This was quite different. For one thing, the call came in from an ex-girlfriend, Genevieve Latour, a petite and brusque woman she'd once met at a Verdun nightclub and had a brief affair with, before both had decided it felt too much like hard work.

"Maddie, that you?" Genevieve began, typically without preamble.

"Who is…? Genny?"

"Latour, yes, Inspector Latour now."

"You got the promotion? Nice."

"Yes, well, I'm not calling for a chit chat. I need an opinion."

"Really? Dealing with extremely cold cases now, are we?"

"You'll see when you get here. I'll send a car. You at the same place?"

The place where they'd made wild, untamed love for three months.

"I'm still here."

"Twenty minutes, Maddie. Be ready."

Was that last comment a dig on her timekeeping?

Genevieve had always been the responsible adult in their micro-affair, organising taxis, setting alarms, booking tickets. In return, Madeleine had rocked her gently to sleep whenever the nightmares came, or the tears.

Twenty minutes on the dot later, a car came to drive her through the battlefields to the nearby village of Brassur-Meuse, dropping her off at a small blockade of squad cars, police tape and forensic tents near a bridge over the canal. Oddly, the tents, which were down on the canal towpath, were unoccupied, and a perimeter had been set up a good quarter of a mile away, ringed with police incident tape. What was going on?

Genevieve barrelled out of a nearby tent. Her handsome but mannish face was immediately familiar, despite the passing years, her diminutive five-foot nothing stature offset by her personality.

"Miss Foss, pleased to meet you," she said, an outstretched hand making it clear what was required. There would be no fond reunion hugs; they must be make-believe strangers. Madeleine could see men bustling around in the background in what seemed to be bomb disposal gear. Had they found unexploded ordnance? What on earth could that have to do with her?

"I've something to show you," Genevieve continued, leading her into a tent where a laptop was set up, surrounded by a fan of long, rusted blades. The screen displayed shots of a ditch containing a partially excavated skeleton – half a ribcage, a skull, a forearm. Some of it was still articulated with ribbons of flesh and sinew, preserved by the dense clay. The arm even had finger bones arranged in a claw formation holding... a rock? A bigger close-up revealed that it wasn't a rock – it was a hand grenade.

"He's a WWI soldier – we know that from the type of grenade he's holding. What we don't know is if he's one of ours or one of theirs. Americans sold ordnance like this to both sides."

"Does it matter?" Madeleine said, in part to annoy her ex.

"Course it bloody matters, Maddie", Genevieve said in a heated whisper. "Because in half an hour we have to finish what he evidently couldn't." She said this indicating the soldier onscreen.

"They're going to blow the poor bugger up. Controlled explosion. We'd like to know who he was before he's dust."

"Okay," said Madeleine, "I'm guessing you reckon he was bayoneted, and you want me to tell you whether it was a French or German weapon."

Genevieve nodded, with the ghost of the first smile Madeleine had seen from her in almost a decade. When she showed her perfectly white teeth, Genny was almost beautiful.

Madeleine sat down to pore through the photographs.
"Who found him?"

"Some kids with metal detectors"

"Did they disturb anything, do any damage?"

"I think they dug with a small trowel."

"Hmm. There's a nick on this rib, but it's partially obscured by dirt."

Genevieve leaned in. "Bayonet injury?"

Madeleine looked at the blades arrayed around her. The French ones did seem to be generally longer and thinner, the German ones short and triangular.

"I'm assuming you don't have the murder weapon?"

Genevieve didn't even dignify that with a response.

"I need to get closer," Madeleine decided.

"You can't. It's too dangerous."

"I only need to move that bit of dirt. It won't take a minute."

Genevieve mulled it over. "You have five minutes. You'll be super careful?"

Was that an edge of concern in her voice?

"Of course."

Minutes later, Madeleine was crouching carefully by the skeleton. For one hundred years this poor soldier had been gripping a live grenade. He had pulled the pin but never had a chance to throw it. Madeleine saw an immediate problem. The clump of earth she'd previously identified was actually a tree root. There would be no moving it. She'd have to extract the whole rib to get at the nick. This wasn't a five-minute job.

Unless... Madeleine looked at the pale fingers clutched around the metal egg that would give birth to a flower of death if disturbed. She could get to that in five minutes easy.

She grabbed her walkie talkie and was about to press the call button when she hesitated. Genny would never let her do this.

This poor, brave soul, whether German or French, deserved better than to be blown to fragments here on this beautiful spring morning. To be killed all over again. He should have a proper burial, and recognition for his act of supreme sacrifice. Madeleine's own great grandfather had perished in the Great War, along with most of his generation of young men. Memories were long in the villages round here – if this man was local, then someone would know his identity.

Turning her body so that her actions would be concealed from long lenses, Madeleine began scraping away at the soil around the hand and grenade, starting with the material nowhere near the safety release. Pressure had to remain on that tiny spring. Otherwise, if this munition were still live, she very shortly wouldn't be.

Here she was unearthing history, saving a man's posthumous life, and defusing a bomb, all at once! To think a senior medical examiner had once told her she'd amount to nothing.

Madeleine's heart was beating furiously, like it wanted to break her ribs, as she scraped away a niche under the grenade and slid her hand into it. With the other hand, she deftly slipped her trowel between the soldier's thumb bone and the safety catch and held it there. The earth above the blade was loose enough, she guessed. She counted to three, then counted to three again, remembering to breathe this time.

Then Madeline pushed her thumb between her trowel and the grenade's catch. In that moment, Genevieve chose to buzz the walkie talkie.

"Maddie? What are you doing?"

The sound made Madeleine rock back on her heels and she almost fell but managed to right herself.

There was an edge of real concern and even fear in her erstwhile lover's voice. It softened Genny somehow, revealing how tissue-thin the defences she threw up against the world truly were. The sound of that fragility did something more to Madeleine. She began to feel a familiar swelling in her chest. Madeleine realised that this was one former lover she would never be entirely free from. She began, slowly, to count down from ten.

Then, saying a lapsed Catholic's silent prayer, Madeleine extracted the grenade from the earth, stood and hurled it with all her might into the canal.

Moments later a blast of water showered her and the unknown soldier. Instant commotion reigned behind Madeleine as figures raced towards her. Genevieve was first on the scene.

"Fucking hell Madeleine. What did you do?"

Madeleine felt almost drunk with adrenalin. "I bought us all the time in the world, Genny," she replied, smiling at all she had just let go.

Survivor

The vehicle came to rest. Startling silence descended. Hot metal ticked against ice, like a clock marking the final increments of her life.

Blood ran down Janice's neck, as she struggled. The airbag hadn't deployed. Janice tugged the seatbelt off and slid onto her side in the upside-down Chevy. She was relieved the crash hadn't killed her but fearful that she was trapped on a frozen Alaskan lake, in a vehicle so smashed she couldn't prise open the door.

She ought not to have drunk so much, and she definitely shouldn't have fought with her sister Grace, who thought Janice was a helpless victim, a single mum bagging groceries with her options dwindling. Stuck-up bitch deserved the slap. But not that it should be her last memory of Janice.

The passenger side, wedged fast, wouldn't budge either. Janice examined her injuries under pale moonlight. Her left ankle throbbed painfully – she couldn't rotate that foot. Her right forearm was gashed. She bound this up using a rag. The wound near her collarbone was small, so Janice ignored it. Triage – like she used to do when she was a functioning member of society, in her student nurse days.

A sharp cracking sound – the ice wouldn't hold the truck's weight. The windshield was cracked but remained in place. Could she kick it out? Janice tried – it wouldn't give. The electrics weren't working; she couldn't wind down the windows. Her previous truck had a manual handle for that. Pride had made her upgrade, and now a payment plan Chevy was going to kill her.

A groan of metal against ice. Janice had mere moments. She dragged herself into the back seat, grabbed her daughter's hockey stick. Abruptly, the front of the Chevy broke through the ice and began to flood. Janice beat the rear windshield furiously, muscles screaming, as ice-water immersed her. The glass shattered; Janice broke through. She kicked hard, straining for the ice-edge, onto which she heaved herself.

Janice rolled over, coughing up freezing water. Retrieving Sophia's hockey stick from the lake, she limped across the ice, using it as a crutch, determined. Whatever happened, she wouldn't die. Janice was stronger than her failed marriage, her troubled teen, her dead-end job, her judgemental sister.

She should have been killed by the accident. Her ex-husband had once said Janice was the toughest woman he knew. Janice wondered if there was something to the old cliché, after all.

Janice was a survivor.

What do you Need?

Reggie Clark was in the shit again. Unemployed, with two young daughters and a frustrated ex-wife, he had finally snagged an interview. Now, forty-five minutes before his chance at the University janitorial position, his car was jacked up at the side of the highway, with a flat. Reggie wished he'd renewed his breakdown cover or packed the right wrench. Reggie watched other traffic roaring by, realising he would have to call Marcia, his ex-wife, for a lift. She already considered him a lost cause. He should call the university and try to delay the interview. What emergency could he invent to save the day?

While Reggie was thinking, a car drew up. The driver emerged, a remarkable-looking woman in, Reggie guessed, her late twenties. Flaxen hair that glowed as if back-lit, pale green eyes...

"Hello Reggie," she said. "What is it you need?"

Oddly, although he didn't know this woman, Reggie felt compelled to reply, honestly.

"I need a miracle."

The woman smiled, revealing pearly-white teeth.

Reggie watched her return to her car, pop the trunk and take out an antique cashbox, which she opened with a gold key kept around her neck. She removed something, then walked back to Reggie and handed him a shiny piece of metal. It seemed to be some sort of adaptor...

Excitedly, Reggie grabbed the wrench and inserted the adaptor, putting the assembly against a wheel nut. It fitted perfectly. After a little resistance, the nut began to unscrew.

Reggie jumped to his feet, but the woman had already

got back into her car and was pulling out.

"Wait!" he called, but, with a smile and a small wave, she left him there. Reggie looked at his watch. He just about had time, if he was quick, to make the interview.

Penelope Higgins was about to lose her temper and start screaming at her daughter Susie, who was having a cataclysmic tantrum in the 7-11, when she felt a nudge in the ribs. Turning to vent her anger in a new direction, she saw a young man smiling benignly. One of those religious nutbags, no doubt. He was carrying an old metal cashbox under his arm. Was he going to try to sell her something?

"Can you not see this is a bad time? Susie, will you shut the f…"

"Maybe this would be of some help?"

The stranger, blonde, with pale green eyes, handed her a small glowing ball, which tinkled softly. It was almost mystical. Susie had quietened and was looking at her mother imploringly. Penelope handed Susie the strange toy. Her daughter began to roll it in her palms, watching the colours change and a strange melody sound.

Penelope turned to thank her benefactor, but he had vanished. No – there he was, outside, striding towards a parked car. Shame – Penelope would have liked to have thanked him.

Penelope realised someone was watching – someone familiar. Mike Fenwick, her social worker, smiling. She gave a timid wave, then headed down the snack aisle while Susie, entranced by her new toy, followed meekly. If Mike had seen her scold or strike her child… the consequences were unthinkable. For Penelope, this was a stroke of uncharacteristic, good fortune.

At one of the expensive modernist homes on the hill, a prime-time drama was playing out. A scattering of police cars and a news helicopter surrounded the entrance. A pool party had been violently interrupted. The host, TV anchor-man Dennis Sloman, was facing the toughest interview of his life. His wife stood before him, furious, brandishing a gun, while the other guests cowered or made a dash for the house.

Selena Sloman shook with rage. She fired off a couple of overhead warning shots.

"Nobody move! I need witnesses. Hubby has been banging a production assistant while I'm at home looking after our three kids. Admit it, Dennis – I might let you live."

The police held back – a negotiator had been called and nobody thought Selena Sloman, former beauty queen and cosmetics entrepreneur, would murder Dennis in front of fifty witnesses. She just needed to get something out of her system. She'd fired off five warning shots, by Detective Rogers' reckoning. Rogers felt unflustered – this sort of thing was happening with ever-increasing frequency. Celebrity drove everyone insane.

There was the negotiator – a lithe woman in her thirties, moving with confidence through the waiting throng. Not someone he'd seen before – Rogers would have remembered that golden mane and those pale green eyes. Oddly, she held a metal cashbox under her arm.

"Detective Rogers," he said, offering a hand, but she walked right past him and into the garden.

"Wait!" he shouted, but oddly, he did nothing to stop her and did not follow.

The woman walked up to Selena, who was oblivious. Selena was busy hearing her husband's confession.

"We slept together twice. It meant nothing. You were never available."

The last word seemed to trigger Selena, who fired straight at her husband's head. The bullet sliced off one earlobe and impacted the stucco wall. Dennis screamed, while Selena fired five times, until the gun was empty. The police readied themselves, as Selena reached into her handbag and found she was out of bullets.

Selena turned; the negotiator was facing her, holding something out. Selena took the fresh bullet and slammed it into the barrel of her revolver. A guest screamed. The police marksmen couldn't take a shot with the negotiator in their line of fire. Dennis yelled:

"Help! She's gonna kill me."

Selena squeezed the trigger. The gun blew up in her hands, a green, smoky shockwave knocking her onto her back while the cops rushed in. Dennis and the remaining guests made a break for the house. Selena was moaning in confusion and distress, but seemingly uninjured.

The negotiator crouched to whisper, "I hope you find your happiness." Then the mysterious stranger stood up and vanished amongst the various policemen and paramedics shouting at one another, and at her.

A tiny golden key turned in a lock, and the green-eyed gift-giver moved on.

Crawling to the Endzone

George's great-nephew Charlie had shown him how to use Facebook in the weeks following Rose's death and George had found this one of the most comforting ways to fill the void. He could post photos of their life together (once Charlie had shown him how to use the scanner), share memories with relatives and chat online to anyone who remembered Rose.

He even discovered he had a long-lost second cousin, Anton Shmuel Goldstein, an American born in Boston, who shared George's pitch-black sense of humour. Anton called old age 'crawling to the endzone', a term from American Football. George called it 'watching the lights go out.'

There was an unending list of things George missed about Rose. The day after her memorial service, he decided to start enumerating them, daily, on Facebook. He missed her readiness with a bandage or ointment whenever he hurt himself. A lifelong klutz, George was always banging his head or stubbing his toe. He'd struggled to open a can of soup yesterday and slashed his hand open on the lid. Bloody and panicking, it had taken him ten minutes, two tea-towels and a trail of droplets before he located the first aid box containing the Dettol and plasters.

He also missed Rose's keen way with a crossword, as well as the fact that she'd never complete his puzzles unless he asked for her help. Rose did the venerable Times crossword while George often got stuck on the Express's much less formidable version. She'd notice him cursing under his breath and rubbing things out. She'd ask, "Need a hand, love?" and he'd shout over a clue (Rose was quite deaf by the time she entered her eighties).

"Organ through which anger escapes... six letters."

"Spleen, Georgie, spleen," Rose would shout back after a moment, peering over her reading glasses as she turned the page of one of her historical novels. Even when she was really ill, Rose had embarked on the new Hilary Mantel. George had got a lump in her throat giving it to her, knowing she'd almost certainly never finish it. Rose had turned down the corner of page 242. There were no folded-down corners thereafter.

He even missed her faith. At least, George missed some of the gospel music she played on Sundays when she was too exhausted to get out of bed and go to church. One of the few white women in the Holy Mountain Mission, Rose had been adopted by the warm-hearted Wood Green Caribbean community and many of them had come to her funeral. George had been embarrassed by how many of these men and women he'd never met before, since he had stopped attending church not long after Rose's third cancer diagnosis.

Three cancers in seventeen years suggested to George that if God existed, he was determined to make a widower out of him, and George didn't see why he had to avidly praise such a spiteful deity. It had been a bone of contention between them, but George had put his foot down. Now he regretted every hour of Rose he'd lost to the songs, the harmonious voices, and the kind black people he'd so assiduously ignored.

Not that he begrudged her those consolations, however illusory. More that he wished he'd just swallowed his pride and shared in her joy. She'd always returned from church beaming, hope renewed.

"Have fun with the happy-clappers?" he'd ask.

Rose would just shake her head, roll her eyes in amusement, and go and put the kettle on.

"You're a determined man, George," said Anton, in a Facebook message one Sunday.

"What do you mean?" he typed back, slowly, with unsteady and arthritic fingers.

"You keep coming up with reasons you miss your wife," Anton replied. "Man... I'd be hard-pressed to name a half dozen."

George knew Anton didn't really believe that. It was part of his shtick that his second marriage was a ball and chain around his neck, when all he ever did was extol Maeve's many virtues in the kitchen, at the flea-market, with a 10,000-piece jigsaw. He would kvetch and kvell, but George could tell he really loved "the old battle-axe", as he fondly termed his wife. Anton was also teaching George Yiddish words and George found them enjoyably onomatopoeic. He was a schlemiel prone to schmaltz, while Anton was a mensch given to kibitzing.

"I'm at reason 98," George said with pride. "What Rose could do with her fingers..."

"Not sure I oughta be hearing this," said Anton. "Keep your bedroom antics to yourself."

"I mean massage," typed George, laughing, and managing to find the 'shocked' emoji. "She could find and release a knot or a twinge in seconds, that girl. A magician."

"Was she a nurse?" Anton asked.

"Home help. Thirty years in old codgers' houses, then nearly twenty looking after me."

"Poor girl," typed Anton, and George didn't know if he was being serious or acerbic.

253

Later that afternoon it seemed to grow weirdly dark in the flat. On the thirteenth floor of his block, George could usually count on a fantastic view across North London. On a clear day you could even see south of the river to the leafy Surrey suburbs. Now, all was lost in a grey-white cloud that blew past the windows like the breath of an immense dragon. George imagined it curled around the block, wreathing the whole thing in smoke. Like Grenfell, he thought briefly, then banished the thought as unworthy. Those people suffered a living pyre, shocking neglect, pitiful reparations, and a long-overdue enquiry. All George suffered was Rose's absence.

He decided to go for a walk, to float out into the atmosphere, and taste that strange dry-ice flavour that London fog often had. He rarely got depressed but sometimes George just needed to shroud himself in silence and quietude for a while.

To walk, to remember, to enumerate the things he missed, to celebrate the memories that remained, to add to his growing collection of overdue thank yous.

You Want it More Vibrant?

I'm a plasterer, and a drummer, and a failure. Well, in the eyes of my father, best friend and ex-wife, respectively, that's what I am. In the eyes of my four-year-old son Alex, I am a superhero, a spy and a giant. At the moment, I'm in plasterer mode, smoothing out a 900 square foot 'feature wall' in one of the fancy new apartments we're building in Brent, overlooking the Welsh Harp reservoir. Lovely view, underground car park, gated and fenced off from the hoi polloi, i.e., Scots construction workers and thrash-metal drummers like me.

With all the frustrations I've suffered lately, I'm happy to have this massive white space to work with, and to be (almost) alone to complete the task. I say almost, as I've managed to sneak Alex in today, to sit quietly in the corner playing iPad games, drawing, or taking photos. He believes himself quite the little Cartier-Bresson. I'll bet you're surprised I know that reference. Hey – I'm a plasterer not a moron, I do read books, you know.

Since COVID-19 descended to wreck all our lives, Alex's nursery closed and I can't get a babysitter until next week, when mum and dad return from their holiday in the Algarve. I thought Marcie would be available to take Alex this week but apparently, she's got plans too important to cancel for her own son. She works from home and is usually a good bet for an emergency drop-off but recently I've seen her on Tinder – can you imagine, seeing your own ex-wife pouting for hook-ups – and she's less amenable.

So, either I sack off this job and lose a week's pay or it's 'bring your kid to work' day. On a normal site, that would be impossible, but all the structural work is complete, so I managed to twist the shift supervisor's arm. Alex was happy to get a yellow hard-hat to wear and his dinosaur facemask doubles as a filter for whatever paint fumes are wafting in and out of the complex.

I fill my hawk up with fresh paste, then climb the small stepladder to the third rung with my trowel at the ready. Apart from the occasional drill-hole where electric fittings will be laid, the expanse is perfectly flat, the block-work immaculate. I look down and see Alex, sitting on a pail like Oor Wullie, intent on his Minecraft masterpiece. Like father, like son. He's no trouble at all. If anything, it's a challenge to wrench him from his digital building work to run around with me in the park. I sometimes wonder if he's 'on the spectrum'.

The plaster goes on thick, then I smooth it in wider and wider arcs, placing my face close to the surface to check it's perfectly flat. Not too close, of course – like most plasterers I've briefly loaned my profile to more than one wall. The plaster's an off-white colour called *Morning Mist*, which has become a bit of rhyming slang amongst the crew on this job. Let's all go and get morning mist.

I'm halfway through the job and have ditched the ladder to work on the lower half of the wall, when I hear footsteps below me, and someone says "Oh." It's said in the manner of a polite person faced with a problem they're going to have to reluctantly deal with.

I turn round and there's the foreman, Mr Brenton, one of the client's representatives, whose name I forget and my mate Sundeep, a Sikh electrician who started on site last week. They're all looking at Alex, still sitting in his corner, engrossed in the iPad.

"Sorry, that's my son Alex. I know he's not supposed to be here…" I begin. I'm not allowed to finish.

"It's entirely against the regs," Brenton begins, "only workers allowed on site."

I try and laugh it off. "I had him mixing up the formula, but his wee arms don't really have the heft."

Brenton, the humourless bastard, doesn't crack a smile, though the others do. Instead, he turns to the client, a slim, salt-and-pepper hipster in his early forties. The guy has a beard and pony-tail combo.

"I'm really sorry, Mr Kazmarski, this won't happen again."

Brenton turns to me. "Mr Baird, I want you off-site in thirty minutes. Take your child home please."

I still have a hawkful of plaster and I'm tempted to see how Brenton looks wearing it.

"You can finish what you've started," he adds, as if it's a concession.

"I couldn't get childcare, and I didn't want to let you down," I say, more to myself than anyone else in the room. Alex is looking up from his game now, watching shyly, confused by the odd mood. An emotional calibration is taking place inside me as I let the rage subside. The client has turned away, and is examining the plaster, admiringly. He looks down at a sample booklet he's holding, showing the different finishes we have available.

"I thought it'd be more vibrant," he muses. Brenton steps in, oleaginous as ever.

"Wait until you see it with all the light fittings. We have some pretty wild colours next door for the show-home. Would you like to see?"

The client nods and heads through to the un-plastered

apartment next door, which is being used as a storeroom for paint and plaster drop-offs this week. Sundeep remains in the doorway, looking awkward.

"Jack, I'm sorry. I didn't know about Alex."

"I know," I reply, bundling my son into his duffel-coat and putting his iPad away in his satchel. Sundeep makes to leave, turning for a final word.

"Pint in the *Grapes* later? We'll be there at six."
I shrug. That seems to suffice and, with a wry smile, Sundeep is gone.

A couple of minutes later, I squint through the newly fitted windows, which still smell of putty and silicon. My throat feels swollen. It might be fumes, but then again, I'm prone to glandular problems. Swallowing, I spot Brenton and the client walking back across the carpark towards the portacabin offices. Alex tugs at my sleeve.

"Alex," I ask, "would you like to make a painting?"

His eyes light up. I take him through to the storeroom apartment and we carry through some pots of paint – deep Cerulean blue, sunflower yellow, poppy red, mint green, lilac, and sunset orange. I don't bother finding brushes or trays as I wrap Alex up in a makeshift apron of plastic sheeting and put safety glasses on him. I show him how to hold the base and handle of the smaller cans and hurl their contents onto the wall. I make the first splash – a huge grin of red like an arterial spray. Alex adds globs of yellow as I throw horizontal lines of blue across the still-wet plaster. I lift him up so he can decorate the wall's upper reaches, then watch the drips run down, like rain on a windowpane.

By the time we leave, ten minutes later, it looks like Damien Hirst has had a mental breakdown in there. Alex giggles as I lick my finger and wipe a splash of orange from his forehead. "Let's go and play football," I suggest, and Alex jumps up and down in a way that makes my heart melt. Marcie's really going to give me hell, but I really don't care.

And the client did want it more vibrant, after all.

Arrhythmia

Johnathan was haunted by his heartbeat. Arrhythmia and the death of three relatives from heart problems turned natural caution into hypervigilance. He would hear the hidden organ throbbing malevolently, pulsing out its weird jazz. Threatening to slow or quicken erratically, threatening to stop. It kept him awake at night, caused anxiety in important meetings, made lovemaking near-impossible. He imagined it as a demonic drummer, forever trying to trip up the band with erratic polyrhythms or strange time signatures.

Doctors fitted a pacemaker. Tiny, state of the art. It didn't work. Now the drummer had a cymbal... ticking electronically away, a hi-hat marking time. Something else to tap out its warnings upon. The drummer kept the pace, relentless, driving the music of his arms and legs, as if waiting for the grand finale. A final drumroll then silence. Every song comes to an end, every drummer lays down his sticks.

Flaming Skies, Frozen Secrets

What do you give a man who's stolen everything? Someone who built a vast empire on one outlandishly brilliant idea: a drug called *Agonía*, derived from a poison procured from an endangered Amazonian tribe, used in their blowpipes to kill capybara and howler monkeys. Reverse-engineered, refined and sold as the ultimate high.

Agonía sends every synapse ringing with world-shattering pain, only to release the user into a blissed-out state of pure relief, lasting many hours. On this ultra-addictive substance Rodrigo Lopez had forged a trillion-dollar empire. Now he wanted his biography written and for some reason he had chosen me, Brandi Simmons, Pulitzer prize-losing journalist, to write it. Flown me out here to his absurd Greenland ice hotel.

"Why me, Mr Lopez? You could have someone with an actual Pulitzer."

Rodrigo, a greying fifty-something with the waistline of someone who lived very well indeed, smiled sweetly. I noticed Rodrigo's shoes appeared to have been made from actual alligator.

"Because you deserved to win – yet lost with such class."

I laughed, remembering tumbling headfirst into a pyramid of half-filled champagne glasses, the reason for the crescent-moon scar over my left eyebrow.

Over the next seventeen days, while I shivered under layers of faux-fur, Rodrigo, as he insisted I call him, told me a series of increasingly tall tales. Entirely fitting his status as a gangland icon, his anecdotes did not disappoint.

Gold-plating his mother's walking frame for her ninetieth birthday, hiding from DEA agents in the sewers of his home village for four months. Encasing his murdered rivals' heads in Perspex and sending them back to their families. Showing his contempt for cocaine by buying Columbia's entire crop of coca plants and having them burnt then compressing the ashes into a gigantic diamond.

I knew this latter tale was pure fantasy, but my research showed everything Rodrigo said contained at least a grain of incredible truth. If he actually allowed the publication of his biography, I knew I had a bestseller on my hands. Fuck the Pulitzer, I'd take number one on Amazon any day.

My visit culminated in a 4am trip to see the Northern Lights shimmering capriciously above the hotel. A green-blue moving curtain of light, like a rip in the firmament through which other, more prefect worlds could be glimpsed. As I was gawping at the majesty of all those charged particles, Rodrigo leaned over from his skidoo, to whisper.

"Now, my dear, I'll show you the reason I'm giving it all away."

I was taken aback. "You're what?"

"I'm giving everything to charity. I'm going to make Bill Gates look like Ebenezer Scrooge."

I was at a loss for words, not a position I often find myself in.

"That's… admirable. But why?"

He laughed at my understatement. One point one trillion was probably enough to end poverty and hunger the world over, with change.

"You'll see. Come!"

Rodrigo tore off, in a spray of snow, followed by his armed entourage (he'd assigned me my own bodyguard, Tuppi). I followed the headlights lighting up the frozen wilderness, under a sky rippling with green and golden waves. I have an aversion to the cold but, having spent two and a half weeks at minus twenty degrees, I was getting used to the exceptional beauty of Rodrigo's giant folly, situated twenty miles north of Kulusuuk.

We reached a rocky plateau that Tuppi, a local, said had been under the ice until the permafrost began to recede. One of Rodrigo's main charities was Rising Tide, a local environmental charity. Rodrigo intended to give them five billion dollars, until the organisation's own chair, Una Brothers, had gratefully declined most of it – they couldn't spend that amount fast enough to cope with the tax burden. Rodrigo had entered a strange realm where it was literally harder to spend money than earn it.

The skidoos were parked in a semicircle around a tented off area surrounded by klieg lights. Rodrigo asked a minion to switch these on as we entered the canvas auditorium. As the place lit up, I was dazzled by silver-grey granite and pristine snow flattened by dozens of feet. A section of rockface, sixty feet long, was covered by a weighted tarpaulin. Rodrigo lowered his hood.

"Under here is the reason why everything I've worked for is utterly pointless. Look."

Two of his henchmen lifted off the tarpaulin, revealing what had been protected beneath.

A living frieze, fixed half in and half out of the rock – the clear outline of a woolly mammoth, embedded in stone, jagged scars across its flank. Behind it a group of humanoid remains, some curled in foetal balls, others lain out flat, almost ceremoniously.

"I've had teams of experts flown in to see this. We found it when we were planning the hotel. They explained it to me. The mass extinctions. Climate on a knife's edge. My eyes were opened about the ice ages humanity has faced, how suddenly they came down, how we somehow survived, by the skin of our teeth. There – that's humanity for you. Where we came from and where we may be going," said Rodrigo.

I read a story in the fossils there, frozen into place by an ice age that had pressed reset on civilisation, ten thousand years ago. A group of hunters, pursuing a dangerous and rare prey, had become trapped during a horrendous storm, with the terrifying creature they had finally killed. They had perished, then been covered in ice for thousands of years, revealed only now. It was a vision of life in extremis, an unthinkable past – perhaps just as unthinkable a future?

"I've done unspeakable things Miss Simmons," said Rodrigo, "I can order the death of politicians and journalists like that." Here he snapped his fingers; was this a warning? No, he seemed more sad than exultant.

"I can buy anything I want – diamonds the size of your fist, Caribbean islands, even a presidency. It's meaningless. I might as well be staring at my own death mask."

I looked at Rodrigo, the world's most powerful man, reduced to a melancholy and apocalyptic pessimist. I had to admit though, he had a point. We'd all seen the news stories – the deterioration of the ice caps, mass extinctions of megafauna, out of control bushfires in California and

266

the Australian outback, hundreds of whales beaching themselves on Icelandic shores because they could no longer echolocate the chaotic currents.

"What now?" I asked, as his men covered up the prehistoric tableau.

Rodrigo shook himself out of his stasis. He squinted towards the first glimmers of sunrise, leaking into the tent.

"I think perhaps breakfast. How do you feel about reindeer sausages?"

I wasn't sure how I felt about reindeer sausages. I'm not sure how I feel about anything anymore. I nodded, smiled thinly, and we went to eat breakfast.

Repentance

When Silas Denham awoke, all was blackness and silence, save the distant buzzing of something mechanical. A rotting cabbage smell filled his nostrils. Silas remembered little from the night before, except the strange young man propositioning him in the hallway. Never one to turn down a blow job, Silas followed him into a guest bedroom and… He could remember absolutely nothing thereafter.

From the rough mattress and the manacles, Silas knew two things. Firstly, he was no longer in his business partner's lakeside retreat. This was somewhere warmer, darker, and much more frightening. Silas ran through possibilities from revenge to blackmail to extraordinary rendition to some barbaric country where he'd done typically shady deals.

Silas sat up, squinting in the gloom. His feet were bare, as were his legs. In fact, he was entirely naked, his greying chest hair matted and sweaty.

"Anyone there?!" he bellowed. The distant machine quietened, without stopping. Keys turned and a metal door shuddered open, emitting a shaft of light. Silhouetted there was the sharply dressed, slim young mixed-race boy from the party, who had given only his first name.

"David?" Silas queried. "What's going on? I have little actual liquidity…"

The man put his fingers to his lips and Silas shut up.

"I'll make this easy for you, Mr Denham," explained David, calmly. "I'll tell you why you're here and what I'm going to do. You'll have time to think it over."

Silas nodded, shading his eyes to see David's face.

269

"Firstly, I am going to kill you. You're probably disappointed, but I'm afraid it's non-negotiable. However, torture isn't really my thing. If you're good, I see no reason to beat you or deprive you of anything else. Is that clear?"

Again, Silas nodded. He had discounted most possibilities. Either David was a contract killer – heaven knows Silas had enemies aplenty – or he was a serial killer. That aside, David did seem unexpectedly... reasonable.

"Why?" he croaked, dry-throated. David handed him a bottle of water. Silas glugged it down.

"It's far too hot here," admitted David. "Sorry about that. That's why I removed your clothes," David said, crouching to take back the bottle. Could Silas move quick enough to kick his captor? He was still too weak; best bide his time.

David leaned back against the doorframe, his face finally illuminated. Silas recognised the long, noble nose and lightly tanned skin. David was handsome – probably how he'd inserted himself into Silas's social group, gained the trust of his business partner Adam, and an invitation to the housewarming.

"You wanted to know why. It boils down to this – you embezzled millions from elderly investors when your retirement resort failed. You hid the profits from other ventures in tax havens and shell companies. You ruined thousands of lives. I intend to show the world how rotten you are inside."

A social justice psychopath thought Silas. Tricky.

"I'm a terrible human being," Silas agreed. "You're preaching to the converted. I did these things because I'm bankrupt. If my wife finds out, she'll finally kick me out and take the kids to Arizona and that'll be my life over."

270

David laughed. "Mr Denham, your life *is* over."

"I know," Silas agreed. "I have no problem with that."

David's face betrayed a flicker of disappointment.

"What do you mean?"

Silas sighed, digging deep into darkness.

"I've been planning to end my life. It was to look like an accident. You're kinda doing me a huge favour. Murder means a massive pay-out on my life insurance. Victoria and the kids will get millions, tax-free. I sold various properties and liquidated offshore funds. My debts will be settled. They'll know what a son of a bitch I've been, but my family will be provided for."

Both men weighed up their situation. David nodded, without anger.

"I'll leave your headless corpse riding the Wall Street bull."

Of course! The RoCK – Rotten Corpse Killer. The serial killer who'd been depositing putrescent bodies everywhere, signs around their necks detailing their venality.

"You're the RoCK?"

David winced. "I hate that nickname. I'm not happy to be colluding in your little scheme but whatever – let's just get on with it," he said, walking away.

Perhaps because he was tired, or because his enthusiasm had waned, David made a significant mistake in not researching his victim's physiognomy. Silas had Ehlers Danlos Syndrome, a collagen deficiency, giving him hypermobile joints, including the abductors and flexors in his hand.

While David was away, Silas folded his left hand down to the circumference of his wrist and slipped off one manacle, then removed the chain from the wall hook. As David returned, with a fearsome-looking blade, Silas swung the manacle as a flail, the heavy metal connecting with David's head, sending him sprawling.

Silas staggered next door. A partially dismembered corpse lay on a metal table. Adjacent, a bloody bandsaw whirred, a hamper of sawn-off body parts nearby. The cloying smell of death pervaded everything. Silas heard a sound and turned just in time to evade David's blade. He barged his attacker towards the bandsaw. Helpfully, David tripped over the coiled chain between Silas's ankle manacles.

Obeying instinct, David put both hands out, slid on the bloody floor, and severed both his arms at the wrist on the bandsaw.

David's screams were horrifying. He slumped down, blood gouting from both stumps, shock quickly taking over.

Silas staggered into a garden bordered by tall fences. The smell of decomposition was overwhelming. Pits had been dug, in which to bury bodies or from which to dig them up. Silas gagged, realising that he must go back inside and find a mobile phone. Everything he'd told David had been true, apart from the decision to die. Silas was quite beyond redemption.

He had intended to go on living, because that's what repentant men do. Silas turned to go and find tourniquets. Both men must remain alive, to face whatever justice their short tenure on this earth could provide.

The Ineffable

"Marty, why do you do all this crazy shit? Do you have a death wish?"

As he struggled to find an answer for his old school friend Anton, all Martin McTeer could think of was a deathbed phrase from his grandfather's passing. When asked by his already-grieving wife, Martin's grandma Johanna, why he appeared sanguine about dying at the young age of sixty-nine, Grandpa McTeer had replied that he was 'anticipating the ineffable'.

As he sat astride his BMX, with its flame-decorated paintwork and custom red tires, Martin understood that he too was intrigued by what lay on the other side of death. Not a death wish, but a death curiosity.

"Ant, why don't you go and check the ramp again?" Martin replied to his friend's plaintive question. Anton shook his head and ran off to do just that.

Marty could have been a smartass and explained that he had 27 million reasons to attempt what he was about to. His last jump, over ten school buses, had smashed the YouTube viewership records of rival daredevils. Moments after celebrating his success and watching the viewer count skyrocket, none other than Scottish BMX legend Danny MacAskill called him to congratulate him on his record-breaking jump. Apparently 'total bampot' was a huge compliment in Scotland.

This, however, was something else entirely. He was about to leap a ninety-foot-deep, fifty-foot-wide canyon. The fact that he'd already jumped this exact distance in training over thirty times, on the dirt course he'd created by his grandparents' ranch, did not detract from the immensity of what he was attempting. Back at the ranch, if he failed, at worst he'd crash into a pile of compacted dirt, designed to break his fall. Sure, he'd broken a clavicle, two ribs, one wrist and fractured his left shin during training, but bones healed when you were twenty-six years old, wiry, and as lithe as a greyhound.

If Marty failed this stunt, captured on six cameras and two drones by the Red Bull film crew, he'd hit a rocky canyon wall at around 35mph, then plunge ninety feet into an icy river, with his bike on top of him. Marty had told his sponsors he'd abandon the jump if he didn't achieve enough speed on take-off, and had a handy device attached to his handlebars to give him that information. He'd already rehearsed jumping off the bike into the river, which was certainly deep enough to break his fall, assuming he judged it right. After all, Marty had made his name on YouTube by back-flipping and spinning off his bike into various lakes and creeks. He'd even shot a clip back-flipping into this very river, just to prove it wouldn't kill him. The clip had scored 22.1 million hits and counting.

Still, it was a little less than encouraging when Red Bull revealed there was a one-minute delay on their livestream, allowing them to pull the plug if he pancaked on the canyon wall. Marty tried to shrug it off; this was merely prudence.

"We're all set-up. Ready big guy?" said the perky PA whose job it was to liaise between the director, stunt co-ordinator and Marty. Her name was Emily, she was perhaps thirty and Marty had already figured out she was single and probably liked him. When you grow up in an orphanage, you learn to read people pretty quickly. Anton had coped as a kid by being sharp-elbowed and belligerent, despite his stunted growth. Marty had played the court jester, a role he sometimes suspected he'd never outgrow.

"Sure. I'll wait for the flag?"

Emily blew him a kiss, then headed back to control.

"See you on the other side!"

Marty stood astride the machine he trusted more than anything or anyone in his life. He'd dismantled and rebuilt the bike so many times, he knew it as intimately as a soldier knew his rifle.

He looked down the immense curve of the fifty-foot ramp, then let his eye carry along the red surface of the runway and up the shorter ramp at the canyon's edge. By the time Marty launched into space, he should be hitting at least 30mph. Even 28mph would carry him across the fifty-foot gap safely. There was always redundancy built into the plan. Marty could land on any part of the down-ramp on the far side, and he'd be fine. Probably.

Nothing short of a bird flying in between his spokes or an exploding tyre could stop him making this jump. It was really just applied physics and mathematics.

Marty saw Anton running his way as the LED counter down below flipped from one minute to 59 seconds. Anton looked flustered as he scrambled up the metal ladder and along the gantry. The wind was blowing hard across Marty's ears and he had trouble making out what his friend was saying through his helmet.

"It's not forty-nine point eight, it's fifty-two point two!"

"What?" Marty shouted, squinting against the glare.

"We used the survey maps from 2012. There was a quake in 2016 and the creek-bed opened up."

Marty laughed uneasily, running the numbers in his head. Two point four more feet. Surely it couldn't be so?

"It's fine, Ant. I can make it. I'll just hit the ramp a little further back."

"Marty, it's not fine. I can draw you a dia…"

An airhorn went off, a flag waved and the protective frame holding Marty's front wheel fell away. Instinctively, he reacted, pumping hard on the pedals as gravity took over. Marty's head was still buzzing with equations that would never be completed as he tore out along the Red Bull branded runway. Seconds later he was hitting the ramp, pumping like fury. He looked down, hardly able to read the odometer. 39.3mph. It wouldn't be enough.

Time stretched like a heartless yawn as Marty tried to prise his feet from the pedals to abandon his flight. He'd have to push down and twist the bike to gain enough air friction to alter the parabola of his fall. Otherwise, both he and bike would hit the rocky canyon wall, rather than the water.

He did none of those things. He simply floated, accepting whatever fate would deliver, the wind and blood pounding in his eardrums, the crowd's cheering an irrelevance.

When, four seconds and an infinity later, his back wheel hit the landing ramp, with just one inch to spare, Marty knew he no longer needed to prove anything.

Whatever it promised, the other side could wait. Martin McTeer would never challenge the ineffable again.

Midnight Shadows

Dave Blackhurst sometimes wondered if he'd been forgotten. He knew the crew were working hard on the reshoots, filming for fourteen hours a day, but it would be nice if someone popped in occasionally. Dave was working crazy hours – starting at ten in the morning and rarely stopping before 3am the following morning. He'd always been a night owl, but this current schedule was more a matter of necessity than inclination.

The Berlin Film Festival had sat on an early cut for months. Now, just five weeks before the festival, they had come back to say they wanted "Midnight Shadows" for their opening gala. This was fantastic but also terrible news – the team had to reshoot thirteen pages, with Dave recutting the picture, then getting the new scenes graded and sound-mixed and delivered within 34 days. Dave had been flown out to Vilnius and set up in a facility called "*Conekt*" (an ironic choice since, despite Lithuania's generally brilliant connectivity, the Wi-Fi at *Conekt* seemed to be as capricious as the weather).

Worse still, a supporting actress, Dame Angela Lowe, had caught Covid-19 during the production, which now moved to strict post-lockdown protocol, making their Sisyphean task even harder, and requiring her part to be recast. This was a terrible shame – Dave had loved cutting Dame Angela's scenes. She was by far the most magnetic on-screen presence, putting Clooney and Blunt to shame. This was fast becoming a "heartsink" project, were it not for the magnificent remuneration Dave was receiving. He'd earn enough on this project to see him through to 2021.

Dame Angela was so fantastic in the film, a noirish vampire tale set in old Vilnius, that Dave had tried to persuade Marty, as the director insisted everyone call him, not to recast. Dave could cut around her. There were script solutions that would explain her sudden disappearance from the picture. Neither Marty nor Mr Schrader (no forced informality pertained to the writer, apparently) were willing to throw rewrites into their maelstrom of difficulties.

Dave couldn't let it go. As well as the official cut, he'd been working on a parallel version, which retained Dame Angela as the historian who knew too much about the Sanguine Society, resulting in her shocking last act murder.

Conekt was so subterranean that all Dave ever saw was a sliver of light from a strip of glass bricks set into the ceiling. All he could hear was the cooing of pigeons pecking at the scatterings of rice from the registry office steps adjacent to the facility house. Nobody brought him coffee or food unless he called upstairs. His bathroom was en-suite. The facility wasn't manned after 10pm but Dave had his own keycard and front door key and could stay as long as he liked. There was even a tiny bedroom, which Dave had used twice so far.

The glass bricks were filthy but the dim blue light leaking through them foretold dawn. He'd really overdone it this evening. Dave rubbed his eyes and rolled back the scene he'd just cut one last time.

Dame Angela, as Professor Trilling, walks into her library, holding a candle, trying to source the disturbance that has awoken her. Behind her, a pale figure emerges from the shadows, moving with feline grace. It's ten-year-old gymnast Lucina, bitten by Count Vladimir, the leader of the Society, a few scenes previously. Trilling spies an open window and feels a chill. She crosses the room to close it, then hears sobbing behind her. Turning, Trilling is startled by Lucina's miserable figure and rushes to embrace her. Lucina places Trilling's ring finger in her mouth and, without warning, as Trilling attempts to soothe the terrified girl, bite down hard.

In Schrader's script, the girl retrieves her mother's stolen ring from the severed finger, and leaves Trilling in shocked agony.

Dave's version hinged on Trilling dropping the candle. Lucina removes the finger from her mouth, extracts the ring, and escapes. Dave cut back to the flame catching the hem of Trilling's robe. In the original cut, Trilling throws herself onto a chaise longe, extinguishing the fire. Dave's version cut from the flame catching to a shot from outside the house. A borrowed bit of VFX inserted flame into the window, as Trilling burns to death. A few screams would be ADR-ed in place of the borrowed sound he'd kept low in the mix, behind the rain and Lucina's bare feet slapping against the cobbles as she runs away.

Dave sat back, his heart pounding, so emotionally tied to the scene that he almost felt the open window's chill and sensed a shadow passing behind him. It would be ridiculous to turn to check he was alone. Horripilation. A wonderful word that perfectly captured the sensation Dave was experiencing, as the tiny hairs on the back of his neck, and the hairs on his bare forearms, stood up in response to his growing fear.

Dave's hand hovered over the mouse, dragging the alternative cut towards the waste-bin. Given that he'd been expressly warned off this version, Dave might be fired if this cut were discovered.

His assistant, Fiona was on set, logging rushes. She was a capable editor in her own right and could certainly complete what he'd begun, should Dave be fired for his impetuousness. Dave should definitely delete the clip.

For a brief second, he imagined Dame Angela sitting in the seat beside him, chiding him for what he was about to do. Dave had enjoyed her visits to the edit suite and screening rooms at *Conekt*. There had always been a sense of ceremony, but Dame Angela was also extraordinarily down to earth, with a surprisingly dirty sense of humour and a laugh like a trucker.

How absurd that he could almost feel a frail hand hover over his own, preventing his own ring finger from delivering the downward right-click that would consign the alternate cut to oblivion. Even more ridiculous to experience a warm breeze on the back of his neck, to hear the breathy tones of Dame Angela mouthing "don't" into his left ear.

This time, Dave did turn round, swivelling in the chair in time to catch a hazy veil of light dissolve away, like the afterglow of a bright light fading from the retina. Dave rubbed his eyes. He was so exhausted and felt the beginning of a caffeine-induced headache coming on. It was no wonder he was experiencing faint visual and auditory hallucinations.

Perhaps he should call it a day and destroy that alternative cut tomorrow (or rather, later today; Dave's sense of time was becoming increasingly confused).

Whatever his exhausted mind experienced, Dave did not delete his cut of Midnight Shadows. The following morning, Fiona found the clip and showed it to Marty while

Dave was asleep in the tiny bedroom off the edit suite. The two exec producers, writer, director, and stars crowded into the small edit suite, with a nervous Fiona at the controls. Darkness fell, a countdown began, and Dave's cut played out.

Contrary to the slumbering editor's fears, everyone loved it. They were excitedly discussing the direction the cut had taken when two things happened. Firstly, Dave woke up and stumbled into the suite in his underpants and rumpled t-shirt to find he was facing a potential firing line of above the line talent. He cursed and grabbed for his trousers, garbling an apology.

"Fuggedit… sorry, I didn't get your name?" Marty said, delivering the first machine-gun volley. Shit, I'm history, thought Dave as he buckled his belt and swept his messy fringe out of his eyes.

"Dave," he said, stifling a yawn. "Dawn Blackhurst".

The diminutive director shook his hand vigorously.

"Dave, this alternative cut… is brilliant. This… I mean Dame Angela is phenomenal, just phenomenal. Benny, get onto Dame A's people, extend her schedule if you can. Paul, can we have more of her? Can you give me a couple more scenes?"

Dave hadn't even noticed the taciturn screenwriter lurking at the back of the group. He was about to offer his hand again, for lack of anything better to do, when the internal phone buzzed. An executive producer answered and received the bad news. There would be no more of Dame Angela. The legendary actress had passed away during the night.

Once the hubbub of shock and alarm had diminished, Marty turned to his team and simply said, "Well that's it.

Dame Angela stays in the picture. We use this cut."

Dave Blackhurst would publicly attribute his radical recut to the unseen hand of the legendary actress. People accepted his assertion in its metaphorical sense, and took it as a tribute to Dame Angela Lowe's talent and charisma.

What Dave would never reveal is that she had whispered the solution to him at the exact moment of her passing. He'd checked the logs – he'd made his decision not to delete the cut at 4:58am. Dame Angela's time of death was certified at 4:56am. Her final fade out had been a moment of sublime creativity.

The Mayor of Little Fittock

The returning officer announced the results of the 2021 mayoral elections in the Devonshire hamlet of Little Fittock. The room simultaneously erupted into cheers and catcalls, the split being roughly 70 percent in favour of the former. Whether you were inclined to condemn or celebrate the result, it was an election that all present would remember for a very long time.

"I hereby announce that the winner of the 2021 Election to the position of Little Fittock Mayor, with one hundred and eighteen votes, is Juniper Lamington III". At this point in the proceedings, the Little Fittock village hall, packed to the rafters with almost the entire two hundred inhabitants of the parish, would normally have quietened as the incumbent handed over the symbolic scroll and staff to the newcomer, who would then make a suitably rousing speech.

However, as Juniper was busy gnawing Neddie Lamington's cloth cap to shreds, having relieved herself on the still-steaming flagstones, there would be no symbolic handover today. Nor would there be a speech, of course, Since Juniper was farmer Lamington's prize-winning goat and goats are nothing if not taciturn.

She did, at least, consent to wearing the resplendent gold chain associated with her office, although that too was subject to a cursory nibble before being abandoned in favour of a dessert of old hymn book.

The election, deemed notable enough to feature in the '…and finally' section of a local news broadcast, was supposed to be a political provocation. For more than a decade, Little Fittock had seen an influx of city hipsters desperate to 'get away from it all' by settling in villages where their money went a lot further and where they were less likely to be robbed, ripped off or choked by carbon monoxide particulates. The elder Tory-voting stalwarts of the hamlet looked on disapprovingly as the new, young residents began to overthrow the old assumptions and moribund traditions.

One of these was the annual election of a mayor from the village's oldest, aristocratic family, the Wilmington-Smythes. Being an advocate of both fox-hunting and capital punishment, Ronald Wilmington-Smythe, entrenched in a long-running feud over right of way with Neddie Lamington, didn't stand a chance on re-election, once the farmer persuaded the committee to allow his favourite goat to stand for election.

Under a banner reading simply 'Get My Goat', campaign manager Billy Harper and his hipster allies ran a lively social media campaign with regular video updates of Jasmine's antics, which generally involved headbutting things, defecating on them or chewing them to pieces. When the targets of her ire were 'Trespassers Will be Prosecuted' signs hung passive-aggressively by old footpaths, or Little Fittock Hunt Gathering flyers, the likes, shares and retweets ensured the campaign became nationally celebrated and Jasmine's election was a shoo-in.

Of course, now that she had won the mayorship, the question remained, how to best employ her? Given that the village's combined population could fit comfortably in a medium-sized wedding marquee, the role was scarcely taxing – the mayor, or in this case mayoress, would open the annual village fête, the agricultural show, welcome visiting dignitaries (few and far between) and generally gad about wearing peculiar robes and a tricorn hat.

Jasmine could not easily be persuaded into the ceremonial ermine, at least, not if you wanted to keep all your fingers, plus she ate one of the three corners of the tricorn hat, so dressing her appropriately was out of the question. The chain of office was fashioned into a reasonably sensible collar, and that would have to do.

At the village fête, she successfully saw off some drunken yobs who had driven over from the neighbouring, and more boisterous hamlet of Greater Fittock, giving their ringleader a decisive butt, which sent him cartwheeling across the village green and into the duckpond.

At the annual farmers' market prize-giving, Jasmine judged the best marrows and onions categories by biting into her favoured selections. These were then extricated from the belligerent mayor's mouth in time for the prizegiving photographs, which were rendered additionally surreal when Jasmine took against the photographer and butted him off-stage midway through his group shot of the great and good of Little Fittock, many of whom he captured merely from the nose up as his body described a graceful arc into the soft fruit display tables.

Unpredictably, Jasmine took offence to the retired rocker and recent village resident Jimmy Page's new cosmic blues direction when she mounted a stage invasion during his set at the Fittock Folk Festival, primarily with the intention of eating the hay bale Page was perched upon. This was deemed ironic by the local paper, given Page's onetime fondness for goat-loving Satanists. The subsequent face-off between Stratocaster-wielding pensioner and cloven-hooved mayor was captured on video and went predictably viral, doing a vast amount to enlarge the event's reputation.

By the end of the year, the Christmas markets were teeming with Jasmine-branded merchandise, including tea-shirts, mugs, goaty-banks (a variation on the porcine norm) and of course, Rampant Goat IPA, courtesy of the micro-brewery that had sprung up behind the Lamb's Head pub. Curried Goat was banned from the menu of the Michelin-starred Fittock Hotel's menu.

Jasmine's ascendancy was incontrovertible and other villages began to follow suit, voting into office prize pork-ers, donkeys and even a chicken called Imelda. None threatened Jasmine's status in terms of media-friendly pop-ularity, largely due to her unpredictable and intractable per-sonality. She even had her own Instagram account, with seven thousand followers.

All in all, once the year was up and it came time to vote once more for Little Fittock mayor, Ronald Wilming-ton-Smythe didn't deign to stand. "What hope do I have against Jasmine?" he opined in a statement to *The Fittock Gazette*, "She's literally a force of nature and although I hold her responsible for all that's wrong with this town, it seems I'm in a distinct minority."

And that is why a goat is mayor of Little Fittock to this day.

Ride Along

It seemed like a good idea at first, agreeing to be one of the test subjects for a radical new concept in online dating. And by radical, PiggyBack Incorporated meant utterly unprecedented. Safi hadn't quite believed what she'd heard when she got the cold call back in September 2020.

"You're what?" she'd said, assuming she must have misheard.

"We're trialling a neurological implant that links two consciousnesses together, allowing complete access to another person's thoughts, feelings and emotions."

"I see. And you think this is a good idea?"

It had seemed a truly terrible notion when Safi had first heard it. Even if it was possible, which it surely wasn't, was it really a good idea to allow anyone at all total access to every accidental, malformed, or deviant thought. How could that possibly make the intimate, terrifying, seemingly impossible task of meeting a life partner any easier?

The research assistant who'd called her explained that she'd be part of a 2000-volunteer study created by the University of Westminster's neurophysiology and neural networking departments. The dating application was simply a sweetener they were using to help them find a group of willing and open-minded (in all senses) participants. It all sounded a bit sketchy to Safi, and she should definitely put the phone straight down.

Yet, somehow, she agreed to receive the literature and a call from one of the lead researchers in a week's time, all the while wondering why a truly forward-thinking group of scientists would resort to something as archaic as cold calling, on the telephone, of all things.

Then, a week later, she met up with Christina, a life-long sceptic of all things technological and, to Safi's surprise, her acerbic friend was weirdly positive about the notion.

"Are you kidding? That's a great idea. For you, that is."

"What are you talking about?" said Safi. "Why for me?"

"Think about it. You're totally neurotic, and surely even worse on a date. But what's causing that neurosis? It's your uncertainty about what the other person is thinking and feeling about you. What you're saying, how you're behaving, even what they think of your eyebrows, for Christ's sake? This way, you'll just know."

Safi shook her head, half-smiling.

"It's not as simple as that," she protested. "They can't just overlay one consciousness over another, apparently. You get overload, or feedback loops or something, as two people go about their days with another full person inside their head looking out. So, they cut out your senses, put you into a kind of coma, then implant you into the head of the other person. You're just a passenger – you can't control your host's actions, thoughts, or emotions."

"Seems a bit one-sided."

"It would be, except you sign an agreement where you take turns with the other person. You spend a certain period inside their head, then you swap."

"You see. That'd be perfect for you. No uncertainty. You'd know in an instant what he thinks of you."

"And he gets to know what I think," Safi said, her doubts building up again.

Nevertheless, one month later, having attended an orientation seminar and undergone psychometric testing, Safi signed her participation agreement and checked her bank balance to find the £2500 first instalment for the trial had already been deposited.

Next, she scrolled through the online catalogue of male participants who had already pre-selected her as a potential partner. There were seventeen in total, which Safi hoped was a decent ratio, although the scientists hadn't told her how many men were in the initial pool of possibilities. This is high stakes Tinder, she thought, narrowing her shortlist to three, then discounting Bob because of his beer gut, and Kurt due to his 'teetotal conservatism'.

That left Lionel, a pale-skinned mixed race 36-year-old man from Norwich, who worked as a cabinet maker and loved jazz, keeping fit and the novels of Haruki Murakami. Lionel didn't sound like a freak, and she'd find out soon enough whether he was or not.

She would be riding shotgun first, as the researcher put it. After her ride along, Lionel would share her experiences. The trial was for three days only, since it wasn't safe to continue the medically induced coma she'd be in for much longer than that. Safi was a little worried about the operation but, as the researcher explained, it was no more challenging than an appendectomy. They'd simply peel back a section of her scalp, drill a small hole in her forehead and insert a tiny neural lace the size of a postage stamp. They would then slide the device over a section of her brain and activate it.

The lace was attuned to the frequencies of a companion device already implanted in the host. It was powered by the heat from her own body and used their phones' 4G to transmit brainwave data. Lionel's lace would use his phone's Bluetooth to talk to her phone, and Safi's phone would connect to her lace. The communication link should take effect within half an hour after implantation.

"I'll just slip off to sleep and then wake up in someone else's consciousness?" Safi asked.

"That's the general idea. Now, a few ground rules. You won't be able to communicate with your host, although your host will of course be able to talk to you simply by thinking. We have built in a failsafe, however, in case you need to sever the connection…"

"Why would I want to do that?" Safi asked, suddenly concerned.

"Oh, various reasons," said the researcher, quickly masking a moment of hesitation. "Some subjects find the whole experience too strange; others experience a sort of psychic nausea. And then there are some who… well, you'll know it if it happens. All you need to do is think of the lyrics of a favourite song and that'll snap you out of it. Do you have one in mind?"

Safi was still a little distracted by wondering what the researcher had considered giving as the third reason for dislocation, but now couldn't help hearing Sting's voice singing a song often mistaken for romantic but actually about an obsessive stalker.

"I'll have *Every Breath you Take* by *The Police*".

The researcher smirked slightly.

"Perfect choice. I'll set it up."

Safi's consciousness came onstream when Lionel was in the shower. *Oh shit*, she heard him think (or was it feel?) *I guess I should have known it'd happen like this.* Lionel managed to tilt his head up from his privates extremely quickly, but Safi still saw enough to discover he was adequately endowed.

I'm so sorry, she started to respond, then remembered he couldn't hear her.

I guess you can't respond. Yeah, think they told me that. Why is this water always going cold? Christ, move it one millimetre and it scalds you! Fuck, there goes the shampoo. Now I'm swearing too much. You probably hate that. I need to finish up and get out of here. I'll just deal with the cold. Ahhh! I wonder if everyone's plumbing is this shit?

Mine is, thought Safi in sympathy.

I've such a good day planned. Tried to think of stuff we might both enjoy that won't make our heads literally explode. Sorry, I'm probably worrying you. And now I'm apologizing too much. And overthinking everything. What did the therapist say? Just be in the moment, don't editorialise.

He turned off the water, stumbled out of the shower. Safi felt the shock of cold air on her penis, a lifetime first. To think, if she'd transitioned a little earlier, she would have felt him washing it. Just as well he can't hear my thoughts, she added, for nobody's benefit but herself.

Then Lionel went over to the mirror, a towel wrapped firmly around his waist and she saw him for the first time. Well, she saw his face. He was even better looking in reality (or what species of reality this was an approximation for). His skin was a few shades lighter than hers. Noble nose, tapering nostrils, thick eyebrows, fullish lips, a square jaw, a muscular neck and shoulders. Best of all, she could feel what it was like to possess those qualities.

Being a man feels somehow more solid, she decided, less fluid. She felt springy and weighty at the same time. Weirdly, looking in the mirror, Safi felt a sensation from beneath the towel that presumably presaged an erection.

Uh-oh. Narcissism or some strange enjoyment of her voyeurism? She shouldn't judge. The sorts of thoughts she was already having. This was dangerously erotic. Hurry up and get your clothes on, Lionel, she thought.

I've taken the day off today, Lionel thought. *I'm going to take you for my favourite walk and then we're going to lunch. Don't worry, it's veggie. I'm not going to make you tuck into a steak. I know some guys would take advantage, to prove a point or some shit.*

Safi felt disappointed that she wasn't going to see him woodworking. It was something she'd always wanted to try herself. Still, he'd just scored all manner of points for not making her chow down a bloody rib eye.

Lionel lived in Putney, as Safi discovered when he glanced out the window to check the weather. Safi saw the river and the unmistakable stone arcs of Putney Bridge. Lionel's flat was compact but tidy and well-designed, with proper works of art on the wall and no piles of dirty clothes. Apart from a few woodworking books and tools, there was no other sign of his day job. Safi guessed he rented a studio somewhere, imagined it being one of those cute spaces built into the arches of bridges, like the boatbuilders at Richmond.

Soon they were crossing the bridge, and Safi hoped Lionel was going to take her along the footpath by Bishop's Park – she'd always like that elegant, unfussy garden with its rose beds, ornamental pond and little kids playing football on the greens by Craven Cottage. It was a little frustrating not being able to direct Lionel's attention where she wanted but then, this wasn't her virtual reality simulation, after all. This was Lionel's actual reality. And what he was choosing to do with his attention, seemingly, was check his phone. Safi was disappointed, until she realised he was flicking between three pictures of her – the ones she'd uploaded to Piggyback's site. She wasn't sure whether to be dismayed or pleased.

Ah, yes, sorry. This is going to seem kinda skeezy. But, no, I just wanted to look at your picture cause… it helps me understand who I'm talking, or thinking, to. Does that make sense? Otherwise, I feel a bit mad, having this monologue running through my head. Wow, she's cute. Look at that booty. I wouldn't mind just… fuck, no. Stop it. God, that sun's bright.

Safi laughed (somehow), as the girl sashayed past, and reminded herself how liable she was to have her attention diverted by a square, stubbly jaw or a broad chest, even in the middle of a business meeting or, yes, a date with someone else. And it was kind of reassuring to discover Lionel had a fairly normal libido. Safi had once dated a man who declared himself asexual three weeks into their relationship, particularly annoying as they had already had sex, twice. She didn't want any weird psychosexual complications this time.

There was a further pleasant surprise as Lionel turned down the steps at the end of the bridge and headed onto the very walkway Safi had in mind. She added imaginary points to Lionel's imaginary total.

The rest of the walk was perfectly pleasant, if not as nice as actually being there in person, in terms of the sensations she was feeling. She couldn't quite feel Lionel's arms as her own, they just felt so much heavier than she was used to, and she felt she could almost feel the blood pulsing in his much more visible veins.

However, Lionel turned out to be a very thoughtful and creative companion, knowing a surprising amount about the history of the gardens and the engineering challenges of the newly completed Fulham football ground rebuild. Plus, he was funny and observant.

At one point, Lionel gestured to a bench full of uniformed schoolgirls, all silently lost in their phones. *Like nuns with their hymn books*, he thought, and Safi could see the image he was painting. They walked all the way to Hammersmith, then on through Chiswick, past the bandstands and weeping willows at Duke's Meadows, then over the Barnes Bridge. Although it was still early April, the day was warm enough for there to be a host of drinkers lined up along the riverside embankment outside the Waterman's Arms. Lionel didn't take her there though, even though she briefly thought a pint might be nice.

Instead, Lionel headed into Barnes village and found a little café with tables outside and a pretty garden where he ate a toasted feta cheese sandwich on focaccia with spinach, sundried tomatoes, and pine nuts, washed down with some exceptionally good coffee. Strangely, Safi knew the coffee was good, although she rarely drank it, finding espresso too bitter. Equipped with Lionel's taste buds, she was suddenly a connoisseur.

During lunch he flicked through his emails, explaining to Safi who everyone was, which ones were from clients, which from friends. The only email Safi noticed he didn't open was from someone called Louise, and even there he seemed to anticipate her question.

Louise is my ex. She said she'd be in touch about returning some tools she borrowed. I should read it, but I don't really want to. She always wants to tell me how unhappy she's feeling and how much she misses me, and it makes me feel guilty and a bit manipulated. I hope that doesn't sound too harsh.

Safi was glad he hadn't left it a complete mystery but

if they ever met, she'd have to do a bit of digging there. Lionel seemed good at compartmentalising and didn't have any more thoughts about Louise at all as he finished his meal. Instead, he sat watching some tiny birds hopping around a bush in the corner of the yard.

For the second part of their walk, Lionel's mind had quietened. He mostly seemed to be looking around, taking pleasure in seeing other people enjoying this rare spring day, the privileged few who were stuck in offices, that is. They walked into the tree-shaded towpath between Barnes and Hammersmith and Safi could feel a slight ache building up in her – no, in his calves, as he quickened his speed. Was he trying to get the walk over with quickly?

I usually speed up here, Lionel thought, there are fewer obstacles, and you can get a good stride going. You're probably gonna laugh, but I started doing meditation and mindfulness from an app recently, and I like practicing here. I just look at things and try not to have any thoughts really, just sensations. You probably think I'm some sort of wet hippy.

Not at all, thought Safi. I like that you're in touch with spiritual ways of being. Of course, Lionel couldn't hear her.

Oh no. It was here, wasn't it?

Something formed – a memory? Except it couldn't be, because Safi had never been for a walk with anyone called Lou, who was maintaining an angry silence and making her feel guilty and bitter. Oh, of course. This wasn't her memory, this was Lionel's. It didn't feel quite right – like a melodrama shaped by his ego.

The same towpath, but a much colder, wetter afternoon. The sky was a steely grey and it had evidently just stopped raining. Lionel's hands were getting wet as he folded away the black umbrella and stuffed it into his coat pocket. He wondered if he should take Lou's hand to mollify her but didn't want to. Let her stew for a bit, after all she'd said.

"Are you sure we can go back this way?"

He couldn't believe she had to ask. Hadn't she lived in Hammersmith for about six years?

"Yeah. It'll be fine."

"There's puddles everywhere."

"We'll walk round them. I'll carry you over them if I have to. Honestly, it's way quicker."

"Couldn't we get a bus?"

"This is supposed to be a walk, isn't it? Come on."

Lionel stormed off ahead, knowing Lou would follow, in her sky-blue suede boots, in the mud, which he knew would only get worse as they reached those places the towpath flooded at high tide, where massive puddles formed that stretched entirely across the path. Fuck it, it was only a pair of boots. He'd maybe get them dry-cleaned for her.

"Lionel! Wait, will you?"

That was the only thing on their first date that Safi didn't enjoy. She felt Lionel's feelings of being belittled and made to feel small. She got it. He hadn't allowed himself to remember the argument in any detail, so she didn't know what had gone on prior to the memory of Lionel deliberately ruining Louise's shoes, but there was enough there to make it feel at least partly motivated. But it was also kind of petty, and a really stupid thing to do.

Regardless, Safi spent the rest of the 72 hours she'd be piggybacking on Lionel's consciousness mostly enjoying his intelligence, his humour, and his honesty.

The following day Lionel spent in his studio, finishing making a sideboard from dark, reclaimed hardwood recovered from old church pews. She loved the whole process of sawing, planing, joint-making, polishing and varnishing, finding it incredibly soothing. She could have done without some of the more extreme out-there jazz that Lionel liked to listen to, but the process of woodworking was fascinating. She'd never had such an insight into someone else's profession before. It occurred to Safi how much we talk about our jobs, yet how little we convey about what it's really like to do them.

On her final day in Lionelworld, he took a zoom call with an American company that wanted Lionel to help design a weird wooden box for a horror film they were making. Even that was kind of interesting, although Safi found her thoughts drifting towards the end.

They had dinner with two of Lionel's friends that night – a white, professional couple who looked like they probably voted Tory, but were otherwise decent enough people. The young woman, Melissa, leaned into Lionel when her fiancé was in the bathroom and asked, with a hint of coquettishness, "So, are you seeing anyone at the moment?"

If only she knew, Lionel thought, aiming that thought at Safi, yet flicking his eyes down to Melissa's cleavage, but without more than a fleeting erotic thought. Safi sensed a history there, but it was very much ancient history, nothing to concern herself with.

But that night, she found herself in bed, slipping off to sleep with Lionel (she somehow always lost her conscious-ness the same time he did, and must remember to ask if that was by chance or design) and his (her) hand reached down for his stiffening penis. Lionel gave it a few cursory strokes but nothing more. Safi was somehow both relieved and disappointed. His restraint was admirable, though. In fact, there was a lot about him that was likable.

She loved that he read for an hour each night, his hands still smelling of the linseed oil he'd rubbed into a set of cabinet doorhandles he'd made on the lathe. The book was *Half of a Yellow Sun* by Chimamanda Ngozi Adichie and he'd only just started it. Sure, he probably normally read books about Colombian drug cartels, and this was just for show, but at least he was trying.

Lionel seemed to be enjoying the novel, and when he was done each night, instead of folding a page corner down, he used a receipt to mark his place instead. Safi had no idea why this was so important to her, but it was.

When she was brought back to full consciousness in the clinical room at the University, Safi felt an immediate feeling of loss and confusion, like she'd awoken from a particularly vivid dream she'd mistaken for reality.

"Don't worry, it'll pass within the hour," said the nurse, plumping the pillows behind her head and checking the pulse at her neck. She was right, and Safi returned to her daily routine, having taken two separate weeks off work for the experiment, with a working week between to let her get back to some state of normality.

And yet, one week later, having gone back to the office and her admin job at the *Burning Bright* charity, a group protecting tigers in India), she couldn't stop herself from wondering what Lionel was up to. She resisted texting him, not because it was forbidden by the experimenters (although it was) but because she didn't want to give him an unfair advantage. In just a few days' time, Lionel would have to immerse himself in her world.

The experience was different this time. Safi felt a presence in the periphery of her senses, like a vague, hazy corona, like distant whispers that might turn out to be the rustling of leaves. That ephemeral sensation, presumably, was Lionel. She half expected him to announce himself when, on the first morning, she poured herself a bowl of cereal and he came onstream. But of course, he could not.

She'd got up at 6am to shower early, having as speedy a set of ablutions as possible. She'd rather not give him a free erotic show on day one of their acquaintanceship.

Hello Lionel, Safi thought when she felt him there. *I feel ridiculous thinking this, but I think it'd be worse if I spoke out loud so bear with me. Have I really got no clean teaspoons? I could just use this one. It's clean enough. I know, I'm a bit of a slob. I do wash up, honest, every day. But maybe just once a day. Ow! Fucking hell. I'll have to knock that nail back down... or call the landlord or something. Yeah, I know. As if.*

Breakfast in bed. I'm a creature of luxury – sue me. I should fit in a run as well. Maybe I will... in a bit. I mean, I did just make breakfast so I should really eat it. I'll go later. Before lunch. Just check Facebook for a minute...

After she'd eaten, Safi surprised herself by making good on her promise, running down to the canal at Brentford, then up a slightly plastic-smelling stretch of the towpath as far as the famous Three Bridges (actually two bridges) then onto the road that led down past Ealing hospital and the viaduct, before turning for home at Hanwell. Only a three-mile loop, but at eight-minute mile pace. She hoped Lionel was impressed, then cursed when she realised that he'd hear her think that.

On day two, she took Lionel shopping for presents for her mum and sister, whose birthdays were both the following week. A top for her mum, a cookery book for Leni. She hoped Lionel wasn't bored, then berated herself for her self-consciousness, then tried to distract herself from further self-deprecation by focusing on the music that was playing in Zara. *The Police. I'll be watching...* no!

Safi dashed out of the store, explaining her reasoning to Lionel's silent presence. Soon she caught another earworm, which saved her from accidentally severing the connection. The cyclical melody emerged from a branch of Lush. *Lovefool* by *The Cardigans.*

That's better. Shame what happened to the singer. Nina. Didn't she die? Check Wikipedia. Oh... apparently not. Who was it then? Someone from back in the 90s. Died a few years' back..? The Cranberries! Dolores. That was it. Shame though. I should have bought something for me, my wardrobe needs a complete overhaul. I wasn't quite ready to give you a sneak peak, you naughty man. God, I sound like a schoolmistress. I hope you don't think I'm a neurotic scatterbrain. That's what my mum called me just the other day. Can you believe it?

Once she calmed her overheated brain down, Safi decided to go to the church in Hanwell, the one her grandmother used to go to. Not to pray or anything, since she was an agnostic at best, just because it was so peaceful in there and it made her feel close to the old lady. Jemima, thin as a twig, myopic to a comic extent (bottle-thick specs) and with a cackling laugh like a crow. Safi missed her so much.

Okay, that's way too maudlin. Let's get out of here. This

place smells musty. I'm meeting the girls later tonight. Cocktails and some sort of futuristic crazy golf. Not my idea – Bella's. You'll like her, she's got a really filthy sense of humour. How am I going to stop her telling you about my love life though? We had a snog once. We were really drunk. I could taste her menthol cigarettes. I'm not a lesbian, really, I'm not.

By the end of her three days, Safi had packed more in than she'd usually do in a month. She wasn't going to be out-done by a boy, after all. She'd been for runs, dinner, cock-tails, even dancing, she'd watched a movie with Christina, who had a truly embarrassing laugh and drew tuts from the well-to-do elderly couple behind them. She'd even cooked a romantic meal for two that she had the pleasure of eating alone. Well, sort of alone.

At the end of day three, Safi felt confident that she'd shown Lionel enough of her world to make up his mind. Whatever he chose to do now, he couldn't complain that he didn't know enough about her. She'd even epilated her legs.

And, on night three, three glasses of red wine in, an hour before bedtime, she decided she couldn't cope with going to bed all smelly and unkempt and decided to have a shower. It was easy enough to wash herself without look-ing down, but she realised that he'd feel every contour of her body as she touched herself. She used a loofah instead of her hand for the bodywash. No need to give away the goods too soon, as granny used to say.

That night she slept a sound, dreamless sleep, feeling a little melancholy as he slipped away from her like the last glimmers of dusk becoming proper night.

After the operation to remove the neural lace, and after the end-of-study questionnaires, debrief and data crunching, there was to be a reunion event at the University. The researchers had hired out a grand ballroom for a dinner and dance. It looked like it had been put together by someone trying to reconstruct a school prom from a pile of 90s teen comedies. Still, it provided a chance for the test subjects to celebrate, ask any final questions of the researchers and, most vitally, meet one another's neural partners.

Piggyback had decorated the hall with pink balloons, red hearts and cartoon pigs styled as cupid, somehow achieving an effect midway between cute and embarrassing. Safi had bought a new dress, crimson, with a lot of cleavage. She'd got Bella to fit one of her amazing hairpieces, and now had long, flowing, shoulder-length locks. Real hair too, none of that ersatz nonsense. A red streak to co-ordinate with the dress. Passing a long mirror, Safi admitted that she looked pretty fantastic.

She hadn't been sure Lionel would attend. Three days before he'd texted to say the event clashed with a friend's birthday. Then, just this morning he'd texted, very simply:

See you there x

One kiss only. Normally, Safi would have considered that perfunctory. However, knowing what she now did about Lionel, she could imagine him taking a moment out from something vital to fire off a quick message, to put her mind at ease. Knowing this didn't make Safi any less nervous when she walked into the huge, panelled, echoey hall, unfortunately. She scanned the room, sidling round the walls smiling thinly at other guests, all uniformly in their late twenties and thirties, all seemingly more comfortable and at home than she felt.

"Hello? Safi?"

The voice came from behind her, deep and resonant, with a bit of hesitancy. She turned, and there he was, dressed to the nines, beaming at her.

Safi didn't need to think. She flung her arms around Lionel, a man she already felt she knew. They had spent only six days together, without a single proper conversation. And yet... he was just so familiar. And Safi had missed him! She had no doubts – Lionel was vitally important to her present and future happiness.

Lionel hugged her back, without any self-consciousness at all. They said nothing as they held one another for a full thirty seconds, way longer than was socially acceptable for two comparative strangers. Nothing needed to be said. It already had been.

Appendix – Random Inspiration

For those who may find it of interest, here are the tales that were inspired by random words generated at www.textfixer.com, or written for competitions using similarly arbitrary strategies to generate story ideas.

I've listed the random words or concepts after each story's title.

Running Coyote and Fallen Star – ferment, duke, murderous, sanitary, Badlands.

Aloha – analyst, explicit, ambiguous, analytical, invention.

Merry Go Round – agency, tragic, examiner, horseback, examiner.

Duet – forbidden, harmony, operatic, cough, goat.

The Pact – biblical, scar, werewolf, lollipop, bridge.

A Cork on the Ocean – firecracker, hell, more, luxury, passenger.

Beeswax – gland, brood, queen, wrestle, teacher.

The End of Money – gigantic, eating, destruction, royalty, federal.

Black Cubes – fertile, bogeyman, rebel, prediction, chaotic.

The Purple Heart – honeypot, controversial, forbidden, drain, goldbricker.

Float Me Down the River – enzyme, adult, bite, desperate, logical.

Agonía – purple, Doberman, belt, confuse, cartel.

Charity – riot, raid, bag, disorientation, department.

Wheatfield with Crows – honey, truth, pity, magnificent, light.

10 Social Isolation Games* – curve, anatomy, poetry, conspiracy, afterlife, bloodthirsty, dismemberment, continental, sentinel, guest.

Saving Face** – grinning, ceremony.

Allies in the Deep – hiss, emerge, devices, bladder, cruise.

Needlework*** – seamstress, vengeance, historical fiction

Far from the Beaufort Sea – beast, primate, naked, drunk, king.

Stardust at the Beehive – host, young, beehive, imaginary, sadistic.

A Sign from Above*** – Stop sign, thrift store, romantic comedy.

In Too Deep – dismember, eyes, shark, bullwhip, noise.

Thermals – hazard, logical, badmouth, pilot, degenerate.

Flotsam and Jetsam – evacuation, horizontal, charismatic, wept, dart.

Import Export – racket, foggy, export, mad, filthy.

Rockabye Baby – gimmick, cradle, blurt, lust, axiom.

Going Down – bachelor, elevator, heating, eight, settler.

Paragon of Pulchritude – compartment, flamboyant, hollowness, hotter, liquor.

Keepsakes – conqueror, ambush, abstinent, collection, vinyl.

Things we Hold Onto – ditch, beautiful, examiner, grenade, whisper.

What do you Need? – happiness, mystical, highway, cashbox, frequency.

Crawling to the Endzone – atmosphere, cloud, jigsaw, bloody, faith.

You want it More Vibrant? – drill, paste, formula, glandular, calibration.

Flaming Skies and Frozen Secrets – alligator, fossil, gangland, frozen, aversion.

Repentance – blackness, silence, bandsaw, decomposition, anger.

The Ineffable – canyon, daredevil, setup, central, orphanage.

Midnight Shadows – downward, filthy, fade, connectivity, shadow.

Frozen Rain – federation, northern, rain, simple, octopus.

The Mayor of Little Fittock – condemn, present, goat, enlarge, cosmic.

Ride Along – neurotic, intimate, freak, cartel, simple.

* I used ten random words for this story, each part of which contains exactly 100 words.

** This tale was a 100-word story, for which I selected only two words.

*** *Needlework* and *A Sign from Above* were both written for the NY Midnight short story and flash fiction challenges, respectively. In this annual contest, competitors are assigned a genre, location, and object to inspire their fiction.

About the Author

Gavin Boyter is a Scottish writer who has been living in London since 1999. Having previously worked in advertising and healthcare, he is now concentrating on creative writing and freelance copywriting. In 2018, he ran from Paris to Istanbul, as described in his 2020 book *Running the Orient*. Boyter is also a screenwriter with two optioned projects in development, including the psychological thrillers *Nitrate* (co-written with Guy Ducker) and *Twenty Questions*. He loves running long distances and will almost certainly never learn to play the guitar properly. This is his first short story collection.

Other non-fiction books by Gavin Boyter

Downhill from Here
Running the Orient

www.gavinboyter.com

Visit *Gavin Boyter's Unforeseen Tales* on YouTube.

Printed in Great Britain
by Amazon

75308284R00181